WENDY JAMES

THE LOST GIRLS

fi

This one's for you, Shaz. With love.

You don't look back along time, but down through it, like water.
Sometimes this comes to the surface, sometimes that, sometimes nothing.
Nothing goes away.

MARGARET ATWOOD—*CAT'S EYE*

'*But where do you live mostly now?*'

'*With the lost boys.*'

'*Who are they?*'

'*They are the children who fall out of their perambulators when the nurse is looking the other way. If they are not claimed in seven days they are sent far away to the Neverland to defray expenses. I'm captain.*'

'*What fun it must be!*'

'*Yes,*' *said cunning Peter,* '*but we are rather lonely. You see we have no female companionship.*'

'*Are none of the others girls?*'

'*Oh no; girls, you know, are much too clever to fall out of their prams.*'

JM BARRIE—*PETER PAN*

PROLOGUE

I am forty-four years old. A happily married woman. I shouldn't be here. I shouldn't be doing this.

But if anyone were to ask me why I'm doing what I'm doing, I'd tell them that it's something that I have to do. That me being out at this time of night—way past my bedtime—drinking myself silly with this virtual stranger is not only inevitable but necessary. That although I'm letting him run his hand down and then up my thigh, and imagining falling into a bed, or onto a table, or being pushed up against a wall, imagining being fucked by him somewhere, anywhere, wherever, before the night is over, the situation is more complicated than it seems. I'd have to explain that despite appearances it's not just base lust; that this is all about fairness, about paying a debt, about redressing past wrongs.

You see, in my head this is all about the past. It's about Angie, about Rob and about Mick, too, in a strange way.

But what if I'm wrong? What if this isn't about them or whatever the hell went on in the past? What if it's just about me? About my life now?

What then?

JANE, MAY 2010

How good would it be if each moment of a life could be contained somehow? If each moment could be made separate, discrete, could be quarantined from the rest. So that there's an end. An over.

Take this particular moment in time, an ordinary morning. Jess, my daughter, twenty-three—grown-up, but a fledgling still in the way twenty-three-year-olds are these days, constantly crashing into the sides of their suddenly-too-small nests—a half-eaten piece of toast in one hand, coffee in the other, hunting for her sunnies, her handbag, her bus ticket, running late for some class or meeting. Rob, dear Rob, coffee in his left hand, newspaper in his right, oblivious to our daughter's noise, her habitual chaos. And there's me, Jane: mother, wife, enjoying my cup of tea and the warmth of the early morning sunshine that's streaming through the kitchen window; looking forward to the busy day ahead, excited about the future, content with my lot, monarch of all I survey.

At least that's how I like to remember it. But it's a funny thing, memory. What if it wasn't really as I recall? What if I wasn't quite as content as the picture makes out? If I were to think long and hard and honestly (though who wants to do that, really?), perhaps I was already feeling vague stirrings of discontent, murmurs that were soon to become something far louder, more insistent, until they became a deafening, all-encompassing roar. And perhaps some of what happened in the next few months would have happened, regardless.

There's no way of stopping the past rising up and making its claim on an already complicated present. If only there were. And maybe there's no such thing, despite what we might hope, despite what we may wish for, as a new beginning.

It's Jess who brings the whole thing back into our lives, who stirs it all up again. It was inadvertent, of course—there was no way that she could have known what had happened, or what was to come. How could she? None of us were warned, and none prepared. This particular morning Jess has said her goodbyes, banging out the front door in her usual last-minute panic, only to rush back into the kitchen seconds later, breathless, eyes wide.

'OMG, Mother! I nearly forgot. There's this woman—I can't remember her name, she gave me a card, but God knows where that is. Anyway, she's, like, this producer, and she wants to talk to you about the Angie thing for a radio documentary. Some crime program she's doing. I told her you wouldn't mind. She's going to call you at the shop—or maybe she said she'd call in at the shop. I can't remember. I thought that'd be best—didn't think you'd like me to give out the home phone number. You don't mind, do you?' She offers her sunniest smile, gives a re-gal wave, and dashes back down the hall without waiting for a reply, slamming the door behind her again. It takes me a full minute to process what my daughter has just told me. To think up a suitable response. And by that time Jess is long gone.

The Angie thing.

Well, what did I expect? That was how we'd wanted her to regard it. All of us: me, Rob, Mum and Dad, Mick. Like it was no big deal. As if it was something we didn't need to dwell on, to make too much of. Of course, we'd given Jess the bare facts, she knew the story—it's not as if we'd ever hidden it from her. She'd read through the collection of yellowing newspaper articles, sighed over the unimaginable awfulness of it all. But to Jess, it was just an old story—a tale she'd tell her friends occasionally. The grief and the terror were all vicarious, thank goodness; it was over well before she was born, long ago, if not far away.

The Angie thing.

But thirty years isn't really all that long ago. Not for the rest of us, anyway.

I'm just about to close the shop when the woman walks in. I've spent the best part of the day attempting an inventory for the auctioneer and, although my effort has been half-hearted, I'm feeling exhausted, and more than ready to go home.

At first I mistake the woman for one of those painful customers who hurry through the door, defiantly within their rights, at 5:29 p.m., wander aimlessly for ten or fifteen minutes, then saunter back out, not once making eye contact. I have a few things to do after closing—a prescription to pick up before the chemist closes, library books to return, food shopping—and for a moment I seriously contemplate telling the woman to piss off, thereby flouting my twenty-odd years of dedicated customer service. But of course I don't do that, can't. Instead I offer her a cool but polite greeting as she approaches.

'Are you Mrs Tait? Jess's mum?' The woman's voice is low and smooth.

'Is she okay?' My panic is immediate and primal, if irrational: the woman is quite clearly not a police officer, nor any sort of official.

'Oh,' the woman says. 'Well, I assume so. I mean, I'm not actually here about Jess.'

I relax, wait for an explanation. The woman is not a customer, that much is clear, she hasn't so much as glanced around, but I can't place her. She's slight, compact, dressed plainly, all in black—jeans, long-sleeved T-shirt, low-heeled boots. Her hair is dark, cut short; her smooth pale skin bare of makeup. She might be my age, but she could be much younger, in her mid-thirties, perhaps.

'I'm Erin Fury.'

'Oh?' The name offers no clues, though she is clearly expecting me to recognise it. I wonder for a moment if the woman is some sort of celebrity, if I've been selected (via Jess, no doubt) for some dreadful reality TV show.

'I met Jess at TAFE yesterday. I'm doing a documentary on murders and their aftermath—focusing particularly on the effect on the victims' families. Jess said there'd been a murder in your family years ago—that you wouldn't mind being interviewed.'

'Ah.' The penny drops—Jess's radio producer. 'Jess did mention something this morning, but I—'

'She gave me your work number, but I was in the area. I thought a direct approach might be better.'

'Oh, well. Actually, I don't really know that I'm all that comfortable with the idea. It was a bit naughty of Jess to say anything without asking me first.'

'Oh, that's a pity. I had a bit of a google and your family's case is particularly interesting because there wasn't just the one crime. We're a bit short on these sort of crimes—serial killings—they're pretty rare here in Australia, so you're something of a find.' The woman's gaze becomes intense, her dark eyes fierce.

'Well, I'm not sure that—'

'Look. I know it's probably not something you like to talk about, and I understand it could be very painful, remembering such a dreadful time, but I'm not doing some sort of sensationalist hatchet job or anything. It'll be a serious radio documentary; I'm currently talking to the ABC and SBS. It's designed to be used as a resource, as well, for other families who find themselves in similar situations. I'm hoping to sell it on to Compassionate Friends and other counselling services.'

'Oh. It sounds very ... worthwhile. But, to be honest, it's not so much that it's painful, it's just that I'm not sure how helpful I can be. I was very young. I only remember bits and pieces. And I'm, well, as you can see, we're in the process of closing down the shop.' I gesture towards the chaos. 'It's a bit of a crazy time for me. I don't know when I'd find the time.'

The woman looks around her, as if noticing where she is for the first time. 'Well, why don't we start now? This seems like as good a place to do it as any. You're about to close, aren't you? So it'd be quiet, we wouldn't be disturbed.' She takes a little red device, no bigger than a mobile phone, from her handbag and waits on my answer—expectant, determined.

For some reason—some reason I will never fully understand, some latent desire to poke around in the past, or maybe just curiosity or even simple boredom—I don't say no. I don't tell this woman that I'm busy, that I'm tired, that I still have an hour of errands ahead of me, and that all I really want to do is to go home, pour myself a long, cold glass of sav blanc, turn on the television and let the exhausting tedium of the day fall away. Instead, I look at my little gilt carriage clock, which has been keeping perfect time since 1910. Twenty-five to six.

'Why not?' I walk to the front door, click the lock and turn the sign to closed.

The woman makes her way to a little reproduction mahogany Queen Anne dining suite in a dimly lit corner of the shop. It's the sort of suite that's become increasingly difficult to sell over the past few years: lovely to look at, but completely impractical—the French-polished timber easily marked, the chairs uncomfortably upright and a little wobbly, the satin upholstery cold and slippery. But somehow the woman seems quite at home in such a setting. She even appears rather therapist-like, in an old-fashioned, clichéd way: calm and focused, slightly distant. I resist the urge to recline on a nearby chaise longue, and sit across from her at the table. The woman has come prepared: she takes a recorder, notebook, pens and a small bottle of water out of her bag, arranges them carefully. Close up, the woman is not plain, as I'd first thought, but beautiful—her eyes large and dark, mouth full, cheekbones high. I wonder whether she's deliberately made herself appear plain, bland. And why.

She clears her throat then speaks quite formally, as if she's reading from a script.

'I'm going to ask you some questions. I will be recording your answers. I'll then make a full written transcript, which I can supply to you, if you like. Our conversation will be edited for the documentary, but I'll get your approval before anything's made public. There are actually a few legal documents that need signing, release forms, permissions, that sort of thing. You can go over them now, if you like, or I can give them to you to take home and read.'

'Oh.' It was too much to take in, all at once. 'I'll read through it later, if that's okay.'

The woman looks relieved. 'Good. Let's get started then, shall we?'

EXTRACT FROM TRANSCRIPT OF INTERVIEW: JANE TAIT

ERIN: So, I've read up a little on your cousin's death, Mrs—

JANE: Oh, Jane. Just Jane. That's fine.

ERIN: Okay. Jane, then. I just want to check that I've got the basic facts right. In January, 1978, your cousin, Angela Buchanan, who was staying with you during the school holidays, went missing after a visit to the local shops. Her body was found a few days later in bushland some distance away. She'd been strangled with her scarf. She was fourteen at the time. Your brother and some of his mates were the last people to have seen her. Yes?

JANE: Yes. And then another girl was found strangled about six months later, in Kings Cross.

ERIN: And the two killings were linked, right?

JANE: That's right. Both of them had been strangled with their scarves. But they couldn't find any other connection between the two girls. The second girl—I forget her name—she was a street kid. Homeless. A runaway from some country town. They didn't know each other; their lives didn't intersect in any way.

ERIN: What made them so sure it was the same killer? Just that they were strangled with their scarves?

JANE: There was something else as well, I think. Some evidence that connected the two killings; we were never told what it was. Anyway, the press started calling it a serial killing—the Sydney Strangler.

ERIN: But there were never any more killings?

JANE: No. Not that I ever heard of—and I'm sure I would have. There were just the two.

ERIN: And the killer was never found? He could still be out there.

JANE: Unless he's dead.

ERIN: Now, if we could go back to the beginning. If you could tell me about the day your cousin, Angela, went missing.

JANE: Everything?

ERIN: Whatever you can remember about that day.

JANE: Right. Well, really, it was an ordinary day. It was the summer holidays. We just did the usual things. You know. Hung around. Watched television.

ERIN: If I could just interrupt for a second, why was Angie staying with you? Was there trouble at home?

JANE: Oh, no. Nothing like that. She'd just come for a week or two. I can't remember how long exactly. She used to live around the corner, but her family had just moved a few suburbs away. She was probably a bit lonely, bored. You know.

ERIN: Oh, okay. So that day you were just doing ordinary holiday things. But at some point your cousin went out and she didn't come back.

JANE: She went up to the shops.

ERIN: Was that unusual? Did she often go out on her own? Even though she was staying with you?

JANE: She was fourteen so it wasn't unusual. Before Angie, before what happened, even littler kids, like me—I was only twelve—went everywhere on their own. We walked to school, walked to the shops. Rode our bikes all over the neighbourhood. It was the seventies. It wasn't like now. The Northern

Beaches, well, it was a bit like the country, really. Kids were safe on the streets. Or so we thought. After Angie died, things were different for a while.

ERIN: I suppose people were scared.

JANE: It changed a bit after the second girl was killed—everyone let out a sigh of relief. That happened a long way from us. You know, in the city, on the other side of the bridge. It wasn't just local any more. It wasn't one of us.

ERIN: No. I guess not.
   So Angie went out ...

JANE: She went up to Ferber's, the local corner store, to play pinball with the boys. She used to go up with Mick, my brother. It wasn't a proper pinball parlour or anything, just a shop with the one machine. Mick was good mates with the owner's son, and there were a few others who used to go up to play.

ERIN: Was playing pinball something lots of girls did then, around here?

JANE: I don't think so. She was the only girl I remember seeing up there, anyway.

ERIN: So was Angie a little bit different, then? What sort of girl was she?

JANE: What sort of girl? It's hard to say, really. She was just ... Angie.

CURL CURL, JANUARY 1978

Angie. Angie is a looker. Or she's going to be. She's only fourteen, but already, heads turn wherever she goes. Male heads, mainly. Golden hair, tanned skin, legs long and shapely, teeth white, straight, a smile that could melt any heart. Just fourteen, and it's not only the boys who are looking, but men—young, elderly, middle-aged—just a glimpse can give a fella that lift that's almost painful, that little zing that straightens the spine, makes a dull day, a dull life, bearable. Just looking at Angie can give a bloke a renewed sense of life's possibilities, even when those possibilities seem to have dried up, to have all but disappeared.

Women look too, but that's different. That's not so simple. Angie's peers haven't really noticed yet, or if they have it's subliminal. They look at her admiringly: maybe wishing for a bit of her spark, her energy, maybe even wishing they could be friends. Young women are looking at her critically, sometimes enviously, wondering how old she is, whether she knows what it is she's got, wondering how they measure up, seeing her as potential competition. They see the way the men look at her, and they don't like it. Older women—mothers, grandmothers—don't like it either, but their reasons are different. They look at her benignly, and while they might feel a slight nostalgic twinge at her youth, the speed and lightness of her tread, the way she's still so at home in her skin, it's the maternal pang that prevails, that slight squeeze of anxiety, that feeling that she's been given too much, too soon. They don't know what's ahead for her, not really, but they know it could be hard. They want to take her home, cover her up, keep her young for a while longer, keep her safe. Keep her alive.

Angie's walking down the street, towards a busy strip a few blocks from the beach that has half-a-dozen shops—a butcher, a baker, a greengrocer, a newsagency, a corner store. Warringah Mall (which will one day be feted as the largest mall in the southern hemisphere) is just a few miles down the road, but it's in its infancy, hasn't yet killed off all the local competition. She's accompanied by her most devoted follower, her cousin Jane. Jane is younger by two years, and shares the substantial whack of genes that all first cousins share—but the two girls couldn't be more different. Jane is a tiny thing, all bone and sinew, a freckled urchin face, mousey brown hair, cut short. Unlike her cousin, who's dressed in the latest summer gear—a crocheted singlet over a bikini top, denim cut-offs, bamboo thongs with red-velvet straps—Jane is unfashionably overdressed. Even though it's the middle of summer, she's wearing a long-sleeved shirt, old jeans, joggers, socks, as if she's intent on keeping those scrawny limbs warm or covered. Jane could be a boy, and to her shame is frequently mistaken for one. She won't always be invisible, of course, won't always pass for a little boy, she'll grow up soon enough, will uncover parts of herself that surprise and delight her, disguise others that aren't as satisfying, alter those things that can be changed without too much trouble—prune this, pluck that. Soon enough she'll be wishing for those angular limbs of her childhood, desperate to retrieve that sense of a physical self that's not too fleshy, too wide, too much.

The two girls are walking along the strip, heading for the corner store, Ferber's. They've been sent to pick up a pack of Benson & Hedges for Jane's dad, a loaf of Tip Top white bread for her mum, a five-dollar note enough to leave change for sweets. Jane has it planned already—she'll buy a pack of chocolate smokes, her favourites. She likes to eat them slowly, pop each paper-wrapped chocolate stick in the corner of her mouth, taking a tiny bite before stretching out her hand and puffing out and up, enjoying the occasional startled glances of passers-by. She'll do this for a while, then peel away the thin paper and chomp down the rest before it gets too soft. Angie will buy a pack of SOSs, which are too hot for Jane, but still she'll swap one of her fags for two of the hard red balls, surreptitiously rolling them into the gutter, not wanting to make her generosity too obvious. Not wanting Angie to guess what her exasperated mother has already figured out—that she'd give the shirt off her back, and her trousers too, to her beloved cousin.

It's like being with royalty, travelling in Angie's slipstream. Not one person, young or old, passes without a smile, without offering up a comment about the weather, the weekend's activities, without attempting some sort of connection with the sunshine that is Angie. At twelve, Jane isn't envious, is more than content to be allowed to bask in her cousin's reflected light. A day like the one they're enjoying—just the two of them, without Mick or his best mate Adam or any of the older kids to spoil the fun, to divert Angie's attention away from Jane—is bliss. They spent the morning watching cartoons in the lounge room. With Jane's dad sleeping after a night shift and her mum out in her salon, doing Mrs Neal's cut and colour, the cousins had a few uninterrupted hours together. Jane persuaded Angie that they didn't need to watch *Sounds Unlimited* and instead they sat giggling at the antics of Road Runner and Wile E. Coyote. They managed to demolish almost an entire packet of chocolate biscuits in the sitting—not the good Arnott's ones that Mum doles out sparingly, but the bag of Nabisco that she buys in bulk. Jane felt queasy after, and only picked at her lunch. But she had made a recovery by the time her father rose, grumpy and hungover, and sent them up to the shop for supplies.

As they approach the shops, though, her cousin's attention shifts. The change is gradual: first Angie's gait alters, her pace is less hurried, but her strides become longer, more fluid, and she affects an elegant slouch. Her expression changes, too, her eyes dart here and there as if she's on the lookout for someone else; her responses to Jane's chatter become less and less focused; her voice sinks and then slows to a drawl.

When they breeze through Ferber's multicoloured flystrips, Jane finds herself abandoned mid-sentence. Angie saunters straight down the back of the store, to where Adam and Mick and some other boys are playing pinball. Jane reluctantly follows her cousin—who seems to have grown a few inches in a matter of seconds. Her stance has changed again, her shoulders are back, bust out, hips swinging. Jane hates the pinball machine, hates the noise and the swearing, hates the dark and dingy area down the back of the shop, with its smell of boys' sweat and sour milk and, very faintly, of mice. She wants to get the cigarettes and milk, spend the change and wander back home. There's an informal but unbreakable time limit that her dad applies, and she knows that too much time spent chatting to the boys will have to be made up for—that they'll have to run all the way home. She sidles up behind her cousin, doesn't even bother to say hello to her brother or the other boys, knows from experience that it's better to stay small, or risk banishment. She leans against the shelves and waits.

The boys have quietly welcomed Angie, relinquishing their places at the Ted Nugent machine to her without complaint, and are gathered around, watching her play. Angie is no more expert than Jane would be, really, but still the boys stand around admiringly, offer up the odd bit of advice, encouragement. Jane can see that it's not the game they're watching so much as Angie. Her brother isn't even trying to disguise it, though the other boys are less obvious in their regard. Mick gazes longingly at his cousin's face, watching her as he comments, trying to make her laugh with some corny joke—his voice, still breaking, raspy one minute and a squeak the next. But today Angie has eyes only for Adam. She resists all Mick's efforts to guide her, brushing him off with a laugh. Jane sees her brother's face flush a deeper shade of red when Adam pushes in coolly behind Angie, puts his hands over her hands, adds his weight to hers.

'Come on, Ange. Just nudge it, like this—not too much or you'll lose it.'

Angie's lips part, her cheeks heat up—though whether it's with the excitement of the game or the close proximity of the boy, it's impossible to know.

Jane is distracted for a little while, watching the scene before her, and lulled by the commotion of the machine—the zinging and beeping, the simulated thrashing on the guitar, the man with the foxtail all lit up and flashing—but soon enough she is impatient, then worried. She marches over, pushes through the male throng, pulls on her cousin's arm.

'Come on, Ange, we have to go.'

But Angie won't be moved; she barely looks at Jane, her mind on the game or on the boys or both.

'You get the stuff and go back. I'll come home later.'

'But …' There's no reason why she shouldn't—Angie is fourteen and Jane has been allowed to walk to the shops on her own for years. It's no big deal.

'I'll be back soon. I just want to finish the game. And you can have my share of the change.'

'But what about …?' She's about to mention the Elvis movie they'd planned to watch, the popcorn they were going to pop, but thinks better of it.

Mick adds his two bob's worth, clearly eager to get rid of her.

'Go on. Piss off, Janey. Dad'll get the shits if you don't get his fags back.'

'Well. I'll come back, will I …?' Pleading now.

Angie's not listening, is concentrating hard on her game. Mick gives Jane a shove.

'Don't bother her, Jane. She's got better things to do, mate. Just piss off home, would ya?'

There's not quite enough change for two packets of chocolate cigarettes, but Mrs Ferber notices the bitten-back tears and says she can take the extra pack and pay the twenty cents later. Jane calls out goodbye as she's leaving the shop, but another couple of boys have joined the crowd around the machine and she can't even see her cousin.

Jane pushes her dad's cigarettes into her pocket, and carries the loaf of bread carefully, so she doesn't crush it. She chomps down both packs of chocarillos without any of the anticipated pleasure. Runs all the way home.

Every day after that, Angie heads up to Ferber's to play pinball. In the beginning Jane accompanies her; they go up together on the pretext of getting something—milk, bread, cigarettes—for Jane's parents. They quickly establish a pattern. Jane will hang around watching for a half hour or so while the bigger kids play the machines. Apart from Angie, it's only boys: Adam Ferber and Mick, a few of Mick's other friends who she knows by sight if not by name. Mostly they ignore Jane. She stands alone in the corner of the store, sucking on a lollipop or an icy pole, waiting for her cousin to finish with the pinball, to come home with her. Every now and then one of the boys will take pity on her, make the other kids give her a go—overturn a milk crate for her to stand on, try to explain the rudiments of the game, show her how to do it. But the other boys—Mick especially—get annoyed, impatient to return to the serious business of competition.

'Come on, Jane,' her brother says. 'You're too small—you can't do it. You need to get the milk back to Mum before she goes bananas. Go on. Rack off. This isn't a game for little kids.'

She's pained by her brother's dismissal, but not as pained as she is by Angie's, who looks past her, then swats at her when Jane takes hold of her hand and tries to drag her away, to force her cousin to come home with her.

'Listen, Jane. You just go home. I'll be back soon. I'll bring you back something good if you go. Promise.' Angie doesn't even bother to look at Jane when she's saying this; her concentration is all on the whirring, pinging machine. And the boys. The boys' attention is all on her too.

It's nothing obvious—it's not like they're talking to Angie all the time, or that she's making an effort to be the centre of attention. On the surface they appear to ignore her, to concentrate on the game; their conversation is limited to throwing insults and cracking incomprehensible jokes. But there's something about the way they say things when she's there—the way their eyes turn swiftly to Angie and then away again. It seems to the quietly observant Jane that all their chaff and banter is actually directed at her cousin. But Angie never gives the slightest indication that she's taking notice. Angie's own conversation is reserved for matters of business—whose go it is, who's winning, who's standing too close.

And then there's the touching. This isn't something obvious either, not something that anyone apart from Jane would notice, nestled into her position in the corner with nothing better to do than observe their antics jealously. There's a whole lot of the normal pushing and shoving that she's come to expect between boys—who are far more physical than even the most affectionate girls, with their constant wrestling and thumping. But this physical contact is quite different and it's not between the boys. It's just a matter of bumping and grazing, easily construed as incidental, accidental—a hand reaching out to pull a lever, push a button, will brush her cousin's arm or occasionally even her breast. Sometimes one of the boys will stand behind her, helping her play—though Jane doesn't think Angie actually requires their assistance. She can't help but notice the way the boys will occasionally push into her cousin from behind and for just a split second their denim-clad crotches push against her bum. Jane notices that during the game, in such close proximity to Angie, her brother breathes heavily, his face turns red—and she's sure it's not just from exertion. Angie is excited in some way too, Jane can tell by the way she constantly fiddles with her hair—pushing it off her face with a sophisticated flick, a gesture copied from some television actress—and on the rare occasions that she speaks her voice is uncharacteristically breathy, her words staccato.

Jane stays, always, as long as she dares, but eventually she has to go back home alone, her parents awaiting supplies. Angie doesn't even bother to turn—her only acknowledgement is a dismissive wave, the vague promise of seeing her soon.

Towards the end of the holiday, Angie drops the pretence of going with Jane, running errands. Instead she heads up to the shop late in the morning or even earlier, when Mick goes. When Jane complains that she has been left out, that it's not fair, her mother chides her, unaccountably on Angie's side.

'Darling, Angie's a big girl. You have to leave her alone. She's spent half the visit with you, you should be grateful. Let her go for a few hours. It's only fair.

'And try not to be clingy,' her mother adds as Jane stomps down the hall to her bedroom. 'It only drives people away. Try to be a little more cool. Now, why don't you invite Lizzy over? Or Sharon? They're nice girls. And it'll do you good to play with someone else.'

But she doesn't want Lizzy or Sharon. She wants Angie.

But Angie, it seems, doesn't want her. Angie has moved on, pulled away. Jane doesn't understand where this distance has come from. Not so long ago the two-year age gap had meant nothing—the cousins had enjoyed the same games, the same shows, enjoyed just being together. But now, it's as if Jane's still splashing in the shallows while Angie has swum out beyond the breakers—at first the deep water doesn't seem so far from the shore, but somehow the swim is more difficult than Jane had imagined, the distance between them vast. She feels as if her arms are too tired, as if she's swallowed water, can't get her breath. Catching up to Angie is taking forever.

JANE

It's evening by the time we finish. The little clock bravely chimes the half hour, seven thirty, just as Erin clicks off her recorder. I'm shocked to discover that the time has passed so quickly, shocked too by how much I've said, how little prompting was required, by how much I actually seem to remember of that strange and terrible long-ago summer.

Despite her initial impression of therapeutic calm, the woman doesn't seem to be a natural confidante: her questions are awkward, her manner spiky, her responses too cool. In a regular social situation I would have found conversation with her difficult, but somehow she's been the perfect repository for what has been an unexpected gush of remembering, a geyser of telling.

When she calls it a day, the shop has cooled in that sudden way that rooms do on autumn evenings, and my feet and legs are numb. The shop has darkened around us, a glow coming in from the streetlight, the headlights of passing cars. I watch as Erin carefully packs away her little machine, her notebooks and pens.

I clear my throat, breaking the silence. 'I hope that was helpful. I mean, there's probably a lot of stuff there that's irrelevant.'

The woman looks up, her face is in shadow, her expression impossible to gauge, but her response is surprisingly enthusiastic.

'Oh. That was fantastic. A great start. Thank you.' She scrapes back the hundred-year-old chair in a way that hurts my heart as well as my ears. 'I can come again tomorrow,' Erin says. 'Are you here on Saturdays?'

When I don't respond immediately, she adds, 'Or we can do it next week. Whenever suits. Just let me know.' It is clearly a question of when, not whether. 'Just give me a call when you're ready. Or if you have any questions.' She produces a business card, gives a wave, and disappears out into the night.

I close my eyes, slump in my seat, suddenly exhausted, reluctant to move. I wonder vaguely about Rob and Jess, whether they've organised dinner, about where I should go to pick up that prescription. I avoid thinking too much about what I've just been discussing and that everything I've said has been recorded, for an unknown audience, for posterity—though there was nothing particularly revelatory in it, just my child's-eye view of Angie, of the day, and not much more than could be gleaned from a newspaper. The experience was weirdly, unexpectedly, pleasurable, but somehow, despite the ease, the feeling of catharsis, I've been left feeling not only tired but raw, exposed. Uncertain.

I pick up the woman's card—shiny red, embossed with *Fury Productions* and a picture of some Roman god, a mobile number, an email—and drop it in the top drawer of my desk before locking up for the night. Maybe I'll call her back. But then again, maybe I won't.

I have every intention of telling Rob about it. On the drive home I contemplate turning it into a funny anecdote—the oddness of the woman, of the entire encounter. It's the sort of story that would have led somewhere once upon a time, down new and interesting conversational paths, into shared memories, observations, amusement, laughter over Friday night drinks, and ultimately a pleasurably early night, or on the rare occasion (our daughter's hectic social life permitting) unbridled passion on the lounge-room floor. But the reality of my homecoming— the house unwelcoming, still in half darkness, my entry unheralded due to the noise of the too-loud television, the messy kitchen, the washing left on the line, the tiresome prospect of cooking an evening meal—dampens my enthusiasm.

I pour myself a glass of wine, almost gulp down the lot in one long sip, then refill it before heading into the lounge room. Rob is prone on the couch in front of the television, half watching some highly irritating cooking show, his iPad propped on his stomach—the television blaring to compensate for his incipient deafness. I don't attempt any sort of conversation under these conditions, just hunt for the remote, mute the TV.

'Hey!' Rob sits up, gives me a surprised grin. 'Janey. You're home.'

Where once Rob's characteristic stating of the obvious would have had me offering a caustically humorous response, tonight I can only manage the caustic.

'Obviously. And it's equally obvious that you weren't expecting me.'

'Eh?' He looks at me quizzically. 'What's wrong? Have you been with your mum? Something happened?'

I sigh. 'No, Rob. Nothing's happened. That's the problem.'

'What do you mean?' He pats the seat beside him. 'Come and tell me what's wrong.'

I ignore him. 'You could've made dinner, Rob. Or cleaned up the breakfast dishes. Brought in the washing.'

'Oh ... I got back late, too. Just thought I'd stretch out for a bit. There's no hurry, is there? It's just the two of us, isn't it? And didn't you say you were getting fish?'

'Well, I didn't. I didn't have time.'

'It doesn't matter, Janey. I'm not even hungry. Toast'll do. Just sit down and have a drink, woman. Relax. Come and watch this—some of this stuff looks really good. And simple. It's kinda Mediterranean with an Asian twist. We should try some of them.'

'Jesus, Rob. I can't see how you find anything about these shows remotely interesting.' There's a sourness in my voice that I hate but somehow can't help.

He shrugs, his face hardening now, responding in kind. 'I like it. But so what?' He turns his head back to the television, speaks without looking at me. 'What's up your arse?'

What *is* up my arse? I return his shrug, throw in a pantomime sneer for good measure, though he's still not looking. I click the volume back up a few notches, sit the remote on the couch beside him, and head back into the kitchen, to my bottle of wine.

By the time I've refilled the glass, he's turned the volume up full bore again. I close the kitchen door against the noise.

Our marriage wasn't always like this.

Once upon a time—and it seems like only yesterday—our marriage had been, if not perfect, then close enough. Not so long ago I would have rushed home to tell Rob all about the interview. He'd have poured the wine, and I'd have poured out my story. I wouldn't have cared that the house was a mess, that the washing hadn't been brought in, that Rob had spent an hour watching mindless television instead of preparing dinner. We'd have made do with leftovers. Or nothing. And neither of us would have cared.

Until just recently I had been blissfully content with my life. I'd been aware of my blessings, and constantly counted them: I had Rob, I had Jess; both of my parents were strong and well, living just around the corner; my brother, his wife and children, not so far away. I had the shop, work that was satisfying and reasonably profitable; if we weren't exactly flush with funds, we were certainly comfortable. I had friends and acquaintances, work connections, a community—a network built up over a lifetime spent in the one place, so dense and tangled that it was impossible to unravel. All this had been my lot, all this I'd been completely happy with.

So where has it come from, this insidious worm of discontent, intent on munching its way through my shiny red apple of a life?

It's true that all sorts of things have changed lately—there have been stresses, complications. There's the shop. The decision to close up, to rent out the shopfront and the factory behind. We'll still be comfortable, more than comfortable, financially. It's a semi-retirement, really—something most people my age would be glad of. This should be a freeing up, a new and exciting phase in my life; there's time and money to do a few things: I can travel, take up a sport, even pursue some new career if I want—it's not too late. But somehow I don't really feel free, don't feel excited. Instead I'm filled with anxiety, a sense of loss.

And then there are my parents: my father's dementia has progressed to the point where we've had to move him into a home. My mother, despite her determination to see this move as a positive, as an opportunity to regain some of her own life, is coping poorly. She's depressed and constantly overcome by an array of minor physical complaints—sciatica, arthritis, blood pressure, bad teeth, indigestion—necessitating trips to doctors and dentists and various other medical professionals every second day. My brother Mick, who's just moved in with her, is supposed to be taking care of all this, but as he's just been retired medically unfit from the police force—PTSD and severe depression—mostly it's me who's having to do all the running around.

It's nothing, really, I suppose, just standard mid-life experiences, not actual crises—not like some of my friends. There have been no tragically early deaths or potentially fatal diseases, no marriage breakups, no drug-addicted children to deal with. My family is secure, healthy, whole. I've been a good mother, a good wife, a good daughter. So why, suddenly, am I feeling as if it's all been for nothing? Why am I feeling as if I've missed something, as if my life has somehow slipped by without me noticing? Why do I feel as if I've been left stranded, breathless and gasping like a fish on the shore, the tide receding inexorably behind me?

Later that night, after Rob has gone up to bed without saying goodnight, and Jess has stumbled home from some shindig or other, I go into the spare room to search for the box. It's here, somewhere amongst the mess, I'm sure of it. For the last few weeks, Rob has gradually been ferrying home all the decades of *stuff* that's been stored at the shop—not just our own, but my parent's and Mick's too—and the room is crammed with dusty boxes and cartons, bursting with years of paperwork, tax returns, records, warranties and instruction manuals for every one of the whitegoods my parents ever owned. There's a box full of my mother's fabric offcuts, another with knick-knacks that Mum didn't want but couldn't bear to throw away, that she's saving 'for the grandkids'—fondly imagining that the fashion for all things retro would one day extend to her childhood thimble collection, the tarnished electroplated silver tea and coffee sets that were cheap and nasty even in the 1960s, her father's old lawn bowls set. There are boxes that contain all the documents relating to Mick's and my childhood—our baby books, full of carefully documented inoculations, weights before and after feeds and eliminations; our school reports, merit awards and, of course, the countless school portraits documenting our evolution from gap-toothed cuteness to the excruciating onset of pimples, braces and, in my case, puppy fat, none of which had been removed from their cardboard frames, let alone proudly hung.

I find what I'm after without too much heavy lifting. A small lacquered pine box with a brass clasp and a prettily looping *Angie* carved into the lid. Mick had made the box in the year following Angie's death. He had kept it hidden, padlocked, worn the key around his neck—his secret stash of all things to do with Angie. Or so my younger self had imagined, though I'd never had the opportunity to properly investigate.

Despite its sentimental value, Mick hadn't taken it with him when he'd left home. I had wondered at him leaving something so conspicuously precious there, but when he'd left, it had been with ill feeling, and there'd been a stretch of years when he hadn't been around much. By that time I had left home, too, and Mum and Dad had transformed my bedroom and Mick's into a spare room and a sewing room respectively, putting anything we hadn't bothered to take into storage at Pop's shop. I had been surprised to find the box there, just last week, and had made a mental note to ask Mick whether he wanted it. But now, my childhood curiosity reignited, I'm going to go through it myself.

Like all good antique dealers, I'm a dab hand at picking locks, and this particular padlock—small and cheap and old—comes apart easily with a paperclip. It's a skill my grandfather taught me and one that has come in handy over the years, mostly in work-related ways.

I delay the moment of opening—heading first to the kitchen to pour another drink, hoping to dull my conscience. This is the first time I've ever used this lock-picking talent for anything other than work, and my heart is racing unpleasantly.

Inside, the box has been lovingly detailed, any exposed timber polished, its base lined with red velvet, padded and tufted with ornate brass tacks. Sitting on top, slightly squashed, is a paper scroll, tied up with a bit of faded ribbon. Underneath lie newspaper cuttings, photographs, cartoon drawings, a couple of handwritten notes. Three marbles—a couple of cat's eyes and a single dark-red honker—roll around on the bottom. I take out each item, one by one.

The newspaper articles, folded and brittle, are ones I'm familiar with—stories cut from the local paper, as well as the big Sydney dailies, detailing Angie's disappearance, the discovery of her body, the ongoing police investigation. Each of the articles features the school portrait of Angie that was to become so familiar, some accompanied by other photos: snaps of grieving friends and family after the funeral, taken without their knowledge, photos of Aunty Carol and Uncle Barry after the inquest, official-looking pictures of my father, in uniform, grim and unapproachable. There are a few later articles regarding the murder of the young homeless girl, stories with lurid headlines warning the female populace about the Sydney Strangler.

There are other photos, faded Polaroids that I've never seen before. They must have been taken during those last few weeks: Angie at the beach, squinting into the sun, wearing her new purple string bikini; Angie in our old garden, a bowl of cereal balanced precariously on her knees; Angie and Mick sitting together on what might be a bed, arms slung around each other's shoulders. In this last one Angie, looking straight at the camera, eyelids lowered as if she's fluttering her lashes, a paisley scarf looped around her neck, is doing her best to look glamorous, while Mick's gaze is only for her. His regard is understandable, in every one of the snaps her burgeoning beauty is undeniable—already, at fourteen, there are traces of the woman Angie would have been, had she lived.

I untie the frayed ribbon on the scroll, smooth out the paper, which is slightly crazed, as if it was once crumpled and then flattened. It's a pencil drawing of a boy surfing. A teenager's sketch, the figure vaguely out of perspective, the surf smudged and blurry, but it has something—it's vivid, energetic, full of life. There's a date and Angie's name is scrawled on the bottom of the page, in dark capitals that make it look more like a record than a signature.

There are a handful of little scraps of paper, smeared and torn at the edges, featuring two delicately drawn cartoon characters, one male, one female, in a variety of comic situations.

The notices for the funeral are there too, carefully snipped out of the paper. I flick through the program—the list of readings and music that had seemed so inadequate as a memorial, and that still seem such a meaningless testament to her barely lived life: the readings from the Gospels by schoolfriends, the hymns that the grown-ups mouthed while the organ wheezed, 'The Lord's my Shepherd, I'll not want; He makes me down to lie ...' Angie wouldn't have cared for the meaning of the verse, would have winced at the discordant rendition.

Buried at the bottom is an article I recognise immediately: it's the piece that Mick put in the *Manly Daily* on what would have been Angie's eighteenth birthday. He hadn't told anyone, but some well-meaning friend of Mum's had cut it out and sent it to her. Of course, Mum had to interrogate him—and couldn't resist telling him (again) that it was time he got over Angie, time he moved on. Inevitably, that had escalated into one of their huge rows, one that ended with Mick screeching off in his blue Brock Commodore and not coming back. He'd been given a posting out at Brewarrina soon after, and when he came home three years later he brought Sarah with him, their engagement a fait accompli. And Mum had given a sigh of relief, no doubt, thinking it was finished. That finally, finally, he was over it, over her. Over Angie.

The memorial in the newspaper must have cost him a packet. He'd had the complete lyrics to the Rolling Stones' 'Angie' reproduced, with no thought given to copyright, and it's long, taking up almost half a column. The memorial is typed in what must have been a pricey decorative font, illustrated with the same two little cartoon characters, this time joined at the lips, and bound with a neatly tied bow. *Angie.* I wonder if Mick knew back then that Keith Richards had written the song not about a girl, but about his drug of choice, heroin. If Mick understood how appropriate it was, this song about a deadly addiction? If he knew then that more than thirty years later those same clouds would still be there, heavy on his horizon, shadowing his life in countless ways?

The box is an odd memorial—not a repository of a life, but a record of death. There must have been another box, boxes even, once; surely Aunty Carol would have made an effort to preserve every bit of Angie's life that she could, all those same bits and pieces that our mother had so conscientiously hoarded, but made even more precious by Angie's absence, her cut-short life. I wonder what happened after her parents died, where it all went.

I wonder, too, who Angie would be now, had she been given the opportunity to reach middle age. It's hard to imagine: she's like Peter Pan, stuck forever in the Neverland of adolescence, forever fourteen. I wonder, as I frequently do, what she would have looked like—whether she would still be blonde, brown-skinned and beautiful, or whether time and indifference would have had its way with her as it does with most of us.

After she'd died, I'd tried hard to look like her. It was a hopeless exercise with my brown hair, my Irish complexion, but I'd done my best: bleached my hair, shaved every body part I could get to and plucked the rest, tried to hide my freckles under my mother's foundation. I'd plaster my face, chest, even my arms and legs if they were exposed, with the stuff. There was no point trying to get brown naturally—if I stayed out in the sun for more than ten minutes, I'd burn and blister and then just develop more freckles. Eventually I'd given up trying to be Angie, had decided to make the most of the (not totally inconsiderable) assets I did have. Those girls who had the looks I craved back then, those glamorous surfie chicks with their long blonde hair, skin burnt dark, who I still see around from time to time, have lost their allure. I'm sometimes shocked to encounter them—matronly, frowsy, weathered. Old. To be honest, I'm really not too bad in comparison—my paler skin has aged well, my hair has very little grey. I look younger—regardless of my slightly thickened waist, the inevitable boob droop—than most of the girls I once envied. It's the revenge of middle age, I guess. A pointless sort of revenge, though—these days we're virtually invisible. We might still be comparing, but nobody else is looking.

I wonder what sort of woman Angie would have been, whether we would have stayed friends. As a child it had never occurred to me to wonder what sort of girl she was, or who she'd become—she was just my adored older cousin. She was just Angie. Who knows how things would have evolved over the intervening years. Angie now? It's impossible to imagine.

I spend too much time on the weekend agonising over the interview, not just going through the things I'd said, but wondering about my motives. Why on earth had I agreed to it in the first place? I have so many other things on my plate, after all, things that need attending to. Now really isn't a good time for this trip into the past. But maybe that's the point—the past is a distraction, a way of avoiding the present, a way of remaining in a world that's certain, contained, over. So unlike the present, or the unknowable future.

My usual strategy is to leave things be. Brooding is something I just don't do. I don't sulk, don't ponder, don't go over and over things, and I'm generally impatient when others do.

It's probably a cowardly thing—if you stick to the surface you avoid all the rocks and reeds that lie beneath—but I've never understood the desire to go back to a moment that's painful or difficult, have never understood others' desire to loiter there. The past is the past is the past is the past, and better left there. And no, the irony of my occupation isn't lost on me.

Perhaps I'm just looking for an excuse to get sad, maudlin, maybe even sentimental. It's not like my memories will actually do any good—it's too late for that. And anyway, what do I actually know? What do I really remember?

Sometimes it's impossible to know whether childhood memories really are memories, or whether they belong to someone else, or perhaps form part of a collective family memory. There's a particular photograph of me as a child, a toddler, sitting on the knee of my great-aunt Glad, an elderly spinster aunt, on one of her rare visits. She'd sat me in her lap and I'd squeezed her massive breast and said in my baby lisp, *Honk honk.* Poor old Glad almost had a heart attack. I remember it so well that I can almost feel the texture of that trussed-up bosom, the flesh soft beneath the stiff corsetry. Can picture perfectly Aunt Glad's horrified look, the way her lips made a perfect circle of outrage, the glistening beads of sweat on her faintly hairy upper lip. Remember, too, my father's twitching lips, my brother's swiftly bitten-back laughter. But there's no way I can really remember any of this; I was only eighteen months old at the time.

Thinking about what happened with Angie, all those years ago, is a bit like that. I'm not quite sure what's memory, what are stories I've been told. And there's no sense, is there, in repeating things I'm not sure about. Telling stories that might not be true.

So, I make a decision: I'll end it, refuse to sign the release. The past can stay past. I need to get back to the here and now.

I ring Erin the following Monday from the shop, determined to put an end to the interviews, to tell her that I'm too busy, that I don't really have anything else to add, and that I'm uncomfortable, anyway, with the whole enterprise. I'd been impulsive, reckless; I should have discussed it with my family first.

But, of course, it doesn't happen quite like that. Somehow the woman, who is polite but determined, manages to ignore or deflect every excuse I make. Too busy during the workday and in the evenings, then why not meet early? she asks. You like to walk in the mornings before work? Along the beach? Sure, no problem, I'll join you. You can talk while you walk, surely? Kill two birds with one stone. It's remarkable how walking can free up the memory. Uncomfortable with the ethics of the under-taking? She is reassuring: think of all the other families who you'll be helping ... And finally I am too weak, too slow, too easily swayed to wriggle out of it. In the end, unable to imagine that precise and contained woman hurrying along the beach beside me, and unwilling to have the precious solitude of my early morning walk compromised by unwelcome company and chat, I agree to meet her at the shop at eight the following morning—giving us a good hour before opening.

I arrive ten minutes before eight, hoping to have some time to myself, but Erin's already waiting in front of the door, two takeaway coffees held awkwardly in front of her, shifting nervously from foot to foot.

She is dressed all in black again, the same outfit, possibly—the monochrome effect relieved by a blue and orange scarf, incongruous and not really necessary in this weather, that's wound loosely around her neck. I attempt some polite chitchat when we first sit down, trying to break the ice, but she refuses to be drawn, her attention all on the little notebook that she's taken out of her handbag. Eventually I give up, savour the silence and my coffee, observe the street outside slowly coming to life. The shop is down the eastern end of Brookvale—which is primarily an industrial suburb, a busy hub of small manufacturers and warehouses. Later in the day the street will be mad with activity, a controlled chaos, as endless trucks are loaded, deliveries received, but this early it's a relatively peaceful scene. I watch as the young hostess at the kitchen showroom across the road and the hotshot new salesman arrive simultaneously—clearly together, but careful to enter separately—just as the young apprentice returns with bulging smoko bags for the factory staff. I watch Chris and Collette Yee, who run what is surely the last remaining privately owned hardware store in the area, arguing softly but frenetically on the footpath; watch the comings and goings of half-a-dozen smokers, pariahs even here, who partake of their poison quickly and without pleasure in driveways and on footpaths. I drink slowly, waiting for Erin to begin her questions. And for a few moments, I don't think of the past I'm about to re-enter, or the future, but remain contentedly in the present.

This particular afternoon Angie heads up to Ferber's just before lunch. She goes alone—Mick went out earlier in the morning—and Angie tells her aunt that she's arranged to meet him and the other boys there, that they'll play a bit of pinball, get some fish and chips for lunch from the takeaway next door. It's been made very clear that Angie doesn't want Jane to come with her. Nothing specific has been said, but it's easy for Jane, sensitive to Angie's every mood, every desire, to tell—there's some sort of shift in Angie's eyes, some lack of warmth or sincerity in her shrugged *Sure, you can come if you really want to*, and so the younger girl retreats, hurt, says she has other things to do, anyway, better things, that she'll see her later. *I'll be back in time for the afternoon movie*, Angie offers, generous in her relief. Jane gives a casual shrug. *Sure.*

Jane has nothing better to do, of course; she mooches about the house, restless and miserable, alternately annoying her mother—*Can you keep out of the kitchen, love, when I'm cooking?*—and listlessly watching reruns of *The Brady Bunch* and *I Dream of Jeannie.* Her dad, when he wakes up in the early afternoon, suggests she come with him for a run to the tip—he has a pile of rubbish to take, and usually a visit to the tip is a treat of sorts: there's bound to be some precious item buried amongst the refuse, just waiting to be discovered. When she declines, his smile is understanding.

'A bit lost without Angie, eh, Janey?'

She gives a forlorn shrug, and he pulls gently on her ponytail.

'Come on, darl. You need to find something to do with yourself when Angie's not around. You've got other friends, haven't you? Other things to do. You can't just wait around for her all day. You don't want to waste your holidays, mate. You'll be back at school in a few weeks.'

She watches the late-afternoon movie alone—although it's only *Jailhouse Rock*, which isn't a favourite.

The trip to the tip lasts hours, far longer than it should, and her dad doesn't get home until after six, red in the face and smelling of beer. Her mother gives him a tight smile.

'So which tip did you go to, darl?' she asks, her voice as thin as her lips. 'The one in Parramatta, was it?' Dad doesn't bother to reply, just heads to the fridge and pulls out a can of beer.

'Mick and Angie home yet?' he asks. His voice has that dark and dangerous edge that Jane dreads, and her mum replies in the negative, gives a long sigh. Her dad says nothing, slamming the back door and stalking out to his shed. He's in a mood, it's clear. Jane hopes the others get home soon, that they're back before dinner's ruined, before he's had time to drink too much more, before things escalate the way they can when Dad gets like this.

Her mother gazes out the kitchen window for a moment and then pulls a face. 'I honestly don't know why I bother,' she says to no one in particular. 'Nobody has the decency to tell me when they're going to be home. I may as well be cooking for a band of gypsies.' She opens the oven, crashes the casserole dish onto the sink, then slops out five servings, taking her own and leaving the others uncovered on the bench. 'Help yourself,' she snaps at Jane, who is watching her mother's odd behaviour with open-mouthed astonishment, then storms off down the hallway. Jane hears the lounge-room television turn on, the sound blaring. Eating in front of the television is usually considered a treat, but Jane doesn't think she'll join her mother tonight.

It's almost seven-thirty—and getting dark outside—when Mick finally arrives alone, and with no idea of Angie's whereabouts. He hasn't seen her since early afternoon, he tells his parents. She'd said she was coming home, she'd promised to watch some stupid film with Jane. Mick's face is pale, his voice shakes.

Two minutes later, their father, his expression grim, lifts the receiver, calls the station.

JANE

Erin is as briskly efficient in her leave-taking as before. She packs away her notes, her little dictaphone, and departs without ceremony or unnecessary conversation, other than to arrange to meet again—same time, same place—in three days' time. I had wanted to ask *her* some questions, about who else she's talking to, what other families, about whether there was likely to be a book as well, but she doesn't give me the chance. Next time.

I am tired. These conversations are somehow physically and mentally draining, and the prospect of the day of work ahead is mildly depressing. I'd once taken so much pleasure in the innumerable tasks of running an antiques business: the pile of silver (plates, cutlery, cups, jewellery) waiting to be cleaned and dated and priced and displayed, the arranging of repairs and restorations, the sourcing of rare objects for valued customers—all these jobs I'd once loved. But today it all stretches ahead uninvitingly—a day devoted to sorting out which pieces will be offered to dealers, and which will be sent elsewhere. Those that aren't even worth the investment of wrapping and boxing will be sent to Vinnies or some other charity store. To make it worse, Mondays I leave early, visit Dad, take Mum grocery shopping. It's a day to survive, to get through, with no rosy patches—other than the prospect of its eventual end. I take a deep breath, get on with it.

The packing seems to be getting more difficult, more intractable, every day—or perhaps I'm just getting slower, desperately trying to stave off the inevitable. I find myself lingering over every piece, avoiding the job that I'm here to do—the simple task of readying the smaller pieces for removal, wrapping them in paper, finding a space in a box, filling each carton, adding a handful of packing peanuts and taping it closed. I'm making a meal of it, as my grandfather would say. By the time Rob arrives to help, around lunchtime, I have barely filled two boxes.

Rob, though eager to hurry the process, is not much use either. He's always been uncomfortable here, the proverbial bull in a china shop, as Pop had always liked to point out. Rob's good with the furniture, skilled and painstaking and careful when it comes to repairs, working with the timber, sanding, cutting, filing, varnishing, and he's good at moving it. His big hands are gentle with anything organic—food, children, small animals—but he's oddly clumsy and sometimes unintentionally brutal when it comes to china and glassware.

I watch him fumble with a silver-topped Victorian perfume bottle that I've had in the shop for several years—a piece I'd picked up while holidaying in Western Australia. The crystal stopper needs to be taken out and wrapped separately and he's managed to work this much out, but the delicately etched silver lid—hallmarked 1887—is soft, and he almost crushes it as he presses down the tape.

He looks up at me guiltily. 'Shit. Sorry, Jane.'

I hold out my hand and he passes it over. I unwrap the top, sigh, push the bent silver this way and that in an effort to straighten out the dents.

'Do you actually like this stuff, Rob?' In all the years we've run the business, it's a question I've never thought to ask him.

He looks surprised. 'Well. I don't actively *dis*like it. I'm not like you, though. I don't—I don't love it. I don't wonder about where it came from, and I certainly don't care who gets it next. It's just stuff.'

'Do you like having it around? I mean—honestly—if it were up to you, would you? Or would you prefer a house full of modern stuff?'

Our house is full of old stuff: furniture, bric-a-brac, worthless-but-quaint artworks. It's been a work in progress since we first moved in and nothing stays for too long—the shop providing an endless supply as well as a repository for things I grow sick of.

'Oh, I dunno. I guess so. I haven't thought about it too much. Occasionally I get the urge to go to Ikea and spend up big. You know. Replace everything with shiny chrome and pale veneers. It appeals sometimes.'

'And do you really care—about it going? All this? The shop?'

He looks guilty again. 'Jane, this is your gig. You know that. It always has been. And I know how much it means to you. I feel bad for you—truly I do. But for me, this change really isn't all that bad, is it? I don't mind getting out of it. I'm a bit jack of all the fiddly repair work, anyway. Running a truck, a couple of blokes— that's easy. It's what I've been doing for years, anyway, but without any of the worry of owning the stuff I'm delivering. If the customers complain, now I can just tell 'em to ring the boss. No skin off my nose. And if we're renting out the shop and the factory, well, to tell you the truth it feels like we're getting money for nothing. It means when I'm sick of doing this, sick of running the truck, we can stop. So, no, I'm not all that unhappy, to be honest. But I guess it's different for you. It's hard now. But maybe—what's the old saying?—one door shuts and another one opens. Maybe you'll find something else. Some other thing you enjoy. You've been doing this for so long. Maybe the change will be a good thing.'

'A good thing? But what can I do? I can't even *think* of anything I want to do.'

He shrugs. 'You could do nothing, you know, Jane. Just for a little while. You could enjoy the break. Enjoy having the opportunity to think about what it is you'd like to do. You could even go to uni or TAFE or something. You've always complained about missing out on an education. Maybe you and Jess could do something together.'

We laugh at the thought, imagining Jess's horror, then get back to work.

I watch Rob eyeing off an art deco lamp, wondering how he might wrap it—the uncertainty on his face is comical.

'How can you be so bad at this? It's not your fine motor skills; they seem to be pretty good, generally.' I prise the lamp base from his hands.

He shrugs, shakes his head, as bewildered as me. 'I dunno. It's some sort of anxiety thing—maybe I should have had counselling.' He's only half joking. 'It's probably tied up with Dad working in retail for all those years, or something silly like that. Maybe I've always been terrified that if I can wrap something neatly I'll end up just like him.' He sighs, wanders over to a worn Jarvi lounge, and sits down, watches me unscrew the shade from the base, wrap the tissue paper carefully around the lead-panelled glass. 'I had such high hopes as a young fella. I was going to be something—not like my old man. Now look.' His grin takes the sting out of the words.

I wrap a few more objects quickly and efficiently, aware of his scrutiny, taking care not to look at them too closely, or to think about who they belonged to, and ignoring the fact that they could do with a clean or polish. By the early afternoon, we have another half-dozen cartons ready for the auctioneer, and I have a sick feeling in the pit of my stomach.

I stop work, suddenly transfixed by a small pewter-topped crystal jewellery box, circa 1874. The crystal is something special—lead-based glass, Hungarian, a rare and complex cut. The pewter—lead too, as it was back then—is in perfect condition, the intricate floral design still intact, and without tarnish or dings. It had come from the estate of an elderly lady, whose German grandmother had brought the box to Australia when she emigrated. Despite my reputed lack of sentimentality, I secretly hate the thought of these precious items—family heirlooms—being sold off as meaningless junk, and the idea of sending this particular piece off cold, without story or connection, to some cut-price dealer makes me feel miserable. And guilty. And overwhelmed.

'Hey.' Rob puts his arm around my shoulder, gives me a little shake. 'It's not that bad, Jane. They're not being sent to the tip, you know. Someone'll buy it. Someone who might even appreciate it.'

I shrug his arm away, annoyed by his too accurate reading of me. His stolid reassurances only make things worse. He's right, as always. There is no reason that the pieces won't be sold off to someone who appreciates them, someone ... worthy.

'It's stupid, I know. But I'm thinking maybe I should write down, you know, any information I have about each thing—to give to the auctioneers. They could pass it on to the new owners.'

'Well, you could, I guess.' Rob keeps his voice light, as if determined to humour me. 'But it might take a while. And I think you've got better things to do right now. Don't you have to pick up your mum from RestView? It's her shopping day, right? And aren't we taking her to the club tonight for tea? I thought you said Mick was going to meet us there?'

'Oh, God.' I'd forgotten all about tonight's dinner. Had been looking forward to a night of no thinking, no conversation, no noise. A night in the rowdy Harbord Diggers bistro, listening to my mother's complaints, her worries about Dad, while trying to avoid falling into the dark abyss of my brother's mood, watching him drink himself into oblivion, just isn't my idea of a relaxed family outing.

Mum is only in her early seventies. Her eyesight's not what it used to be, but it's nothing that specs can't rectify, she has an arthritic shoulder, and a bit of sciatica in one of her hips, but really, compared to many of her peers, she's not doing too badly. Her blood pressure's fine, there's no sign of diabetes, no heart problems. No cancer. But since Dad's decline she's lost confidence, has gradually become more and more dependent on me and Mick, and in a lesser way Rob and Jess, to help her run her life.

She's stopped driving, and is reluctant to walk too far in case her sciatica worsens—never going further than the park at the bottom of her street, where she occasionally walks her spaniel, Toto. I had imagined, stupidly it turns out, that Mick's move back home would mean that I'd be relieved of some of my duties, but in fact Mick is just another responsibility, for me and for Mum. Mum's attitude to Mick doesn't help. Despite all the evidence to the contrary, his PTSD diagnosis, his retirement from the police, his ongoing psychological treatment, the medications that render him barely able to function, the fact that he stays in bed fifteen hours out of every twenty-four, rousing himself only at drinks o'clock, Mum appears incapable of seeing that Mick is actually ill. Ever hopeful, she's convinced that Mick's condition is nothing more than the inevitable unhappiness connected to his recent split from his wife, Sarah, and their two little kids. A misery, she's certain, that will be easily overcome once the divorce and the accompanying custody arrangements are finalised.

Mum has already been at the home for hours. Despite my assurances that I'm more than happy to pick her up on the way, she has caught the bus—a fifteen-minute car trip that somehow expands to two hours on public transport. We have all told her—me, Rob, Mick, the nursing staff, Dad's doctors, her own doctors—that it's not necessary and not good for her to spend so much of her time here with Dad. It's of no particular benefit to Dad. In fact, according to the nurses his blood pressure readings are sometimes dangerously high when Mum's around, and it's definitely no good for Mum—physically or emotionally. She's meant to be getting back to some semblance of a normal existence after months of providing Dad with almost twenty-four-hour care, combined with the stress of constant specialist visits. She should be out on the golf course, back to her afternoons at the club, doing some sort of volunteer work, playing bridge—not spending most of her time here at the nursing home. But she sighs and looks irritated whenever this is suggested. *I don't have to do the heavy lifting any more. I don't have to cook for him or clean up after him. But he's still my husband, while he's alive. I can't just abandon him, can I?*

In my more cynical moments I wonder whether it is in fact Dad who has abandoned Mum, in his retreat to this nether world, but at other times, I can so easily understand her unwill-ingness to let him go, to give up. After all, what sort of a life does she have without him? And when I translate this to my own circumstances, when I think of myself being so dependent on Rob, some time in the not so distant future, I feel chilled to the bone. I don't want to experience that neediness, that sudden falling away of everything solid. Not at that age. Not ever.

Instead of her husband, Mum has Mick—vastly demanding and entirely lacking in gratitude. And Mick would be a harder man to live with, I think sometimes, than Dad ever was, even when he was younger. Dad had become gentler, easier, after he retired, had cut down on his drinking, taken up exercise—oh, he could be selfish all right, and a bully on occasion, but at least with Dad there had always been some sense of appreciation and loyalty. Mick is completely oblivious to Mum's endless ef-forts to make his life easier.

When I arrive, Mum is standing behind Dad, slowly brush-ing his still-thick hair. It's bizarre to see him sitting so passively, as if he's enjoying it, when as far back as I can remember he has hated having his hair touched, has avoided haircuts in the same way most people avoid a visit to the dentist. Ironic then, that he ended up married to a hairdresser. He has always worn his hair as long as he could, even before he retired, and always joked that he only became a detective so he could let his hair grow and wear plain clothes every now and then. Mum is chatting away to him as she brushes, and she isn't being careful, even I can tell that she is just pulling through the tangles quickly and vaguely in a very un-hairdresser-like manner.

'... and she had the nerve to complain that the tree is shading her French windows—you know the ones they had put on last year when they built the deck. Mick says she's probably within her rights to ask us for half, as the tree roots are on our—'

She jumps a little when she sees me in the doorway, as if startled, though I had rung to tell her I was on my way. Mum frequently looks startled these days.

'Oh. Hello, darling.'

My father is sitting facing the window, awake, though his eyes are closed—the beautiful view out over the Pacific wasted on him. I kiss him on the cheek, give him an awkward hug, but there is no response, and no sign that he recognises me. I could be hugging a tree.

'How is he?'

'Well, I thought that perhaps he might respond, Janey. I really thought that telling him about the Stantons asking us to pay half so they can have that tree lopped might have some effect—that sort of thing used to make him so angry. And you remember how he could never abide Mervyn Stanton. But there was nothing. He didn't even open his eyes.' She puts her brush on the table and gives a hefty sigh. 'I really don't think there's been any improvement. Despite all that medication.'

Dad's dementia—if it really is dementia—is baffling even his specialists. His blindness and deafness appear to be psychosomatic, his muteness may be selective, as there's no indication of any physical trauma or deterioration, but there's no way for anyone to know how much he actually takes in. He can toilet and feed himself—though his lack of vision means he requires considerable assistance—but his connections with other humans have become non-existent. He is dignified, but unreachable, as if his soul has deserted his body, leaving his physical remains behind him like an empty shell.

His decline occurred with stunning and frightening rapidity, proceeding at a rate of knots. This time last year, he'd been fine—still fit and interested in life, still ready for a drink with his old copper mates, a spontaneous trip down the coast. He swam regularly, and had even run in a veterans' mini marathon not long before—though his knees had suffered for a few weeks following.

The blindness came without warning. There had been no complaints about darkening vision, cloudiness, no bits and bobs floating across his field of vision: he had simply woken up one morning declaring that he could see nothing, had stumbled out of bed, fallen over and broken his arm. He had been taken to numerous specialists—ophthalmologists, orthoptists, neurologists—but none had been able to find anything wrong with him. The doctors had explained that the cause might not be organic, that it was possible that the problem was psychological. Initially Dad had refused to believe them: it wasn't that he didn't *think* he couldn't see—he couldn't fucking see. But eventually a psychologist had made a diagnosis; Dad was suffering from psychosomatic blindness—for which, unfortunately, there is no particular cause nor guaranteed cure. The best the psychiatrist could do was to hazard a guess.

'It could be connected to some sort of childhood trauma—psychological or emotional,' she explained. 'Or it could be physical. Believe it or not, even a knock on the head, mild concussion, has been known to have this sort of effect years later. Can you recall a head injury when you were a police officer?' He couldn't. 'Well, it could be something else entirely.' The psychiatrist didn't actually shrug; she didn't need to.

But was there a solution, we'd wanted to know, can it be fixed?

'It might right itself—or it might not. There's no way of knowing.' Another invisible shrug. End of consultation.

Dad's vision didn't return, and Dad, too afraid to walk with a stick even when guided, insisted on a wheelchair, which he installed in the kitchen, where he sat, day in, day out, listening to the radio, staring out into the darkness. It wasn't long after this that he began complaining that his voice was going. At first he insisted that it was getting rusty, that it hurt to speak, but after another round of visits to doctors (ear, nose and throat, audiologists) with no diagnostic joy, he came up with his own explanation—he had nothing to say, so he was saying nothing.

At first, he wrote notes—laborious, virtually indecipherable—when he wanted something, but soon enough, not only was he not speaking, he wasn't hearing or responding either. To all appearances it was as if he had become catatonic. Despite the best efforts of the specialists, no physical problem could be found, and once again it was up to the psychiatrist to attempt a diagnosis: conversion disorder, which would once have been labelled hysteria.

'I've seen one or two functions go before,' the doctor told us, 'but not this particular cluster—it's quite atypical to have all three at once in an otherwise healthy man. We'd usually see it in conjunction with advanced dementia.' The diagnosis was of no help, after all, nothing more than a description. Dad is suffering from psychosomatic blindness, deafness and aphonia—an interesting cluster from a clinical perspective, no doubt, but a tragedy for everyone else involved. Again there's no prognosis—he might recover spontaneously, and then again, he might not.

Pretty soon it was evident that without a full-time nurse, Mum wouldn't be able to cope. Disregarding her reluctance, and thanks to Dad's huge network, and his generous health fund, we were able to get him settled into a decent nursing home quickly and relatively painlessly.

Dad's room has a view of Mona Vale Beach; it's clean and spacious and sunny, and the food seems decent enough, but even so, it's a wrench to leave him there. The nursing staff are compassionate and competent, and they cheerfully ignore aspects of his condition, insisting that whether or not he responds, they'll continue to make the effort, make sure he's spoken to, communicated with.

'We think it's very important that the lines of communication are kept open, so to speak,' the matron explained. 'Even though it seems that your father isn't taking anything in, we can't be sure. We'll put the television on during the day, or the radio—let us know what programs he might like—and our staff will be in and out constantly. We'll chat, keep him up to date with all the news in the home. We have volunteers who come and read to the residents once a week or so, too.'

The home insists on having a selection of family photos

arrayed about the room. 'You never know,' the matron said hopefully, 'just what it is he might be seeing, what he might be aware of. And who knows, the external stimulation might help. And if his sight comes back all of a sudden, or even if it's there now, or if only one part of him is still conscious, perhaps he'll be comforted knowing he's surrounded by pictures of you all, of the people he loves. We don't really know what's going on in that head of yours, do we, Mr Griffin?' the nurse raised her voice cheerfully, as if hoping that this might do the trick.

'The doctors explained it might be a while before there's any effect, Mum.' I try to keep my voice light and encouraging, despite thinking that the medication is unlikely to have any effect at all, that at best he is just another guinea pig providing a trial, and at worst the drugs are placebos to keep Mum happy. But it's no use pointing any of this out—Mum will bristle at any negative comments from me, even if at heart she agrees. 'Well, there's no harm in trying, is there? I'm just going up to talk to someone about tomorrow night's menu. I don't know how many times I've told them that he doesn't like potato soup. You have a chat with him, love.'

When she leaves I angle a chair into a puddle of late-afternoon sunlight and sit beside Dad, putting on a smile as I take his hand.

'Hey, Dad. Has Mum been torturing you again? She's got you where she always wanted you, I guess. Helpless and uncomplaining. She'll be giving you a short back and sides next.' I'm horrified to find myself speaking in that gratingly officious, too-loud voice favoured by nurses and patronising relatives.

Dad says nothing, his fingers limp between mine. I grip his hand more tightly, take a deep breath and try again. 'I've been packing up the shop today, Dad. It's a bit of a nasty job, really. It'll be good to have it done. We've got a tenant signed up and everything now. He moves in in three weeks. A health food store. Hard to imagine, eh?'

The most devastating thing about it all is how much Dad still looks like himself. He's shrunk, sure, as any body will when it takes in only the minimum nourishment required to stay alive, but somehow there's still enough muscle tone in those once-powerful shoulders, enough bulk has been retained to give the illusion of him being physically the same man. But his expression or lack of—the lips that are always slightly parted, the blank, glazed eyes—makes it clear that the man himself is no longer there, or not in any meaningful way. I can keep my face neutral, my conversation chirpy and positive, but there's a constant pain somewhere deep in my chest that overwhelms me whenever I see him. My father's gone—and it looks like he won't be coming back. Despite what the nursing staff have said about how important company is, how it's possible that conversation, or even just his family's physical presence, might trigger some sort of response eventually, today I can't bear it. I need to get out of here.

When Mum gets back, her mission satisfactorily accomplished, I hurry her up, telling her that I need to get back quickly today. And for once she doesn't argue.

'Good idea, darl. If we leave now we can get to Coles before the after-school rush. I just can't stand it any more,' she tidies away the brush, straightens the photographs, gives Dad a quick peck on the cheek. 'Being around all those bad-mannered, overindulged children. Running amok. Throwing tantrums. *I want this; I want that.* I want to slap their bloody mothers.'

It surprises me how quickly the shopping is done. For once Mum's list is easily filled, and none of the items seem to induce the usual agonising over price and content. A visit to the meat counter can sometimes last half an hour as Mum goes through the cuts, their relative per-gram cost, fat ratio, iron content, colour—anyone would think she'd been a butcher—and her expertise on fruit and veg is unparalleled. But today even the toilet paper is chosen without the usual excruciating wrangling over a multitude of competing factors—price per roll, the comparative length, strength, thickness and comfort of each brand's sheets. The only moment of pain comes when she can't resist commenting on the few items that I have thrown into the basket for myself.

'Do you really need all this cheese, dear?' she asks, pushing my three wheels of brie to the far end of the trolley so they won't be confused with her groceries at the check-out.

'It's on special, Mum. And you know how much Rob likes his cheese.'

'But it's not just for Rob, is it, Janey?' she says it with that twinkly smile that's meant to indicate that what she's saying is only light-hearted, just a little tease. But I know that smile well, know that it is, in fact, a comment on my eating habits, my self-indulgence, my need to lose a few pounds. I smile back just as sweetly and say nothing, but toss a couple of packets of Tim Tams into the trolley as we pass by the aisle end. My mother's lips purse, and she gives a little sigh, but resists.

She's not exactly nasty, Mum, certainly never outright, but where I'm concerned she's rarely got anything positive to say. If it's not my weight, it's my daughter (*Do you think perhaps Jess is just a late bloomer?*), my mothering (*It's because you worry too much, do too much, she can't make any decisions*), my choice of clothing (*Oh, I suppose you're still young enough to wear your skirt above the knee—anything goes these days*), my hair (*A little longer might be better for your jawline, darling—give it some definition*), my garden (*All these shrubs! Why don't you get some annuals, darling, or even some bulbs? You could make it quite pretty without too much effort*), even my little Golf (*It's such a compact car ... I suppose being cramped up doesn't really matter for short trips*).

I'm not quite sure what possesses me, perhaps I've been lulled into a false sense of security after the relatively painless shopping trip, but on the drive home I tell Mum about the interviews.

I know that any conversation about Angie will mean venturing into depths that Mum would prefer to leave undisturbed. But it's too bad. There's something down there that needs to be let up, given light, given air.

'You're what?' Never one to miss an opportunity, Mum gives a slight wince as she turns to look at me (the cramped car seat, her sciatica). 'You're talking to someone about Angela? Whatever for, Jane? And anyway, what does she want to know?'

'She's making a documentary for radio. About murders and their impact—the aftermath—on the victims' families.'

'But why would she choose Angie? Why that particular murder? There have been plenty of other murders, surely.'

'I don't really know. I think she—she met Jess somewhere. At TAFE, I think.'

'Oh. Jess.' I'm too busy watching the car in front of her to actually see it, but can imagine the comprehensive nature of my mother's eye roll.

'It's actually been kind of ... interesting. Talking about it all, I mean. I haven't thought about it for years.'

My mother's sigh is equally comprehensive.

'Well, I don't see why you should start thinking about it now. What good is that going to do? It's something I'd really rather not be reminded about, thanks all the same. We've all moved on, haven't we? Got over it. Why dredge it all back up?'

'Mum, I know it was a long time ago, but Angie was murdered. It's not really something we should stop thinking about. And they never caught the guy who did it. Who knows, maybe something good will come out of it.'

'What do you mean? Surely this woman isn't trying to solve the case? That's not something you should be getting involved in.'

'No, Mum. I told you—the show's really about the effect on the family. The long-term psychological and emotional impact.'

Mum doesn't speak for a moment. 'I don't want to seem cold, Jane, but I can't understand why the woman is interested in speaking to you. If Angie had been your sister, I'd understand. God knows you wouldn't want that sort of tragedy in your own family. You saw how it destroyed Carol and Barry ... but it was different for us,' and now her voice has a familiar pleading tone.

'It was different: Angela was just your cousin.'

'Mum, it still had an effect on us. On all of us.' The producer's pat line trips off my tongue: 'And if it helps other people in similar situations, well, surely that's a good thing?'

But Mum goes on as if I haven't spoken. 'I know it was terrible—a truly terrible thing, an unthinkable thing to happen to anyone. But Angela *wasn't* your sister. She wasn't a part of *our* little family. We were all sad, and it was a terrible time, but we got through it.'

I say nothing, know this is all about Mum, about her unacknowledged, desperately repressed feelings of guilt.

'We were all fine,' Mum continues. 'We *are* all fine. It didn't change anything, did it?'

I don't reply to this either—it's so clearly a statement, not a question.

I'm not expecting her to tell Mick. Mum isn't one to let the Angie genie out of the bottle in his presence, but she brings it up the moment we walk in the door.

Mick is sitting in the dining room, which is dim and cold—blinds drawn, lights off—a half-drunk longneck of beer on the table and three empties beside it, though it's not yet four o'clock. 'Hello, darling. How's your day been?' Mum switches the dining room light on, her voice breezy, cheerful. She picks up the empties as she passes the table, saying nothing about the damp beer bottles making rings on her precious cedar table.

'Hey, Mum. Jane.' Mick blinks, dazzled by the unexpected brightness, but doesn't stand up or make any sort of move, though it's clear that there are groceries to bring in, things to pack away. He stays slumped in his seat—his body and his expression weirdly static.

'We've got dinner tonight, remember. You were going to come.' I call out from the kitchen as I stack the tinned food in the pantry, keeping my voice casual.

Before he can respond, Mum chips in brightly, 'Oh, it doesn't matter. I was thinking I'd prefer a night at home, anyway.

There's a show on the telly I wouldn't mind watching. That dancing show—I think they might be up to the finals tonight. You know the one ...'

'You hate that show, Mum. You made me turn it off last week.' Mick's voice is low and flat, edged with something hard. Mum pauses in front of the refrigerator, her eyes wide, the egg carton balanced precariously in her hand.

I take a deep breath. 'We'll come and pick you up, Mum. It's no trouble. And you too, Mick. You should come.'

'Oh, no. Really, I'd rather not, Janey. I'm too tired. You don't want to go, do you, Michael?'

'Whatever you want, Ma.' His reply is innocuous enough, and Mum sighs, carefully moves an egg from carton to shelf.

Mick comes into the kitchen, leans against the doorjamb, watching. Mum finishes dispensing the eggs, closes the fridge door, then turns around to face him.

'There's something you should know, Michael.' She pauses, takes a breath.

'Yep. No doubt. Plenty of things I should know. It's common kn—'

'It's not a joke. It's—well, your sister's just told me that she's been talking to someone. About your cousin. About Angie.'

'Mum, I—'

'It's for some ridiculous radio documentary. I've tried to tell her that it's a bad idea, that she shouldn't be doing it—maybe she'll listen to you.'

I'm not sure whether I'm more shocked by my mother volunteering this information or by her blatant attempt to enlist Mick against me. If there's one thing my brother doesn't need, it's an excuse to think about Angie. Another excuse to drink, feel maudlin, to contemplate the wasteland that is his life.

It's more than likely, in Mick's current state, that this will precipitate some sort of explosion, some display of temper at the very least, but instead he gives a little laugh—a genuine laugh.

'So Ms Fury's talking to you, too, eh, sis? Getting your side of the story as well? Typical bloody journo.'

I yelp with surprise. 'You mean *you're* being interviewed? Shit. She didn't tell me she was speaking to anyone else.'

'Yeah. Well, I expect they like to keep their sources separate—like police witnesses.'

Mum is gazing at Mick, clearly horrified. 'But Michael. Why would you want to talk to her? Talk about all that? I don't understand. My God ... Your Father would—'

'This has got nothing to do with Dad, Ma.' Mick speaks quietly, but I can sense the rising anger, and leap in to change the conversational direction.

'So, how did she get in contact with you?'

'She rang me.'

'She rang you? How'd she get your number?'

'How d'you reckon? Same place she got yours, I'm thinking.'

I can't resist admonishing Jess, stopping her at the door when she gets home that night. It's past eleven when she makes her noisy entree, and I'm overtired and irritable—in the end we'd all gone to the club, and the evening had been every bit as draining as I'd anticipated.

'What possessed you to give her Uncle Mick's details? You should've asked me first. It was silly. It could be dangerous in his condition.'

'Oh, come on, Mum. You'd have said no way. That he shouldn't be stressed.'

'That's because he *shouldn't* be stressed. There are good reasons for that, Jess.'

'Look, I warned what's-her-name about his mental state, okay. But she kept calling me, said she really needed another perspective for the program to work. I filled her in, told her to approach him gently. Anyway, if it was going to upset him he was perfectly welcome to say no.' She shakes her head, clearly not impressed with my reasoning. 'He is actually a grown-up, you know, Mum. He can make his own decisions. And anyway, it's all cool, isn't it?'

But I'm not so easily diverted. 'He was drunk when I took Granny home this afternoon. You don't think there might be a connection? I just don't think it's a good idea for him to go dredging all that stuff up right now. He doesn't need *more* bad memories ...'

'Oh, come on, Mum, when is Uncle Mick not pissed? Honestly. What difference will it make if he talks to this woman? He's already fully fucked.'

'Oh, Jess.'

'Oh, Mum.' She puts her hands on her hips, considers me squarely. 'I know you think this has nothing to do with me. I know I wasn't even born when it all happened.'

'Well, it's not *that* exactly—'

'But I reckon what happened to Angie back then is still really big in your head. Much bigger than you let on.'

'What makes you think that?'

'The way none of you ever discuss it. Ever. What happened. Angie. The whole thing. And you know what? I reckon that's fully fucked too.'

'Oh. So now you're a psychiatrist, are you?' The arrogance of the post-adolescent child.

'It's not rocket science, Mum. Maybe it's time you got it sorted. Maybe it's time you all got over it. And it affects everyone, you know, not just you. Jeez, Mum. God knows what effect it's had on me—all these unresolved issues of yours. I'm probably gonna end up some sort of basket case. Now, I don't know about you, but I'm stuffed.' She gives me a quick hug, blows a kiss as she trips down the hall. 'Don't let the bedbugs bite.'

I wonder then whether my daughter's right—whether it is, in fact, much bigger in my head than I realise. Whether that's why I'm keeping it to myself, why I'm not telling Rob.

Rob had known Angie too. He hadn't been an actual friend, he was older, not a part of Mick's group. But he'd worked for our Pop so he'd known her well enough to be questioned by the police about his whereabouts on the day she disappeared.

I can't really remember much about Rob at that time: he was seventeen, tall and good-looking, kind but remote, practically a grown-up, and no more available to me (other than as an object of distant admiration) than the members of Sherbet or Hush or the Bay City Rollers. And he certainly didn't take any particular notice of his employer's youngest granddaughter, the little scrap of a child that I was then.

But he'd noticed Angie—I'm sure of that. Everybody noticed Angie.

I actually asked him what he thought of her once—years ago, when we were first going out. We were at Rob's place—a dingy shared flat above a fish and chip shop across from Dee Why Beach. It was Sunday, we'd just had lazy, sweaty, summer sex, and were lying at each end of his bed, limbs entwined, sharing a joint and feeling languorous and open to one another, to anything, in that state when absolute honesty seems not only easy but imperative. We'd been talking about Angie for some reason, discussing the murder, remembering what she'd been like, about how half the boys in the neighbourhood had been in love with her at one point or another.

'Did you fancy her too, Rob? Did you have a crush on Angie?'

I wasn't sure even then what my motive was in asking him that question—a dangerous one for any girl to ask. Perhaps I hadn't had a motive, at least no motive beyond the obvious, beyond simple curiosity. I was eighteen, Rob was twenty-three. The few boyfriends I'd had were all locals. Every one of them had either known Angie or known of her, and all of them had thought she was something else. I suspected, though I hadn't asked them outright, that some of them had found an added attraction in my being the murdered girl's cousin. In fact, I had wondered whether this was the main attraction for some of these boys. A death is one thing—tragic, sad—but closeness to a murder victim, and the victim of a serial killer no less, added something else, some sort of allure that I had half-consciously exploited, but didn't want to question too deeply.

But Rob was different to most of the other boys I knew. First, he was older, and though he'd known Angie, the connection had only been slight. And he was my grandfather's employee, which meant that, regardless of her age, any attraction to Angie would have been compromised, somehow illicit, forbidden. Still, I had no way of knowing what he'd thought of her—and I was curious.

Rob had taken his time answering my question, had run his hand up and then down my leg, as if mesmerised.

'Rob?' I asked again, more urgently this time. 'Did you? Did you fancy her?'

He had said something that I couldn't quite make out, something preceded by an odd stoned giggle, and when I looked up, trying to gauge his mood, his answer, I couldn't actually see his face, but could see one of his ears, sticking out slightly from the side of his head, burning brightly red.

'Oh, Rob. You didn't? Really?' I assumed that his blush was an indication of his attraction, felt my stomach lurch, was preparing for the inevitable disappointment.

'What? Oh, no!' He looked up, as if bewildered, his entire face red. 'Fuck, no. Bloody hell, Jane. I know everybody says she was the best thing since sliced bread, but I can't say that I really ever took all that much notice of her, to be honest. She had a reputation as being a bit of a … tart. I'm sure she wasn't,' he added hastily. 'But she wasn't my type at all. And anyway, she was a bit young for me.' He had spoken carefully, as if fearing my response. But I wasn't angry. Far from it. Instead I was exultant. And suddenly aware of myself being deeply, seriously and gratefully in love.

Deep down, I'd worried that I'd never find a boy who would like me simply for myself, and not because of my connection to Angie. All through my teens, every boy I went out with appeared to get some perverse thrill out of my being the cousin of that 'murdered chick'. The myth of Angie wasn't just in my head: three, four, even five years later, her reputation, dead and alive, seemed always to precede me. Out of loyalty to her memory, to the life Angie didn't get to live, during my teens I'd worked hard to become the sort of person I imagined Angie might admire. Not only had I tried to look like her, I'd done my best to be like her—assuming a brash, cool persona that was an awkward fit with the old me, the real me. I feigned an indifference to schoolwork that I didn't really feel, gave up sport, hung with girls I didn't really have much in common with. I had even gone for boys that I thought Angie might have liked: blond surf-obsessed boys who I found both boring and intimidating. Although my mother occasionally bewailed my academic decline, no one really noticed that I was so essentially altered—I was a teenager, after all, and profound and sometimes disappointing changes are par for the course.

So, in a way, Rob's admission that he hadn't even liked Angie had pulled me off the slippery psychological slope that I was hurtling down. With Rob I was able to relax about being myself: I let my hair grow back to its natural brown and had it cut short. I wore the clothes I was most comfortable, most myself, in—ditched the short skirts, the midriff tops, the high heels, the jeans that left me breathless. I ate enough to stop feeling hungry, took up tennis, spent less time basking on the beach, listened to the kind of music I enjoyed. It was too late (or so I imagined) to rethink my attitude towards university or a career, and I'd already decided to take up Pop's offer of full-time work at his shop. But instead of seeing that as a stopgap—or a dead-end—I decided to take it seriously, regard it as a real career, to put my heart and soul into the business. Rob had given me a sense of self-worth that had been lacking, and I'd never once probed Rob's judgement of Angie, his statement that she'd been a bit of a tart. Never challenged it. Never even referred to it again. It was enough to know that it was me and not some ersatz version of Angie that he was interested in.

And I don't imagine that Rob would have given Angie another thought from that day to this, had we not stayed together.

He'd have moved on eventually, maybe set up his own business elsewhere—his dream had been to move up the north coast somewhere, to some seaside village as they were twenty years ago, to do a cabinetmaking apprenticeship. But of course, that dream had been replaced by others once we got together.

I'm not sure why it is that I'm reluctant to tell Rob about these interviews. I tell myself that I'm not keeping secrets, more that I've made a decision not to bother him. If I'm honest, maybe I don't want to bother myself. Rob would be far too interested. He'd want to know what it was all about, why I'd agreed to talk, what I was saying, how I was feeling. He'd want to check all the legalities, to ensure that I wasn't being exploited, or saying the wrong things. Right now I'm enjoying this solitary journey into the past. And I'm enjoying keeping it all to myself. I'll tell him soon enough, it's bound to come up in conversation eventually, no doubt Jess, or Mick, or even my mother will let slip, but for now I'm happy to keep quiet about it for a while longer. Not quite a secret, but not quite shared.

It isn't until her third visit to the shop that Erin actually looks around, takes in the surrounds. I'm busy talking on the telephone to the estate agent who's handling the shop and factory leases, arranging a visit from the new tenant, who wants to measure up for fittings, new floor-coverings. Erin wanders about the place while she's waiting for me, looking at this and that, picking up the odd piece of bric-a-brac and examining it closely. She handles each object gingerly, as if it's likely to bite her or run away. She weaves her way through the still densely packed furniture, towards the back, and is lost from sight momentarily. By the time I've finished on the phone she has reappeared, is making her way back to the desk, treading slowly, carrying something in her hand. When she reaches me, she holds out a small mushroom-shaped timber object, gives me an enquiring look.

'It's a sock darner,' I explain, smiling at her bemusement.

It's a pretty piece, turn-of-the-century Australiana, homemade, whittled from pine and decorated with orange and black stained pokerwork flowers. In addition to being useless, in this age of cheap cotton socks, it's also worthless. I picked it up at a garage sale aeons ago—and have no idea of its origins, though the clumsily burnt lettering on the bottom reads *Kelly*, which I assume was the owner's surname.

'A sock darner?'

'You put the sock over it, a holey sock or stocking, and then darn it.'

She still looks blank. 'What's darning?'

'You kind of weave the missing fabric back in with a cross-hatching stitch.' I can vaguely remember my mother's attempts to teach me to darn as a child, but unlike crocheting and knitting—which seem to make periodic comebacks—darning is definitely a lost art.

'Wow. I'd actually assumed it was some ancient cooking implement. Like an enormous pestle.' She gives an embarrassed smile.

'You can have it if you like. It'll just be thrown out otherwise. I've had it for years.'

'Thanks. I like it. I'm sure I can find some interesting way to use it.' She laughs, and it comes as something of a surprise, high-pitched and giggly, at odds with her usual demeanour.

'Oh?'

'It's cute. A conversation piece. And the name, *Kelly*—' she hesitates. 'Anyway. Thanks.' She gives the room another considering look. 'So, you're packing up. Are you closing down or just moving?'

It's the first time she's shown any interest in anything outside the story of Angie, and I explain the situation as briefly as I can.

'That's hard. After all these years. You must be sad.

'It is. And yes, I am a bit sad.'

Erin looks down at the darner again, her expression suddenly serious. 'You know, I don't think that I could work somewhere like this. Be around all this … old stuff. I mean, this meant something to someone once. Someone must have spent so much time carving this, sanding it, drawing the flowers, colouring it.' She traces the pokerwork with a long pale finger. 'And it was for someone they loved, I guess. A mother, a daughter, a sister. A lover. And now it's just a meaningless bit of junk that nobody wants. We don't even know what darning is any more.'

'Story of my life, Erin. Meaningless junk.' I grin, but she doesn't return the smile.

'Actually, on second thoughts, I don't want it. I don't really need any extra stuff in my life right now.' She thrusts the darner back at me, her voice businesslike, brisk. 'Now, do you mind if we just get started?'

The news doesn't come in the usual way. They're a police family after all.

The news arrives via her father, who hasn't been home for the last few days. He'd joined the search, spent nights at the station, blatantly ignoring the directives of his superiors who told him to stay home, be with his family. Wait.

Jane hears his heavy tread on the front steps, rushes to open the door. He pushes past her, his face set, grim.

'Where's your mother?'

Her mother is lying down in her darkened bedroom, where she's been since the previous afternoon.

The day before, Jane had gone with her mother to visit Barry and Carol, driving to Balgowlah with a lasagne they'd made especially, and a cake—a peace offering, comfort—but the two of them hadn't made it over the threshold. When Uncle Barry had answered the door, Jane had been shocked by his appearance— the usually neatly dressed man was wearing a pyjama top over suit pants, his hair was dishevelled, his eyes wild. He had accepted a hug from his sister, and had gone to usher them through, but Carol had screamed from elsewhere in the house, her voice echoing down the long hallway, that they weren't to be allowed in. Her mother had offered the food and Barry had accepted it, along with a final despairing squeeze from his sister and her attempt at reassurance: 'I'm sure there'll be good news soon.'

Jane had hurried down the steps and along the driveway after her mother, whose shoulders shook with uncontrollable sobs. Her mother had paused before starting the car, taken some deep breaths in an effort to compose herself.

Just as they'd pulled away from the kerb, they'd watched, stricken, as the casserole dish was flung through a front window, hitting the cement driveway with a *thunk*, the food and china exploding in a red mess, swiftly followed by the cake. They'd quickly driven away, but not before they'd heard the curses that were hurled after them. When they arrived home, her mother had gone straight to her bedroom and locked the door after her. She hasn't come out.

Her brother has been closeted in his room, too—or so Jane assumes—though possibly he has taken off out the window. There is no way of knowing. He has not answered her knocks at the door, her requests that he let her in; she has spent hours with her ear pressed up against the keyhole, and has heard the sound of desolate crying in between long periods of silence. He has only emerged once or twice, his eyes vacant, red-rimmed, has brushed past her as if she were invisible, to go to the toilet, or get a drink, or to grab something from the fridge. She has heard the sound of retching, too.

Jane has had to look after herself: occupy herself, feed herself—tinned food, toast, cereal until the milk ran out—last night she had to put herself to bed. Although there have been occasional calls from her father, checking that they are all okay, there has been no one to alleviate her misery, her anxiety, no one to give comfort or support—or even provide patently false words of hope.

She has spent the day—the longest ever—tiptoeing through the house like a ghost. She has wandered aimlessly from room to room, deliberately dragging her fingers along surfaces that ordinarily she would not touch—the sharp metal edge of the window frame, the flaking rungs of the clothes airer, the rough orange brick surrounding the fireplace, the abrasive surfaces providing a welcome distraction from the unrelenting base note of fear. It is strange how quickly she has grown used to the paralysing dread—how it changed from a feeling of terror—so sharp and painful it took her breath away—to more of a dull ache, a feeling of terrible inevitability.

Occasionally she cries, violent spasms of weeping that leave her exhausted and vaguely guilty, uncertain whether the tears are for her lost cousin or for herself, trapped in this nightmare version of her old life. The house itself has become cold and alien; without the constant ministrations of her mother, with no active inhabitants, it has developed a smell—sour, rank—the smell of sweat, of dirty dishes, unwashed clothes, of fear and unhappiness.

When her father arrives Jane is glad momentarily, relieved to have him home, confident that he will soon put everything right, that he will be able to sort out her mother, to reach Mick, to restore Angie. But her father goes straight into his bedroom, shutting the door. She presses her ear close, but can only hear the deep rumbling of her father's voice, her mother's shriller, louder, but still far too muffled to make any sense. Jane scurries to the relative safety of the lounge room when she hears her father leave the bedroom. His footsteps move further down the hall, and she peers around the doorway, watching as he forces her brother's locked door with a savage shove from his shoulder. Her father closes the door after him, and though she moves quietly down the hall she doesn't need to press her ear to the keyhole—wherever she runs in the house she cannot escape the pain in her brother's animal howl.

JANE

Lately, I've been wondering what it might be like to live some-where else. To not know every turn in every road, every house in every street so well that you could draw a map, or walk the entire district blindfolded. To be new. To feel the way you feel on holidays, to have that nervous anticipation, that feeling of not knowing exactly where it is you're heading, or where you'll end up. To have that sense, for a short while, anyway, that home could contain something unexpected—an uncharted room, an undiscovered garden—could throw up a question you just can't answer.

Before Angie died, I'd never wanted to move. My childhood was secure and happy, the circumference of my life contained, known, constant. Even my parents' occasional talk of relocat-ing—a bigger house, a better suburb—was nothing short of terrifying. But after Angie's death, our tight little world sud-denly seemed to contain previously unknown and completely unexpected unpleasantness.

People don't wait long. Only weeks after the funeral came the little jabs, the barbed expressions of concern, of sympathy. The *what ifs*, the *if onlys*. Barely any time at all went by before the remarks became slightly thornier: *It's the sort of thing you never get over; your mother must feel so terrible, so responsible.* And then the politely veiled questions that embedded themselves somewhere in my soul: *I suppose there was nothing anyone could have known or done? No sort of warning?* Eventually, they come out with it, always camouflaged in the briar-tangled clichés of well-meaning solicitude, so softly that I was never quite sure that they'd really said it, the thing they'd been desperate to say from the start: Do *you think that maybe she did something—that she brought it on herself? That she was asking for it?* It was always cloaked as a question, but I was never deceived.

Mrs Wishart, down the road, a benign presence before this, who always offered up a cheery good morning as I passed her house on the way to school, or a friendly spray from her hose as I cycled past on a hot summer day—not someone we really knew, but there, familiar, a part of the suburban landscape—suddenly she was stopping me, determined to talk about what had happened, to find out what she could, by whatever means.

'Oh, you poor things,' she'd whispered, her bony hand clutching my wrist as if she could sense my desire to run away, to escape. 'Your poor mother. Now, how is she holding up? You wouldn't think such a thing could happen. Not here. And it never has before. And your dad a policeman, too. So dreadful. I doubt that any of us will ever sleep peacefully again if they don't catch whoever did it.'

Up close I noticed that her eyes weren't full of kindness, but were cold and mean. I could sense the accusation in her words, even as she professed her sorrow, just as I could sense the accusation in all their words. I pulled my hand free. Ran.

There were numerous others too, not the people we really knew—the friends and family who were involved, who saw how we were falling apart—just acquaintances who would once have given me a friendly grin over the counter, or the front fence, who were now eager for my conversation, my news.

For the first time in my life, I wanted to move. I desperately wanted to be elsewhere. Anywhere else. But—as Dad pointed out—there was nowhere else to go. Wherever we went, whatever we did, it wouldn't change anything. What had happened had happened. Angie was never coming back.

So we stuck it out. As you do. Dad and Mum had their work, their friends, their place in the community. Despite our sadness and notoriety, and the suspicion surrounding Mick in that first six months, we stayed put. And soon enough our family's trage-dy was last week's news, last month's, then last year's. Eventually, everyone else moves on, people forget. In my first year of high school, my relationship with Angie distinguished me amongst my peers, as well as amongst the older girls who'd known Angie, and those who knew Mick. The cousin of the girl who was murdered—I was vaguely famous, respected, looked after, was never bullied or teased. The air of tragedy that surrounded us kept me safe—though the event itself was rarely referred to or discussed with me directly.

Now, thirty years later, though Angie's death is still talked about occasionally—even newcomers have heard about the Sydney Strangler—I doubt there'd be more than a handful of people who know or remember that I have any connection to it. Who know that Angie was my cousin. Thankfully, that knowledge has all but disappeared.

And there'd be no one left who knows or remembers the rest of the story. The real story: that Mick ran away after the funeral, that Dad wouldn't make an official police report about his disappearance, but unofficially every cop in New South Wales was on the lookout for him, that he was found up the coast a week later. That Mum had taken to her bed for months after Angie's body was found. That Aunty Carol refused to talk to any of us for the rest of her life. That both Uncle Barry and Aunt Carol outlived their teenage daughter by only a few years. That in ways that it's hard to put your finger on, our family was never the same. That none of us—not me, not Mick, not Mum or Dad—was ever the same, after. I'm not sure that we were precisely grief-stricken, we were stricken, that's for sure, but it was with something else. Guilt and shame, perhaps. And when I say we, I don't mean me—not that much. Though I'd loved Angie dearly, and missed her terribly in those first few years, I was young enough to get over it. But not Mick, not Mum, not Dad.

And that desperation to leave, to start again, that left me too. For years I've lived in this same house in this same suburb, with the same job, the same man, my family all within cooee, utterly happy and content—never considering other possibilities, other places. But now, now I don't know what's happening. I'm thinking about Angie again, and all of a sudden, I'm imagining being someone else, somewhere else.

A coincidence, perhaps? I'm not so sure.

I spend hours, days, fantasising about what it would be like to live elsewhere, start over, be someone else. Or to discover the person I was really meant to be, perhaps. But where exactly would I go, I wonder? And who else would I be, anyway?

I've been to enough post-divorce auctions to have heard a thousand stories of women who've decided to leave, to start anew—at my age, sometimes even older. I've heard from and about those women who leave when their children grow up and move out. It's becoming a trend, apparently, for mothers to get that last child through their final exams, to push them out of the nest, and then up and leave. In many cases they take nothing with them—they don't want their share of the car or even the family home, they don't want the furniture, or any of the stuff they've accumulated over the decades of marriage and childrearing. But I wonder, what happens next? Does finding a new lover, moving to a new town, changing jobs, cars, routines, taking up swing dancing, hang-gliding, horseriding—does any of it really make a difference? Or do you wake up every morning still trapped in your own head, carrying your own past, your own bad decisions. Even surrounding yourself with everything new, starting afresh, don't you still just remain yourself?

I had been out for dinner recently with Shaz, my best and oldest friend. Shaz was visiting from Coffs Harbour, staying in a nearby hotel, sorting out her elderly mother's estate after moving her into a home. The night was one of moderate indulgence for two women rapidly approaching (or denying, maybe we were already there) middle age. We drank two bottles of champers over dinner and then headed to a pub across the street. Our conversation was intense, wide-ranging—several years' experiences had been condensed; we indulged in the usual reminiscences as well as the inevitable 'where are they now?'

conversations (*She's doing a Law degree? You've got to be kidding. She was as dumb as dogshit!*). This led to a maudlin conversation on the state of our own lives—whether we'd done what we'd wanted, whether we were happy, whether happiness was even a possibility. Had we been seduced by others' expectations? Duped by our own? Were we prisoners of our own particular moment in history? The younger generation of women seemed to have lives that were so infinitely full of possibility; their choices vastly outnumbering those available to us in those long-ago times, the eighties. Or were all these possibilities paralysing? Confusing? My Jess, for example, wasn't exactly milking all these opportunities, or realising her true potential. As far as I could make out, she was just coasting, though in a thoroughly enjoyable, responsibility-free way.

Shaz, who recently separated from her husband of fifteen years, spent some time agonising over the consequences of that decision. 'I don't really regret it, Janey, but, you know ... To be honest, Derrick's actually not a bad bloke, when you get down to it. He put up with me for all those years, didn't he? And he was always—you know—so keen on me. I think I've just been greedy. Wanting something else. Wanting something more. And what have I got now? A lovely house, a career that's going nowhere, and two teenage sons who treat me like a maid. There's no one to help with the bills, no one to take the bins out, no one to snuggle up to at night. Glorious independence, eh?'

In return I drunkenly blurted out all the doubts I'd been having about shutting down the business, about our impending 'retirement', about the persistent feeling of boredom—the strange weightlessness—that was afflicting me. And then, in what was almost as much a surprise to me as to Shaz, I owned up to a vague feeling of envy for Shaz's newly unpartnered state.

Married years before most of my friends, I had always maintained an unbreachable, mildly defensive, almost pathological loyalty to Rob—even in conversation. Whatever my own true state of mind, I'd never expressed any doubts to my friends, never complained, never whined, about either husband or marriage. I knew this apparent devotion was frequently a source of irritation, and was sometimes the butt of not-so-subtle teasing, but such loyalty had seemed a necessity, a bulwark against the sometimes critical, always sceptical, judgement of my footloose and fancy-free peers during those early years. Now, after years of being annoyed by my close-lipped loyalty, Shaz seemed appalled by my tentative expressions of doubt.

'What do you mean, you're not sure you're happy? You and Rob have always been my great white hope as far as marriage is concerned. You get on so well—you always have. I mean me and Derrick, we were okay, I guess, but we never really—I dunno—*liked* each other in the same way. You two just ... well, you just dig each other, if you know what I mean.'

I knew what she meant—Rob and I *do* get on, we *do* like each other. But.

'The thing is sometimes, lately, I don't know—there's just nothing happening between us.'

'Are you talking about sex? You mean you've been together for more than twenty years, and it's only just now that nothing's happening?' She sounded incredulous.

'No. It's not the sex. It's just. I dunno. Maybe it's because we've spent so much time together. It's like I don't have anything to say, any more. I've sort of run out of energy, or interest or something. I keep wondering, isn't there something more? Maybe there should be more.'

My explanation was incoherent, but it was as much for my own benefit as Shaz's.

'Jesus, Jane. What? What else is there? What the *fuck*—oops, sorry—' she smiled brightly at the clearly fascinated patron at the next table, who hurriedly looked away, 'are you talking about? You can't be having doubts, Jane. Not when you've got what everyone else wants.'

'It's not doubts, exactly. It's just ... I feel ... unsettled. Maybe it's just selling up. It's made me wonder about everything. I mean—what have I been doing for the last thirty years? What if there are other things that I should've done? Or could've done. If you know what I mean.'

The reasoning sounded lame even to me, and the look Shaz gave me verged on disgusted.

'You know, I've always thought you were smarter than the rest of us, Janey. But this just sounds just like classic mid-life crisis bullshit to me. Don't be fooled, sweetie. It's just a—what do you call it?—a mirage. A fantasy. It's no different to what happened to me. I thought something seriously bad was going on in my marriage—told myself Derrick didn't understand me, that he was holding me back, keeping me from being who I really was, all that shit. It'll pass—believe me. What you need is something else to focus on while you feel like this.'

'What do you mean?'

'Don't you think you might just be bored in general? There's a simple solution: get a hobby. Or a new job. Something like that.'

But I don't want a hobby, I thought. *I don't want a new job. That isn't the problem. The problem is bigger than that.*

'You've got the perfect opportunity. To change things, I mean. Just don't do anything … rash. Anything you might regret.'

'Like what?'

'Oh—you know—like having an affair with a younger man. Leaving. That sort of thing. It won't help, you know. You just have to face it.'

'Face what?'

'The fact that you're not young any more. That your youth has passed and you can't get it back. And that that wrinkly old bag you see in the mirror, she really is you.' Shaz emptied her glass in one noisy gulp. 'You know what you could do? You could see a doctor.'

'A doctor? What for?'

'*Botox*, sweetie.'

'Oh, for God's sake.'

Shaz ducked expertly when I threw a paper napkin straight at her head.

'Or maybe you could get some pills. Prozac. Something to lighten things up again.'

'I'm not fucking depressed, Shaz.'

'No?' She raised her eyebrows. 'You sure?'

'I'm sure. Anyway, why would I need pills when there's this?' I picked up the bottle, filling both of our glasses to the brim.

Shaz took a sip, then gave me a funny look. 'Remember when we were kids and I got into all that occult stuff and started giving out free palm readings?'

'Actually, if I remember correctly, they weren't free—you made us cross your palm with silver.'

'That'd be saliva—which of you mean bitches ever had any money?' We laughed like the crones we are, getting another sideward glance from our trying-hard-not-to-look neighbour.

'Anyway, don't you remember me telling you that you were going to be an alcoholic? You were really pissed off. Looks like it's coming true ... You'd better be careful.'

'You also said I was going to marry a film star and live on a Greek island.'

'You got Rob. You live in Curl Curl. Close enough, I'd say. Now, isn't it your shout, you lousy cow?'

The evening ended reasonably sedately, if late, after a cocktail nightcap at some swish wine bar, and with me lurching from the taxi half a block away from home, then tripping on the root of a tree and sprawling headlong onto the footpath. When I recovered from the shock of it, I discovered that I'd twisted my ankle too badly to walk, and had to call Rob to come and retrieve me. It was, to put it mildly, rather humiliating. Happily it was a long weekend, so I wasn't forced to hobble to work—instead I spent the days recovering in bed or on the lounge. They were very reflective days. There were a few things I'd forgotten about our evening out, but I remembered our dinner conversation well enough to ponder what I'd said to Shaz. To consider whether what I'd told her was merely drunken invention or truth, and if truth it was, to consider what I could, what I should, do about it.

A fortnight later, the ankle fully recovered, I indulged in another out-of-character drinking session, this time with my much-younger gym buddy, Fran. Fran works as a solicitor for the Department of Public Prosecutions, she's single, childless—and on the surface our lives are poles apart. Actually, it's not just on the surface. Fran is well travelled, educated, she has no desire for marriage, kids, we move in very different circles. But we've discovered—over coffee—a sort of kindred spiritedness, which is as pleasurable as it is unexpected. Somehow we view the world similarly, though our lives run in parallel grooves. We laugh at the same things, admire or dislike the same people, the same ideas. Unlike mine, which is leisurely at best, boring at worst, Fran's work is gruelling, and she likes to party hard when she gets the chance. Usually our nights out are midweek, and involve a meal and conversation, but this particular week we did something quite different—and for me, quite out of character. I'd begged her to take me to a club, to dance. I hadn't been dancing since I was young—other than the odd wedding—and even then it wasn't something I did regularly; Rob and I have always been more comfortable in pubs than nightclubs. Fran had been surprised, but eventually agreed, had even sacrificed her usual Friday night pursuit of male company (strictly casual) to humour me.

Instead of eating out at our favourite tapas place, we spent the earlier part of the evening having pre-drinks, as the children call them, at Fran's chic harbourside apartment, all leather and chrome and smooth modern surfaces—so different to my own worn chintz and aged timber. We shared gossip about various gym characters—the instructor who's pregnant, but not to her husband, the woman in our pump class who's lifting bizarrely heavy weights and appears to be in preparation for Movember. Thus fortified, we made our way—me in perilously high heels and a cute but slightly too-short borrowed dress that I somehow managed to squeeze into—to a nearby nightclub, the sort that has a block-long queue at the front door—a queue coolly bypassed by my experienced friend. It's the sort of club I didn't go to even when I was young.

Once inside, I gave myself up to the spirit of the place. I didn't much like the music, which I'd ordinarily dismiss as noise, but I made the best of it, attempting to dance in a way that didn't raise too many eyebrows. Trying hard to blend in. I was surprised to find, as the evening wore on, that I was occasionally approached by much younger men, men I would normally call boys, young enough to be my children. Though I knew their enthusiasm was largely due to alcohol-induced blurred vision, I let myself enjoy the experience, dancing and drinking until I could barely stand. I'd resisted any cougar-like foolishness—and there'd only been one close call. Happily, I'd been discovered in a dark corner and rescued by an exasperated Fran.

'No, Jane. This is not a good idea,' she'd said, prising a vodka shot from my fingers and handing it back to the charmingly drunk young man who had been all too happy to provide for a lady in need. 'You should pick up someone your own age, honey,' she'd added sweetly, before taking my arm and dragging me reluctantly away. 'Time to go, I think, Cinderella.'

She'd caught a taxi home with me, had had to get the driver to help me up the front steps, had unlocked the door and led me inside, and parked me—semi-conscious—on the lounge, leaving a sleepy and bewildered Rob to sort out the aftermath.

'Jeez, Jane, what's going on?' Rob had teased me the following afternoon, when I'd finally dragged myself out of bed, every muscle and every organ aching from the previous night's excess. 'Are you trying to relive your misspent youth? Not as much fun now, is it? It takes too long to recover. You'd be better off taking up golf. Or bridge.'

I'd taken the chaffing good-naturedly, laughed along with him as I downed my third Hairy Lemon for the day. But my laughter had a panicky edge. Drinking. Dancing. Boys. What the hell *was* I thinking?

For the first time in years I dream about Angela. It's a happy dream initially. Me and Mick and Angie at the beach. We're at South Curly in my mind, scene of so many childhood memories, but it's a dream landscape—there's no cliff, no lagoon and no end, the sand stretching further than the eye can see. In the dream I'm only young, six or maybe seven, although in that timeless way of dreams, Angie and Mick are the age they were that last summer. We are playing that game that children love, covering one another with sand, shaping it around the entire body, beginning at the feet and working all the way up until only the face is visible. I am the first to be buried, and Mick and Angie work quickly, scooping the sand over me, patting and shaping it until I can't see my prone and captive body, but I know that I'm inside the perfectly sculpted form of a mermaid. Angie collects dripping seaweed and arranges it around my head to make long hair, while Mick finds shells to decorate my elegant tail. Despite the beauty of the sand sculpture, once it's complete, I smash my way out of the increasingly claustrophobic sand sarcophagus. Escape is infinitely satisfying. It's Mick's turn next. Angie and I cover him, spreading his arms wide, carefully manipulating his legs, expertly forming the shape of a surfboard, a wave, beneath him. After Mick demolishes his casing, it's Angie's turn. Mick and I throw sand over her, enthusiastic and indiscriminate, with no design in mind. We don't stop when we reach her head, but keep on heaping sand over her smiling face, over her nose, her eyes, her mouth, piling the sand on and on and on until she's completely covered, until she disappears.

But despite all our work, in the end there's no mound, no Angie—the sand is utterly smooth. Mick and I busy ourselves in the pristine sand, building castles, digging tunnels, our cousin forgotten.

And when the tide comes in, there's nothing to slow the water's progress even momentarily; not a ripple on the smooth surface of the beach, no indication that anything or anyone was ever there.

ERIN: So can you tell me what happened next? After Angie's body was found? I mean in terms of your family. With your parents. Mick. Your aunt and uncle.

JANE: I've been thinking about it—trying to remember. It's hard to describe, but what I remember most is this feeling of being really isolated. And not just from outsiders, but from one another. I was really upset about Angie, but more than that, I was really lonely. And for some reason, I was scared, too. I remember feeling scared, most of all.

ERIN: Scared of what? Scared of the murderer? I guess the whole community was worried.

JANE: They probably were—I mean, I'm sure they were. I remember Mum drove me everywhere for ages—but for some reason the fact that there was a murderer out there, maybe close by, was never really on my mind, although it probably should have been. Maybe I was too young to understand properly. No, I was terrified that everything was going to fall apart. Oh, we all seemed to settle back down to being a perfectly normal family—Mick went back to school, though he left later that year. I started at high school. Dad kept on being a cop.

But everything was crazy. Mum was completely out of it, and Dad was hardly ever there. And whenever they were together they were fighting. I don't remember what about—half the time I'd be sent outside. I was sure they were going to get divorced. Mum was carrying so much guilt, I guess, even though she wouldn't ever admit it. Dad's drinking was out of control and he was just so angry all the time. Something to do with being a cop, I think. He always told us how he'd tried so hard to keep all the bad things away from his own family, but he'd failed—and with Angie he'd failed spectacularly. Because what had happened to her had happened on his watch, more or less.

And then Mick was always in trouble with Dad. I don't know what was going on there—they'd always got on so well, but after Angie died it wasn't the same. It was almost as if Dad hated him—as if they hated one another. And it kept getting worse, the more Mick went off the rails, the more angry Dad would get, and the worse Mick would behave. Sometimes it was frightening. You know—physical. They had a few punch-ups. Poor old Mum—it's hard to imagine now.

ERIN: How did your mother cope?

JANE: She didn't. Not at first, anyway. I think she actually went mad for a while. She basically closed the salon for a couple of months. Didn't do anything at all, really. She was still making dinner for us occasionally, but that was as far as it went. Most of her time was spent in her bedroom, or in front of the television. The only time she ever went out was to go to the doctor, and I think now that that was just to keep up her supply of tranquillisers—Valium or whatever. She was completely doped up. Pop—her dad—would come over every now and then to try to help, but he was pretty hopeless when it came to anything domestic. He could barely boil an egg. I used to do a bit—I'd do the dishes, clean the bathrooms—but it was too much for a twelve-year-old. In the end it got pretty bad—the house was filthy, we never had any clean clothes. Dad threatened to get a cleaner at one point, but Mum wouldn't have it.

And Mum behaved as if nothing had happened. We had to behave as if nothing had happened too. We weren't even allowed to mention Angie's name, to talk about it around her. Looking back, it was completely bonkers. We'd all had counselling—I don't know who arranged that—and I remember that the psychologists had told us quite clearly that discussing what had happened was the healthiest thing. That the only way to lessen the trauma would be to face it. But Mum wouldn't let us. It was absurd, very *Fawlty Towers*—'don't mention the war'. Only it wasn't funny at the time. It wasn't funny at all.

ERIN: If we could just go back a bit. What happened with your aunt and uncle—I guess you saw them at the funeral ...

JANE: It was pretty terrible. We were asked not to come. Uncle Barry rang and told Dad. That's probably what sent Mum right around the twist. Funerals are important, aren't they? A sort of public closure. We went anyway. We came in late and sat right up the back and left early. I can remember Mum dragging us out in the middle of the last hymn, almost running. Everyone would have noticed. Half the community would have been there, just having a squiz—and everyone would have seen that we weren't up the front with the rest of the family. I didn't really understand at the time, and to be honest some of it's a bit of a jumble, but I've pieced it together from what other people have said.

I really don't think we ever saw Barry or Carol again. Mum posted back all the clothes that Angie had left at our place. I kept one of her scarves as a sort of memorial. She'd started wearing those hippy silk scarves that summer—I guess there was some actress or singer or something she liked who wore them ... The one I kept was new; she'd only bought it that week, so Carol wasn't going to miss it. I've still got it.

ERIN: And your brother. He was under suspicion?

JANE: He had the police breathing down his neck for a while. And that put incredible pressure on him, I guess. I wasn't really aware of it at the time—Dad tried hard to protect me from all that—but looking back it must have been terrifying. Mick and Adam Ferber and the other boys who were at the shop had been the last ones to see her. So they were all interviewed. And then they were interviewed again. And the police were always trying to find gaps in their story. They probably went easy on Mick because of Dad, but it was clear that he was a suspect in the beginning.

ERIN: Did the police have any other evidence, or was it just that they were the last to see her?

JANE: I don't think they had *any* evidence, really. There were signs that Angie had had sex. They didn't know if she'd been raped—interfered with, as they used to call it—or if it was consensual. There was evidence that she'd had intercourse sometime in the days before her death, but they couldn't tell exactly when. No DNA tests back then.

Dad got a solicitor in the end, but in the beginning it was pretty nasty. They'd call Mick down to the station, and turn up at odd hours to ask questions. But there was no way it could have been him. He and Adam had been together all afternoon. And it couldn't have been any of the other boys either. Angie's body was found miles away—at the bottom of a gully in some bushland near Palm Beach. They didn't think that was where she'd been killed—there was evidence that her body had been moved. But none of them had cars and I don't think any of them were old enough to have a licence at that stage. So there was no way any of them could've dumped her body. But the cops kept on hassling them anyway. There were older brothers, older friends with cars, so I guess there was always that possibility.

ERIN: And what about people you knew, locals? Were they suspicious of Mick?

JANE: Look—I'm pretty sure they were, they must have been, but I was probably too young to notice. We had the press camped on our doorway for a few days, they kept hovering for weeks, and Dad had warned us not to say anything at all to anyone— just in case. But I don't remember anyone I knew asking about Mick particularly, or saying anything nasty. I remember people saying how terrible for Mum—how bad she must feel—and I remember people saying some pretty off things about Angie— but no one really said anything to me about Mick.

ERIN: And then the other girl was found ...

JANE: Yeah. That changed everything. It was the same—what do they call it?—the same modus operandi. There were certain differences, she was older, she'd taken heroin, but the scarf thing was conclusive.

ERIN: And how did that change things for your family?

JANE: Well, I suppose it brought it all back again for a little while. It had died down before that—people forget so quickly—but then it was huge, all the Sydney Strangler business, in the press, and suddenly everyone was talking about Angie again. But it also meant that Mick—that all the boys—weren't under suspicion any more. The police established pretty quickly that none of them had been anywhere near the Cross—so that ruled them out for Angie's killing as well.

ERIN: It must have been a huge relief.

JANE: It really was. After that, somehow things really did seem to get back to normal. Or sort of normal, anyway. That seems terrible, I suppose. I mean, it didn't bring Angie back, but when that other little girl was murdered everything got better for us. When she died it meant we could get on with our lives.

CURL CURL, JULY 1978

After Angie's death Jane spends much of her time at home sitting in front of the television, sometimes entire days are spent immobilised on the lounge, moving only to change the channel or find food.

Once upon a time, before this, before Angie, Jane would have been out all afternoon, roaming the streets, visiting friends, but now she avoids leaving the house. Back then she was just one anonymous kid on the street, doing what kids do, but now it seems that everybody knows her. And everyone wants to talk to her, to ask her questions she really doesn't want to answer.

So most afternoons she stays home, though there's no one to talk to and nothing to do. Even when her mother's not in her bedroom, she's vague, listless, can't be engaged. Mick, who would once have provided some sort of companionship in the afternoons, is either absent or locked in his room doing God knows what. The house is always cold, the pantry always empty. The television shows are boring—too young for her in the early afternoon, and then too old and dull once the news begins. It's okay when her dad is home; he can be relied upon for some conversation, at least, or a trip to the shops. Occasionally, if he's home before dark he'll even take her over to the Abbott Road tennis courts for a hit.

Sometimes, when the loneliness of home is too much to bear, Jane walks straight from school to Pop's shop. He's never anything less than glad to see her. However busy with customers, he will always poke his head around the door to the office, his cigarette dangling, his wrinkled face breaking into a snaggle-toothed grin, and ask her to *make him a cuppa, there's a good girl.* She might need to buy herself some milk, and a packet of bickies too, if she's hungry. There's five dollars in the money tin—she can spend the change on herself if she likes. And Jane's happy to wander up to the Greek cafe on Pittwater Road and get a pack of Milk Arrowroot or Scotch Finger biscuits and then boil up the ancient porcelain kettle with water from the bathroom handbasin, being careful not to scald herself when she pours. Her grandfather likes his tea black with two sugars, served in an old enamel mug that Jane suspects he never washes. She usually brings back a carton of chocolate milk for herself—not trusting the stained cups on offer—as well as the biscuits.

Once the tea is made, Jane helps her grandfather with odd jobs, rearranging various items, dusting, answering the phone and occasionally minding the shop while Pop ducks out to do this or that, sometimes to give Rob, who has just started working for him full-time, a hand with a heavy delivery. On quiet days, Jane likes to sit in the office on the tatty vinyl recliner that her grandfather keeps in the corner, angled to capture a slice of afternoon sun. She half listens to the slightly fuzzy talkback radio programs her pop keeps the radio tuned to—she's forbidden to move it from 2UE—and flicks through some of Pop's funny old books. Victorian novels with fabric covers, gilt-edged pages, and heroines who find God and a husband simultaneously, or *Reader's Digest* condensed versions of classics, the odd Mills and Boon. At the end of the day Pop will usually drive her home in his ancient green ute, but occasionally he gets Rob to drop her off on the way to a job, and she gets a bumpy ride home in the van. Jane likes Rob; he's dark and tall and good-looking and quietly kind. And he's distant enough in age for her to develop a pleasurably hopeless crush on him.

This particular afternoon her grandfather closes the shop and drops her home earlier than usual, the lure of a deceased estate in Palm Beach outweighing the chance of any late Friday afternoon custom.

He doesn't come in, just sends his love, and tells her to be a good girl and help her mum, before driving off without a backwards glance.

Jane fills the sink, is ready to attack the huge stack of dishes that teeters precariously on the bench, when she hears her father's familiar footfall on the front verandah. She pulls off her rubber gloves, rushing to open the door before he can use his key—it's a race that would usually provoke some light-hearted tussling, but today he is clearly not in the mood, today he is upright and official in his uniform (unusual in itself), he's wearing his gun-belt, and presumably his gun, his nightstick jutting awkwardly from his hip, hat under his arm. She can tell straight off that he has some news—and she's sure it must be bad—he has a grim look to him, his shoulders are slumped, his eyes look baggy and tired. He doesn't comment on her super-speedy opening of the door at all, just steps through the doorway, gives her hair an absent-minded tousle.

'Why are you in uniform, Daddy? What's wrong?'

He looks at her properly then, takes a breath, attempts a smile. 'It's been a big day, kiddo. I'm just a bit under the weather. I could do with a beer. Reckon you could go and pour me one?' Pouring her father's beer is Jane's new job—one she enjoys and one she's becoming quite proficient at. Her father used to go to the pub with his workmates after knock off and sometimes on the weekends, but now he rarely drinks with his mates. Instead he settles down alone in the kitchen or the lounge room every afternoon, drinking first beer and then whisky, until long after Jane has gone to bed. When he drinks he starts out cheerful enough, but then descends into a brooding silence, and sometimes becomes a frighteningly dark presence, volatile and sometimes vicious.

He walks into the kitchen, takes a long slug from the glass of beer that she's poured so carefully.

'Where's your mother?' He hasn't even noticed the perfect proportion of foam to amber.

'She's in the shed. Doing Mrs O'Lachlan.' Mrs O'Lachlan, an elderly neighbour who still turns up every Wednesday for a set and rinse, regardless of her mother's excuses, is a notorious chatterbox and finder of last-minute imperfections. Her mother won't be back inside for an hour at least.

'Mick in his room?'

'I guess so.'

Her father heads down the hall, glass of beer still in his hand, he taps on the door, rattles the doorknob. 'Open the door, mate.'

She can't hear Mick's reply, but the door is unlocked, and her father goes in, pushes it shut. She waits to hear the click of the lock in the keyhole, then tiptoes up the hall, presses her ear against the door, heart pounding. She can hear only isolated words, her father's voice mostly, deep and calm, reassuring; her brother's—higher, tinged with anxiety—less frequent.

She gives up, and moves back to the kitchen, busies herself washing the dishes, as she waits for her father.

They emerge together. Her father goes straight to the fridge and pulls out two cans of KB, throws one to Mick. 'Here y' go, son.'

Her brother's eyes are red, as if he has been crying, but he gives Jane a small smile.

'What're you doing, Jane, washing up? Mum'll think you've gone mad.'

Her father tousles her hair again. 'D'you think you could go get your mum, love? I can't face that old O'Lachlan bat; she'll start going on at me about the Dunstan kid's music again. Just tell Mum I need her for a moment. Tell her I've got some news.'

Jane rushes out to the shed, interrupting Mrs McLachlan, who has embarked on some longwinded complaint. 'You've got to come in now. Dad says it's urgent.'

'Oh, God, what does he want?' Her mother gives an irritated sigh, apologises to a curious Mrs O'Lachlan, and reluctantly follows her daughter back to the house.

'Why are you wearing your uniform, Doug? What's hap-pened?' Her mother's irritation has changed to thinly disguised panic.

She sees Mick leaning against the bench, drinking beer, and her eyes widen, sensing the unusually relaxed atmosphere. 'What's going on?'

'There's been another one found, love.'

'Another one what?' Her mother's face pales, she grips the side of the bench.

'Another girl.'

'What do you mean? Another girl?'

'A young lass was found in the Cross this morning. Murdered. She was strangled with her scarf. Same perpetrator. No doubt about it.' Her father's face is stony and he doesn't blink when he speaks.

'Good grief. Oh, that's—oh, the poor thing.' As her mother sinks down onto one of the kitchen chairs, Jane feels her own legs weaken, her stomach lurch.

'Who was she—the girl? Oh, God, it's—,' her mother covers her eyes momentarily, stifles a sob.

'She was just a ...' he hesitates, looking over at Jane, '... homeless girl. They haven't established her identity yet. There'll be photos put out, I suppose. She was found in an old warehouse. Been dead a few days.'

'Dear God. Her poor parents. The poor child.' Her mother shakes her head. 'But I still don't understand. Why are you back so early? I thought you were on till late tonight.'

'I was at a meeting in town when the news came in. Carruthers told me to go straight home. They're putting me on leave for a while—during the initial investigation, anyway. I'm too close—they don't want me near it.'

'You didn't find her, did you, Daddy?'

'No, it was nothing like that, sweetheart. It's just—she was found close to the city. Our detectives will be investigating. And I can't be involved because of Angie.'

'And how does this affect Michael, Doug? This changes things, doesn't it?' Her mother is looking at her father, pleading.

'It changes everything.' Her father moves across the room to her mother, claps his hand on her shoulder. His voice seems suddenly light, hopeful, though his expression remains grim. 'He's in the clear.' He looks over at his son. 'Completely in the clear.'

Killer at large:
Murdered teen second victim of Strangler

A police spokesman has today confirmed that the recent murder of teenage prostitute Kelly McIvor is almost certainly the work of the same person who murdered Angela Buchanan earlier this year. In a chilling reprisal of Buchanan's murder, McIvor, who was found dead in a Kings Cross warehouse last Friday, had been strangled with her own scarf. While police are unwilling to elaborate on any other links between the two killings, they are satisfied that the same person or persons are responsible for the two murders.

McIvor, known to Kings Cross locals as 'Little Kell', was a heroin addict, a tragic member of what the Rev. Daniel Davies of Reach Out claims is part of a 'growing army of hopeless and homeless' in our major cities. Kelly, formerly of Dennington, Western NSW, was reported missing last November, after running away from home.

Although police say they have no evidence that the murderer of the Sydney teens, already nicknamed the Sydney Strangler, is likely to strike again, they have issued a general warning to girls and young women.

'While we don't want to create a panic, we're advising young women to exercise caution. Stay with a group, make sure your friends and family always know where you are. Just be sensible.'

Police are investigating numerous leads. Anyone with information relating to either murder is urged to contact Detective Sergeant Raymond Shepherd, NSW Homicide squad, 277 730.

ERIN

Erin Fury. It sounds so ordinary, but this time the name is significant. Her preferences have changed over the years: Kathy was discarded long ago and she'd be hard-pressed to recall all the others. At first she'd gone for the glamorous, the exotic—Cassandra, Juanita, Evangeline—but lately she'd tended towards the more conventional—Sophia, Anna, Isabel. Erin is an oddly genderless name, innocuous enough, compact and with a certain Irish lilt that she likes. It's also eminently forgettable—Erins aren't a dime a dozen exactly, but they're common enough. And Fury, that has an Irish feel too. Wasn't there some Irish folk band back in the eighties? She remembered her mother playing some song over and over in the years after Kelly died, remembers her warbling along with the record. *When you were sweet sixteen* ... There was some story attached, some bullshit romantic story of her mother and father's early relationship, their 'courting' days, as her mother euphemistically referred to them. After the warble, her mother would inevitably start crying.

So, the name is plausible. It would never occur to anyone that the name was a tautology, no one would see the connection between the first and second: Erinyes. The Furies. No one would ever read anything into her name, full stop. Still, it gave her a certain degree of satisfaction that a name that was chosen for her so long ago has a link to these mythical creatures. She was meant to be one of them: an instrument of truth, of justice. And perhaps, if it's necessary, of retribution.

Even she was unsure, initially, why she'd come back, what she'd come back *for*. Her return was spontaneous: one afternoon she'd simply walked out of Paddington station into a typical

London day—the sky low, the drizzle incessant, the misery palpable—and felt an urge, irresistible as it turned out, to be properly warm again, to see that vast blue dome above her, to discard the coats, umbrellas, the air of grim perseverance. To go home.

As always there was nothing much stopping her from moving on. In London, her flat came furnished, her own belongings were minimal and easily discarded, her job was eminently resignable. She had no real friends—oh, there were some work colleagues she drank with occasionally, a neighbour who waved hello. But there was no need for protracted farewells, no promises to stay in touch, no reassurances of her eventual return. No one would miss her.

No one had missed her here, either. No familial ties, and no physical home to return to; for Erin, home is something that belongs to the past, a fantasy. But the moment the plane touched down, she was filled with an almost immediate sense of security, of knowing this world and the way to be in it, a sense of relief that even the long wait at customs, the taxi queue, the uncertainty of her future (so what's new?) couldn't eradicate.

It was only when she asked the taxi driver to take her straight to Kings Cross and had him drop her outside a hotel on Bayswater Road that Erin understood: she was going to do something she should have done years ago. She just hoped that something good might come of it, some questions might be answered, that there would be some sort of resolution, for herself if not for her sister.

She'd never actually been to the Cross before. An absurd thought, considering something like ten years of her life—a previous life—had been spent in this city, and not so many miles away. But she'd managed to avoid it, though she'd been to other red-light districts, lived in them and played in them, in cities all over the world. Somehow it had been possible in those other alien cities to enjoy what was on offer, but there could never be any pleasure for her here, she'd always known that. It could only be a place of darkness and despair. And of almost unbearable wondering.

But now, the wondering had become the focus, urgent, inescapable. The wondering was why she'd come.

She booked a room, took her luggage up, showered, lay down and tried to sleep. But despite her exhaustion, the inevitable jetlag, she was keyed up, restless. She dressed and headed back out into the mid-morning sunshine, decided to begin her sightseeing sooner rather than later. Her sightseeing was not like that of other tourists—all the locations she wanted to visit were highly specific, circumscribed by what she knew about her sister's brief time here, her sister's death. And that's limited too—she knew nothing beyond the little she remembered, augmented by what she'd been able to glean from the papers. At the time, her mother had asked very few questions of the police, had kept the details to the bare minimum, seeing little sense in fanning the flames of her own pain.

All Erin had was an address, a few locations, a couple of names. She spent the rest of the day tramping the streets, visiting the places that until that moment had been nothing more than that—names. She walked along the strip of road that Kelly was said to have worked. During the day the street was just a thoroughfare, busy with traffic, thronged by pedestrians. There was nobody loitering here, no one waiting to be picked up. At this time of day everyone—from adolescents in hoodies to suit-clad professionals—was walking purposefully, heading somewhere.

The street where Kelly died was no longer a dirty, derelict back alley—a place where drunks went to piss, junkies to shoot up—but a respectable residential street, with potted topiaries and well-tended window boxes, and the warehouse had been converted into a complex of funky townhouses. It took her an age to get directions, but the Reverend Davies' shelter had been replaced by a gym, and according to the friendly—and long-time local—manager, the reverend himself was dead, posthumous accusations of child abuse dimming his once-burnished halo.

There was no longer any trace of her sister, no evidence that she ever existed. There were no answers here.

It was late afternoon when she arrived at the police station in her final bid for information. She asked the constable at the front desk if there was anyone around she could talk to about the old Sydney Strangler case; provided the date, the names of the officers involved. He directed her to a screwed-down vinyl chair in a brightly lit corner, told her he'd make some calls. While she waited, she flicked through an old police journal that had been left amongst a pile of women's magazines. It was an industry journal, obviously not meant for the general public, the stories alternating between the utterly gruesome and the unutterably dull. One article, detailing the successful use of DNA in a robbery investigation, captured her attention. It was surprisingly interesting—the writer had a talent for storytelling, the narrative was vivid, coherent, full of fascinating facts and the occasional witticism. She flicked to the end, curious about the author: Detective Sergeant Michael Griffin of North Sydney LAC. He was an attractive man in his mid-forties, his head shaved, jaw square, mouth firm. Even from the photo it was clear that his eyes were his best feature, they were unusual eyes for a man, heavily lashed, wide set, smiling, a luminous amber colour. And they were eyes that were immediately familiar—seen once, long ago, in another man's face, but never forgotten. *Lion eyes.*

At her mother's request it is just the simplest of funeral services: there are no hymns, no eulogies. Instead there are the one-size-fits-all expressions of love and sadness, along with the unavoidable platitudes about God's infinite plan, the false promises of hope, of resurrection, of eternal life.

The man keeps his distance, but Kathy notices him. There are so few people that it's impossible for him to blend in, or remain invisible, though he's trying his best, she can tell. There's something odd going on with him, the way he hangs back, the way he stays seated after the too-short service, observing, but not making contact with anyone, the weird way he keeps his sunglasses on even inside the church. Most of the other adults, the ones who know them—the school Principal, a few primary school teachers, a couple of parents, her mother's bosses, old friends—and even a few who don't, wait to pay their respects as they exit, though it's clear that it's painful for everyone involved. They all do their best to offer something, even if it is just a significantly lingering clasp of the hand.

There are others who make no effort to offer their condolences. There are the gawkers—locals who've come to satisfy their curiosity, or to be seen. And there's the press—the man from the local newspaper, who'd been at their door the moment the news had come through, and the Sydney journalists too, with their feigned sadness—all itching to get a shot or a story. They don't come too near, keep a respectful distance, but they can't keep their eyes off the two of them, they're waiting like hyenas for a breakdown, tears, some out of control emotional outburst that they can write about for their drama-hungry readers.

But this man is neither gawker nor press, she's certain of that. He's sitting alone in a pew at the back of the chapel, as if waiting for them to leave. He is a tall man, straight-backed, his shoulders broad and powerful beneath his dark suit.

She only gets a glimpse of his eyes by chance, when he takes his sunglasses off for a moment, and swipes his hand across his face as if brushing away a headache, pain. They are distinctive, what she thinks of as lion eyes: an almost translucent yellow colour, so heavily fringed that they appear oddly feminine in a face that is otherwise all masculine hard edges. They're eyes unlike any she's seen before, eyes she'll remember forever. When he looks up he meets her curious gaze almost unwillingly—and quickly looks away again.

Later, when she asks who he was, her mother shrugs, says she didn't notice him, hasn't got a clue, he's probably just another slimebag from the press. But Kathy doesn't think so, there was something that made him different—something to do with his solitariness, his upright stance. Something in those eyes.

It was only a fleeting moment, but the memory of that intense gaze has stayed with her all these years, even when the memory of so many things she'd imagined would be unforgettable—her sister's face, her mother's, the sound of their voices, their touch—seems to have dissolved, to have evaporated.

Lion eyes.

She was still staring down at the picture when the young officer called her over, explained with an apologetic shrug that the two detectives she was looking for were both long gone—one retired, moved to Queensland, the other dead. He'd asked around, but there was no one else who was around at the time—no one left who remembered the case.

She left the hotel phone number—just in case—and asked if he'd mind if she took the journal with her—she'd started reading one of the stories, and was finding it particularly interesting, would really like to read to the end, she explained with her best good-citizen smile. Distracted by the noisy entrance of several outraged teenage girls, he waved her away. *Sure, whatever.* She rolled up the magazine, zipped it into her bag.

She doesn't really believe in coincidences, but this was a sign—perhaps the sign she'd been waiting for.

The connection excited her, once she'd worked it out—though working it out hadn't been all that difficult—googling the author of that journal article had brought up numerous references to that long-ago crime. The surname should have been familiar to her but for some reason she'd never thought much about that other family, she'd had no time to consider any story but her own. But now she wondered—perhaps there was something they could tell her—perhaps there was some connection between the two deaths that no one else had discovered. Perhaps someone knew something vital, something they didn't even know they knew. It was clear that she was at a dead-end: there were no traces of her sister here or anywhere, it was as if Kelly had marked her route with breadcrumbs. But this other girl, the first victim, Angie, she had had family and friends; her path would be better marked, might still be visible, might even lead Erin to the truth. Why not? After all, she had nowhere else to go, nothing better to do.

Finding them had been easy and connecting with them simpler than she'd ever imagined. It surprised her a little that they hadn't moved away in all those years, that they'd all stayed put—the same suburb, the parents still living in the same house, for Christ's sake. Her instinct was to move on as soon as things got hard—and lately, even before, in anticipation. It was something she'd inherited from her father, she supposed, this inability to settle, to stick, to see things through. An incapacity to even see the point. *Why would you?* They reckon there's no escaping yourself. But she's not sure that's true. There are means of escape, if you look hard enough, ways to become someone else.

But this family, who were living the lives they'd been given rather than lives they'd been forced to choose, who appeared to desire nothing beyond their own limited realities—it was incredibly simple to discover not only their whereabouts, but so much else about them: their interests; hobbies; schools; workplaces; their connections, friends and family; the concerts and shows they were likely to attend; the cafes they frequent. How she'd enjoyed setting up this roundabout route—making it seem entirely random, serendipitous, rather than a carefully planned campaign. Something about it appealed to her sense of intrigue. In another life (and she's had a few, so why not?) she would have liked to have been a spy, working deep, deep undercover, rarely rising to the surface. There'd never be any anxiety about her getting lost in the alternative manufactured life, of becoming contaminated, getting too involved. That would never—could never—happen to her.

It was a stroke of luck, really—her decades-old media training, the years she'd spent working in the field. She'd never imagined it would provide such a perfect cover. But when she'd discovered via Facebook (oh, the young, and their irrepressible urge to overshare) that the youngest member of the family, Jess, was at the local TAFE studying media production, immediately her brain had started whirring, churning through the possibilities. Obviously, she had looked for the cousins first, Michael and Jane—such storybook names—but neither of them had much of an online profile. Jane had a Facebook account, rarely used, and Erin had tracked her to the business, a family business, Brookvale Furniture, which her grandfather had founded sometime in the fifties. A family business—imagine that! It was like something out of a novel. Erin's knowledge of antiques, of any furniture, is limited. She has no house, nothing to buy or sell, and doubts she could feign interest, let alone passion, so there was no way that avenue was going to provide any sort of access to the family.

Michael, author of the serendipitous article, proved to be a dead-end, too. A call to his former station revealed that he was on leave, but it was impossible to find out anything else about him. Despite her best efforts, there was no possibility of anyone giving her his phone number or email address and he had no Facebook, no Twitter, no online presence at all.

But Jane's daughter, Jessica—now, she was a find. It had been a simple matter for Erin to offer up her services to the media unit at the TAFE, to let them know that she'd be happy to give a talk on her industry experience to the students—and they'd accepted without too many questions. Her media credentials are solid enough, she'd used her real CV—she'd worked in a number of regional radio stations, then for 2UE for a few years in the late nineties, and had been associate producer of several English-language programs in Germany, had been on the production team of several New Zealand radio documentaries. She was pretty confident that the TAFE would jump at the offer, that no one would bother to check her name. Though it would be easy enough to explain if they asked any questions. But she was offering a free-of-charge lecture—why would they?

This labyrinthine approach appealed to her sense of mystery as much as her by-now instinctive need to cover her tracks, to keep her real self distant, untouchable, invisible even. Of course, she had a back-up plan, was prepared to contact the family on some other pretext if this particular lure didn't work. And if the connection was ever made, it might look like the weirdest type of synchronicity, but no more than that. Just the universe making another of its perpetual jokes ...

The class had gone smoothly—Erin knew more than enough to fill the hour lecture, to make it interesting and informative, and the girl had been there. Erin had recognised Jess from her Facebook photos, though her hair was an unexpected shade of tangerine. Erin had given her spiel, answered the expected questions, and had waited until the end to make her invitation (which she'd made sure to discuss beforehand with the tutor). She'd explained that she was making a radio documentary, that she was hoping to interview the families of murder victims, to discuss the long-term and ongoing effects of losing loved ones in such a terrible way.

'I really hope,' she'd added earnestly, 'that no one here has ever had any such experience—and statistically it's highly unlikely—but if you have, or if you know of anyone who has, and who would be willing to talk to me, you can see me after class, or if you need to think about it, you can get in touch later. Your wonderful tutor, Cilla, has all my contact details.'

But Jess hadn't hesitated—apparently she hadn't felt the need to consult first, there'd been no hanging back, no umming or aahing, she'd been quite casual about it—a little too eager, even. The girl came straight over to her at the end of the class.

She was small, and (notwithstanding the tangerine) naturally dark-haired and dark-complexioned with black brows that beetled over startlingly big brown eyes, and a tangle of lashes. She was dressed in regulation student apparel, the sort of thing that Erin had never worn. Skinny jeans, a too tight T-shirt, Converse gym boots. She had a tattoo around one wrist—some sort of Aztec pattern—and Erin could just glimpse the edge of another on her upper arm, peeking under the edge of her sleeve.

She was pretty and friendly and brimful of confidence—the type of girl Erin had felt intimidated by when she was her age, the type of girl who had everything Erin didn't: family, love, security, a pain-free past and a future where the possibilities loomed larger than the threats.

'Hey.' The girl gave her a toothy smile, the result of thousands of dollars of orthodontia, no doubt. 'You mentioned your documentary—that you're looking for subjects ...?'

Erin raised her eyebrows slightly, encouraging but not overly eager. 'Do you know someone?' She made sure there was the faintest trace of scepticism in her voice.

'Well, yeah. I do. Actually it's my family. I mean—I'm not one hundred per cent sure that they'll want to talk, but there was a ...' She paused, as if suddenly aware of the silence in the classroom, the few lingering students pricking up their ears.

'Why don't we meet in, say, half an hour?' Erin gave her best teacherly smile. 'Is there a college cafe?'

The girl's relief was obvious. 'Oh, no, we can't go there, the coffee's horrendous. You wouldn't want to give it to your grandmother. Though come to think of it, I'd probably give it to mine. But just across the road, at The Pitt Stop, they've got the best coffee.' She flashed her million-dollar grin again. 'See you there then, half an hour.'

The girl was completely unsuspicious. When Erin asked her about her family tragedy, as she put it, Jess didn't hesitate, speaking frankly and unsentimentally as she chomped her way through a pile of chips.

'Well, it wasn't really my tragedy. It all happened way before I was born, in the seventies. It was my mum's cousin, Angie, she was only fourteen or fifteen. She disappeared on her way to the shops and they found her body a few weeks later. She'd been strangled—and maybe raped.'

'So, you're not offering to talk to me, then?'

'Nah. But my mum might. Angie was staying with her when it happened, and Mum and her brother were really close to her.

You might be able to talk to Uncle Mick too. And Grandma.' She sounded slightly less certain.

'What about the girl's immediate family? Her parents? Her sisters and brothers?'

'That's the thing—her immediate family are all dead. She was an only child and then her dad had a heart attack about five years after the murder, and I think her mum got cancer not long after.'

'Do you really think your mum would want to talk to me? It wouldn't be too painful?' Erin tried to sound both doubtful and concerned.

The girl slurped on her double-chocolate fudge smoothie. 'Well, it's worth a try, I reckon. In fact, it'd probably do everyone good to discuss it. It's one of those family things that, you know, it's not a secret or anything, but no one really talks about it. Granny hates anyone mentioning Angie at all. Anyway, I think Mum might do it.'

'What about your uncle?'

'Yeah. I dunno about him. He was crazy about Angie, apparently. And he's a bit, well, he's kinda unpredictable. He's been sick. He's just split up with his wife and moved back in with Gran.'

'So how do you think I should approach them? Should I get you to give them my number ... see how they feel about it?'

'Oh, Mum'll never call you, she's slack that way. Look, she'll probably get the shits with me, but how about I give you her number? I'll mention it to her, say you're going to call. Or maybe you could call in at the shop or something? I'll give you the address. She'll be less likely to say no if it's all sort of spontaneous.' She scribbled down some numbers and an address on a scrap of paper, handed it across the table. 'So is this just for radio?'

'I guess there are other possibilities, but yeah, for now it's just radio.'

'I mean, she wouldn't do telly—I totally know that. But radio shouldn't freak her out too much.' She paused, thinking. 'And I can tell Uncle Mick, too, if you like. I'll give him your number—he really would kill me if I gave you his. But you never know, he might talk to you. And I reckon he'd have an interesting take.'

'What about your grandparents? I'd like to get as many family members involved as possible.'

'Gramps would have been the one to talk to—he was a cop, so he knew everything that was going on. And there are probably things he knows that no one else does ... stuff about the investigation. But it's too late. He's got some dementia thingy going on. Actually, it's really weird what's happened. Twelve months ago he was fine, he was this really fit old bloke—going to the gym, doing laps down at the beach pool—but then he started saying his sight was going, it was like he was blind, and then he stopped talking, and now he can't communicate at all. The doctors can't explain it—he's got nothing physically wrong with him, not that they can find, anyway. He just sits in his chair and does nothing all day. It's like he's a vegetable. Poor old bugger. It's totally fucked. He'd hate to see himself, now. I hate to see him now.'

Erin loaded her voice with concern. 'Is he still living at home? That must be a lot of work for your family.'

'Nah. He's in a home—they just moved him in recently.' The girl supplied the information without prompting. 'You hear so many horror stories about these places, but it's pretty nice, really. It's right on the beach in Mona Vale. I don't know if you've ever seen it—RestView? And his room has an incredible view. Not that he would know.' She gave a resigned shrug, took a final noisy slurp.

Erin allowed a respectful pause. Then: 'And what about your grandmother? Would she be willing to talk to me?'

'Granny? I dunno. Gran really doesn't like to dwell on ... the past. Nor does Mum, really. But Gran's worse. Mum says Gran was completely devastated when it happened. Had some kind of breakdown. It was the guilt, I guess. I mean, she was responsible for Angie; she was staying there. And Carol—Angie's mother—never ever forgave her. Anyway, now she refuses to discuss it. The couple of times I've asked her about it she's said it should be forgotten.'

'So, there's definitely no point asking her?'

'Well …' the girl waved her hand vaguely. 'Look, maybe she would. I can't really say. It's hard to tell with Gran. Maybe you could ask Mum when you see her. I can pass on your number too, if you like. Do you have a card or something?'

'I'd appreciate that.' Erin passed her one of the business cards she'd had made.

'Fury Productions—cool name.'

'I'm really grateful for this, Jess. It's not that easy to connect with people who've been through this sort of thing. It's generally not something people advertise. And they don't necessarily want to talk.'

'Actually, there was some other girl who was murdered, too. It was like this serial killing thing. The Sydney Strangler. It was a big deal at the time. Mad scary shit. Mum's got these cuttings hidden away. Both of the girls were strangled in the same way, but other than that it was totally random. The other girl was from somewhere else and they found her body in the Cross, I think. And there wasn't any connection between the two of them—they didn't know each other or anything. The other girl was some sort of street kid, or maybe there weren't street kids back then? A junkie maybe? A prostitute? I don't know her name or anything, but I'm sure you could find out. You could contact her family, too, couldn't you? Maybe they'd be happy to talk about it. But I guess, that sort of girl … maybe she didn't have anyone who cared, anyway.'

Erin kept her voice even, her expression blank. 'Yeah. Good idea. I'll do some research, check into it.'

'Anyway, I gotta go. We've got a screenwriting class next. My favourite. I'm doing this thing about a girl who gets sent to boarding school and goes through a portal in time and finds herself in Ancient Greece—or maybe Egypt—I haven't decided yet. With all this family history I should probably write a bloody crime series.' Jess rummaged in her bag, pulled out some cash, but Erin waved it away.

'My shout.'

The younger woman didn't argue, shoved the notes back into her handbag before Erin changed her mind.

'Oh—and if you want to google the case, I'm sure you'll find out more. There are all sorts of wackos out there running true crime blogs. Mum's cousin's name was Angela Buchanan, Angie. And I think it was 1978.'

Erin smiled and thanked her for the details, though it was information she wouldn't need. She already knew all the important names. All the dates. They weren't something she was ever likely to forget.

Erin rents a serviced studio apartment in Manly. It suits her perfectly: bland and anonymous, with no stickybeak neighbours, her only connection a brisk young property manager who couldn't care less whether she is alive or dead, as long as she pays her rent on time. It's close enough to the family to keep travel to a minimum, but not so close that she's likely to meet up with them unexpectedly. It's not cheap, but then she doesn't intend to be here for long. A month, two months at most; surely if there's anything to find, she'll have found it by then.

Getting a job at the nursing home had been a breeze, too. They're so desperate for reliable workers that women of a certain age are welcomed with open arms and very few questions. She didn't have to forge references or qualifications; unqualified was fine. They'd phoned her only two hours after she'd dropped off her résumé, on which she had made it clear that she was willing and available to work the afternoon or evening shifts, more specifically, the shifts after visiting hours.

'Can you start tomorrow?' she was asked. She could. The pay surprised her—it's better than she imagined, more than she's been paid for her time in quite a while. Not that the money's any sort of consideration, really.

'It's not work that you need training for so much as work you need a *feeling* for,' the nurse who'd been in charge of her induction had enthused. 'You're not a nurse so much as a companion. A carer. Of course, there's always the occasional accident, and you may have to change someone, clean them up, but in the main, if you're doing the afternoon or night shifts you'll just be responsible for checking that they're fed their supper, toileted, medicated and put to bed, that they're safe and comfortable, that they're sleeping okay. Not a lot happens overnight—oh, there's the occasional patient who passes on. People do tend to pop off in the wee hours.

'We pride ourselves on engaging with our residents as humanely as possible here at RestView—treating them with dignity, being empathetic to their situation. So if you've got the time, and usually you will—we don't skimp on staff here, unlike some other places—you can read to them, tell them stories, sing to them. Just provide some sort of adult stimulation. Something to help them feel that they're still connected to the world, that their lives have meaning, purpose. Now, it may feel odd at first, so many of the poor dears can't speak, let alone hold any sort of conversation, and there are a few who can be a bit aggressive, but you'll find that you'll be able to establish a good relationship with most of them. Some of them tend to flit in and out of consciousness: they might be catatonic one day and you might get the story of their life the next. You'll be surprised by what you learn. They're worth listening to—some of our old folk have led very interesting lives.'

The stories of interesting lives. She'll be listening. That's why she's here.

Her interviews with Jess's mum, the sister, Jane, had gone surprisingly well. She had been willing, had volunteered more information, and more readily, than Erin had expected. But Erin had been disappointed, too. The woman's memories were those of the young girl she'd been. What she knew about the day of her cousin's disappearance, the circumstances leading to it, had been interesting, but nothing more. There was nothing that contradicted the story that was in the newspapers, no gaps or inconsistencies. And she wasn't hiding anything, that much was clear.

Erin figures that the further she spreads her net, the more likely she is to succeed, the more likely she is to find that *something*—a picture that doesn't fit, information that doesn't add up. She'd rung Jess only hours after she'd spoken to her mother and talked her into handing over her uncle's mobile number.

'Look,' she'd reassured Jess, 'I'll just leave a message. My phone number. If he doesn't want to get back to me, he won't. And if he does, it's all good.'

The girl had interrupted, surprisingly anxious.

'Yeah, but you do know about his condition? He's got PTSD, which means he's kinda mental. We all have to be extra careful not to upset him. Even little things can set him off. And he drinks.'

'It's okay,' she'd made her voice as soothingly professional as she could, 'I've actually done a bit of counselling, in a former life. I know what not to say.'

The thing is, she doesn't; all her carefully wrought professionalism seems to crumble into a heap when she actually speaks to him. She'd prepared a simple phone message, rehearsed it—as always she leaves as little as possible to chance—*Hi, this is Erin Fury of Fury Productions. I'm making a documentary ... blah blah blah.* But his voice message—a short and simple *Hey. Sorry I can't talk. Leave a message*—spoken in a voice that's low and deep and smooth and sort of humming, disarms her, and the message she leaves is fragmented, not quite coherent. It happens again when he calls her back. She's surprised by his gently polite response—had prepared for battle, for some heavy persuasion at the very least—and his keenness to meet her without further ado confounds her. He's not convinced, he tells her, that these interviews would be a good thing for him to do—he has some issues that he's currently sorting through. But he'd be happy to meet for coffee first and talk about talking. She arranges a time and a place, too eagerly, her voice embarrassingly high-pitched and breathless, with a slight quaver she can't control.

At first, when they meet, she has herself under control. She's dressed for business in her usual black, her hair pulled back in a loose bun, her makeup minimal. She arrives at the cafe ten minutes early, finds a table at the back, orders peppermint tea, arranges her notebooks and pens, makes herself look as busily professional as possible. She's on the lookout for him, but when it's half past the hour and he still hasn't arrived, she assumes he's changed his mind, begins to pack up her notebooks, prepares to leave. Just as she's pushing back her chair, he walks in the door. He's the sort of man that everyone notices—men and women. He's big, good-looking, fit—and he's instantly recognisable as a cop. Something about his stance, the way he scans the room, some indefensible barrier that surrounds him. She's noticed it before with cops in uniform, the way their very presence is intimidating, authoritative, the way it brings a hush, a type of collectively drawn breath, and a furious determination to look entirely innocent that only makes everyone look furtive. But this man has the effect even without the uniform. He carries something else with him, too—a darkness that's at variance with his tawny good looks. Conversation around the cafe is suddenly subdued, and when he heads unerringly to her table, those distinctive eyes having homed in on her with a weird certainty, the waiter (who had been far more casual when it came to Erin, sitting alone) scurries over to serve him immediately.

'God.' He pulls out the chair opposite Erin, squeezes himself into the corner. 'Sorry. I went to the wrong fucking place.' The smooth voice takes any sting out of the profanity. 'I heard what you said, Cafe Royal, all right, but for some reason I went to one further down the road. I was getting all steamed up about *you* being late, and then I looked down at the menu, realised I was in the wrong place. The psych told me I should write everything down. But you'd think I'd remember a cafe. *Jeee-zus.* I'm really sorry. If you've got somewhere else you have to be, we can do this another time. It's the PTSD,' he adds, 'it's just a total brain fuck sometimes.' He stops, draws breath, looks right at her for the first time. 'Shit. You are Erin, aren't you? I *am* talking to the right person?' His wide smile—with those golden dark-fringed eyes crinkling at the corners—is as unexpected as it is endearing.

'No. I mean, yes, I am Erin, and no, it doesn't matter that you're late. That's fine. I was … I'm just grateful you could come. Really. I mean, I think, having spoken to your sister, to Jane, there are probably some things you could add to the picture. That is, if you want to … if it's okay.'

In contrast to his liquid tones, his calm authority, Erin's voice is pitched higher than usual, her response garbled. She is fidgeting too, which is most unlike her, moving the sugar pot in small jagged circles. She puts her hands in her lap, clasps them together. Takes a deep breath.

The waiter is hovering, eager to take their order.

'D'you want another cup of whatever that is? I'll have coffee, a double espresso. And a big piece of that honeycomb cheese-cake. And Erin—you'll share, won't you?' The man is clearly used to making decisions, for others as well as himself, and she doesn't argue, though she has drunk more tea than she has room for, and doesn't usually eat cake.

'Okay,' he says when the waiter goes, 'you want to talk to me about my cousin's death? Is that right? For some sort of documentary?'

She nods.

'Fair enough. But I want to know why.'

'Well, the documentary's about crimes and their aftermath— the way these sort of violent, unexpected deaths impact on the whole family. My aim is to interview as many people as I can. That's the idea, anyway.'

'No, I mean, why my cousin? Why *this* particular murder?

There are plenty of other murders, plenty of other families who could fill you in on their ... feelings, surely.'

She speaks slowly, assuredly, careful not to let herself get flustered. 'To be honest, it was just a coincidence. I was doing a class and your niece was in it. It's the way these things happen ... I mentioned what I was doing, she responded.'

'Right. Purely coincidental? We're just one family of many?'

'I'm hoping so, yes. Although your sister is actually the first to agree to talk to me.'

'It's just I've been burnt before: there've been a couple of other journalists, wanting to talk to us about the Sydney Strangler business. Trying to get big publishing deals on the back of our story. Parasites. I have to say I'm not a fan of true crime writers. I've been involved with them through work, too. They're generally smartarses, always think they're one step ahead of the cops, then get themselves mixed up in all sorts of things, and cause more trouble than the story's worth.' Adds darkly, 'I'm surprised more of them don't end up getting shot. Those *Underbelly* blokes, for instance.'

'No, no, it's nothing like that; I'm not trying to solve any crimes. I'm not even focusing on unsolved murders, necessarily. This is, well, it's for therapeutic reasons as much as anything. I figure I can sell it on—a resource for other families.'

'Right. A resource. How to survive a loved one's murder? That's lovely.' He looks as if it's anything but. 'Mostly people don't, you know.'

She sighs. 'Look. It has to have some sort of commercial potential, something beyond a single airplay. But really, I'm in it for the story—I'm genuinely interested in what happens to the surviving members of the family after something like this. We generally only ever hear the initial part of the story. About the murder itself, about the investigation, maybe a trial. But what happens after, to everyone involved, everyone who's left? How do they live? Do they ever get over it? That sort of thing.'

He says nothing, considers her for a long moment. She has

to force herself to look back, to keep her hands still.

'Okay,' he says finally. 'I'll talk to you. But I don't want you discussing what I say with anyone else from my family. Or anyone, full stop. Not before the program goes to air, anyway. This stays between us.' There's a hardness to him now, his air of amiability has evaporated.

'I wouldn't anyway,' she's swift to reassure him. 'It wouldn't be ethical. And I'll make sure you're happy with the final edit.'

'I don't care about being happy,' he says, not smiling, eyes hard. 'That's not ever going to happen. It just has to be the truth.'

ERIN: Now, if we could just go back to that morning. If you could tell me what you remember.

MICHAEL: Yeah … I … It's weird. You know, I've told this story so many times. It's hard to remember that it's true. That it's not just a story. It's hard to connect it to myself any more.

ERIN: I think that's a very common response to trauma.

MICHAEL: Yeah. I guess. Though I kinda feel like that about my entire life these days. That I'm not connected. That it's a story.

ERIN: Oh?

MICHAEL: But apparently that's just a symptom, too.

ERIN: A symptom?

MICHAEL: Of PTSD.

ERIN: Oh. Of course.

MICHAEL: Yeah. Sorry. That's not relevant.

ERIN: Well, actually, in terms of discussing the emotional aftermath, maybe it is. So the PTSD? That's just to do with the police work?

MICHAEL: That's what they're saying. And that's what I'm saying.

ERIN: But?

MICHAEL: Well, to be honest I've been rooted for a lot longer than that. The police force was probably just the … er … proverbial icing on the cake.

ERIN: So when would you say it began?

MICHAEL: The day Angie died, probably. There's been a heap of other stuff, too, since. Obviously. But I reckon that Angie dying, well, that was the start. I was never really right after that. I dunno how I even made it into the force in the first place. I guess having a father who was an inspector helped.

Anyway ... we should probably just keep going. What was the question again?

ERIN: If you could just go back to that morning. The day she went missing. What happened the last time you saw your cousin. What you can remember about that day.

MICHAEL: Well, my memory's a bit hazy. About the exact details and all that.

ERIN: But you gave a statement to the police, didn't you? At the time?

MICHAEL: Yeah. I did. But, you know. My dad helped me out. Prepped me, you could say. Made me write it all down so I wouldn't get muddled—so I'd always give the same answer. It was bloody terrifying—I wouldn't have had any idea what to say otherwise. My memory wasn't all that clear even then. He went over it with Adam too, to make sure we had our stories straight, that they matched up, so that they wouldn't be able to trip us up.

ERIN: Did you need to get your stories straight? Were there inconsistencies?

MICHAEL: Not really. It was just, well, we were young blokes. A pretty, young girl had gone missing and we were more or less the last to see her. It didn't matter that she was my cousin. Actually, that made it worse, probably. Dad knew we were going to be suspects. He made sure the two of us kept our stories tight and together. That we didn't say too much so we couldn't come unstuck.

ERIN: So what you told the police—the statement you gave—it wasn't actually correct?

MICHAEL: Oh, it was pretty right. Look, I was a cop for more than twenty years, I know how confused people's memories are, how hard it is to stick to one story, all the little things that escape you. Everyone forgets things, even when they're telling what they think is the absolute truth, sometimes they forget important things, and then they come back later. And I know now something I didn't know as a kid—that those gaps are sometimes crucial as a cop. It's like getting your foot in a door: the gap can open it all up. Even if it's just a not-quite truth, not quite a memory—that's not going to worry the cops. Sometimes— more than half the time, probably—people are lying big time. But even when they're not lying the cops are looking for it. That gap. And I guess Dad knew if I changed my story, even if I admitted to not knowing or forgetting, they'd have the opportunity—they'd have their foot in the door before you could take a breath. Even though I was just a kid.

ERIN: Well, can you tell me as much as you can about what you remember about that day?

MICHAEL: Okay ... So, this day, I went up to Ferber's a bit earlier than usual. Angie was going to come up later, have some lunch. I had been waking up pretty late all holidays. I'd always been an early riser before that, but it was teenage hormones, I guess. If Dad had been at home he'd've hauled me up earlier, found something for me to do, but Mum always let us do whatever we wanted during the holidays, more or less, as long as we weren't bothering her. Angie had been at our place for a week or so, which had been pretty cool. We'd always been close, y'know, even before that—like brother and sister. But, I dunno, those last few weeks we'd got really close. We weren't doing anything—just hanging out, drawing, watching telly. Angie was making a bit of an effort to hang with Jane too, but it was hard. She was that much younger. But we couldn't afford to have her getting the shits—telling Mum we were leaving her out. Mum would've sent Angie home if there was any sort of fighting, any trouble. The whole point was that we kept out of Mum's hair. So we'd stay at home most mornings and then go up to Ferber's in the afternoon. We had this competition going—me and Adam Ferber and a bunch of other boys—mostly blokes from school.

So anyway, this day—it was a Sunday—I went up to Adam's place at about ten. We played a few games of pinball and went over for a swim and then when we got back to the shop Angie was there. She'd already been there for a while. She and a couple of the other boys—Jason Dunne, Darren Stokes, I think— were in the middle of a game.

ERIN: You actually seem to have a really good memory of this day ...

MICHAEL: Well, like I said, I've told this story that many times, it doesn't even feel like it was me any more. It feels more like a story than a memory. Like a movie I watched once.

ERIN: So what happened next?

MICHAEL: Well, we played a few games, and then around two the rest of the boys headed off, and Angie said she was heading home too. The shop closed at three on Sundays, anyway.

The Ferbers lived above the shop, and Adam had this bedroom that was sort of separate to the rest of the house—up above the garage. There was a landing outside the window and a dodgy little metal staircase—like an old fire escape. It jutted out over the access lane behind the shop, where they got deliveries. So we'd go up there and hang out. Sometimes Angie would come up for a while, but not that time. It was pretty casual, you know. But that day I remember Angie saying that Jane had had the shits pretty bad that morning—that she'd wanted

Angie to stay with her … so I assumed she'd gone back to keep her company. Anyway, I stayed at Adam's for the rest of the day. It was after seven when I left.

ERIN: But what were you doing all that time?

MICHAEL: Nothing. We were just, you know, hanging. Adam'd get things from the shop, he had a stash up there. Coke, chips, packets of biscuits. Sometimes we'd nick a pack of cigarettes, smoke ourselves sick. We'd read his older brother's *Penthouse* magazines. Comics. Listen to records. I remember Adam had just got into the Sex Pistols and he had their latest album. We thought we were pretty rad … The time always seemed to pass pretty quickly.

ERIN: Were Adam's parents around? Didn't they come and check on you?

MICHAEL: Nah. Mrs Ferber didn't have a clue what we were doing. And anyway, Adam's parents always went to the club Sunday afternoon, so we could pretty much do what we wanted.

ERIN: And were you worried when you got home and Angie wasn't there?

MICHAEL: Well, yeah. I hadn't thought twice about it after she left. I'd assumed she was there—and all that time Mum and Dad thought she was with me. I think Dad called the cops straight away. Before he even rang her parents.

ERIN: And why did he call the police? Weren't there other possibilities? Places she might have gone? Why did he assume the worst?

MICHAEL: Because that's what cops do. They always see the worst so they assume the worst. Look, at first we thought that maybe she'd met up with some of the kids her mum had wanted her to stay away from—her old friends from the local high school—Manly Girls. But she hadn't been trying to contact them or anything while she was here—she'd really just been hanging with us. So it didn't seem all that likely.

ERIN: And what happened after?

MICHAEL: Yeah. Well, that's a blur. Barry and Carol came over, and the cops were there. I dunno who arrived first. I think Barry and Dad went out driving around, looking. It was just complete panic. I've seen it in other families when something like this happens. It's full-on crazy stations. No one knows—no one knows how to behave, or what to do. What to feel, even. Though I guess it was a bit different for us because of Dad being a cop. He knew the ropes—he could tell us what to expect, what was likely to happen next. And probably the police were more sensitive at first—keeping us informed about what they were doing.

ERIN: What do you remember about those first few days after she disappeared?

MICHAEL: I remember, well, I remember it being God-awful. Interviews with the police. Waiting. Everyone trying to stay calm, but everyone hysterical. Mostly what I can remember is just lying on my bed. Howling. Being completely out of it. It was ... it was horrendous. But at the same time it was unreal. Or what's the word? Surreal. Like this couldn't really be happening to us.

ERIN: And then what happened—after they found her body?

MICHAEL: Well, I went pretty crazy to be honest. I locked myself in my bedroom for a day or two—and then I just upped and ran. Climbed out the window and took off. I got on a train, and ended up in some godforsaken coastal town. I dunno what I was thinking. Well, I wasn't thinking, was I? I thought that if I could get away from everything it couldn't really have happened. It wouldn't be real. Angie wouldn't be dead.

Mick doesn't think about leaving in any practical sense. He's beyond rational thought—doesn't plan where he's heading, how he'll get there, what he'll do when he arrives. He waits until the household is quiet and he can hear his father snoring. He has already collected all the money he can scrape together from here and there—emptied his mother's purse, taken the spare change his father leaves in the fruit bowl, raided Jane's moneybox and his own, stolen the change his mother left out for the milkman. It's not much—not even fifty bucks—but it'll do. He'll make it last. He doesn't dare open the front door, knows his dad will wake the moment he pulls it to and isn't game to leave the door ajar overnight, instead climbs out the window. He jogs to Brookvale and catches the Wynyard bus, then walks up to Central, standing dazed in front of the departure board, wondering whether he should head north or south, what's most sensible, what he can afford. In the end it's almost random, or chosen for him, fate, however he chooses to look at it, there's a Brisbane train leaving in twenty minutes, and that's the one he'll catch.

He's not even halfway through the journey and he's had enough: the seats are uncomfortable, the incessant rattling of the carriage is getting to him, he can't switch off his mind, he can't even drop off to sleep. He gets off at Macksville, which is nowheresville as far as he's concerned. No one else alights and the tiny station is deserted apart from a weary porter, who shuffles back to the ticket office the moment the train pulls away, without even acknowledging him. Beyond the station the town itself is still in darkness, dawn is some hours away. He's sure he's not tired, but he stretches out on the station bench anyway, his backpack under his head. His mind continues to buzz for a few minutes, but then settles, lulled by the distant roar of the incoming tide, rhythmic, comforting, familiar, and soon enough he's asleep.

The young porter shakes him awake at sunrise, 'I'm finishing my shift soon, man. If I were you I'd get up before the boss gets in. He can be a bit of an arsehole about people sleeping at the station.'

Mick is surprised to see that the porter is barely older than him, and that his voice is tentative, almost apologetic. Mick sits up, runs his hands through his hair, shakes his head in an effort to clear it.

'So, where do I go to get something to eat around here?'

The boy gives a bark of laughter. 'It's not even six o'clock. Nothing's open yet.' He gives Mick a curious look. 'What are you doing here, anyway?'

Mick doesn't have the energy to concoct a story.

'Dunno. Just needed to get out.' He shrugs. 'I'd had enough of the train. And this seemed as good a place as any.'

The boy shakes his head. 'Man. I wouldn't leave Sydney for this shithole. You shoulda kept going up the coast. Got off further north—or kept going to Brisbane.'

'There's a beach somewhere here, isn't there? I thought I could hear the surf.'

'There's a river—the ocean's miles away.'

'It doesn't really matter. This is as good as anywhere else, I guess. I just needed to get away.' He stands up, stretches. 'So where're the nearest shops? I guess I better wander up and wait for something to open. I'm starved.' He doesn't have any idea where he's going to stay, what he's going to do here, but he tries hard to act confident, to not appear as lost as he feels.

The older boy considers him for a moment, 'Listen. If you can wait another ten minutes you can come home with me. Mum usually cooks me a hot brekkie when I do this shift—and she won't mind doing another. There'll be nothing open here for hours yet. I don't live in Macksville—we're over at Scotts.'

'Scotts?'

'Scotts Head. It's a few k's south of here. And it's on the coast.'

The boy's name is Shane, he's sixteen, has just left high school. The job in the railways is okay, he tells Mick, it's boring as bat shit, but it's paid for his car (a nipple-pink EH wagon) and leaves him plenty of time to pursue his real loves—surfing and music. He and some mates have got a band together, they've got some gigs, just local, but they're going places, he's certain of it. Even if they don't go together, he'll be getting out of here as soon as he can. There's nothing happening in Scotts—or in Macksville or Nambucca or any of the nearby towns—they're all shitholes unless you're after a dull seaside holiday or a nice quiet place to retire.

'What about you? What are you doing? Run away from home or something?' He asks the question casually enough, but Mick has had time to work something out while the other boy was talking, has constructed a plausible alternative existence.

'Nah. Got kicked out. Had a row with my old man. Mum died a few years ago, and he's been hitting the piss pretty hard. He loses it occasionally, and I clear out. Usually I go and stay with a mate, but this time I thought I'd head up the coast for a few days. Something different.' He's roughened up his speech a little, deepened his voice, he squares his shoulders, pushes out his chin, trying to look older than he is.

'Sounds like you've been through some tough shit, man.' The other boy's sympathy is matter-of-fact.

Mick nods, sighs. 'You got that.' Agreeing is easy, no acting required. He turns his face to the window, his vision suddenly blurred.

Shane's mother, *Lorraine, but everyone calls me Lonnie, pet*, is considerably younger than his own, and plumply pretty, warm, hospitable. She can see that he's ravenous and offers him up seconds and then thirds—bacon, eggs, tomatoes, sausages, the sort of fry-up that's reserved for special occasions at home—without comment. He's quickly made aware that her soft exterior conceals a quick mind, that she's nobody's fool, sharp as a tack.

Unlike her son, she doesn't accept his story at face value. Her questions are casual, but their very simplicity is deceptive—he knows she smells something fishy, and he has to work hard not to trip himself up, to keep his answers consistent, stay cool.

He manages to escape the meal unscathed, his story and his dignity both relatively intact, then takes up Shane's invitation to walk down to the beach with him, just to check out the waves—*I'm not going to swim, Mum, I'm not that much of an idiot*—before he hits the sack.

They wander down the road and through the scrub to the beach. It's a long strip, blue and inviting, and after a bit of a yack about the conditions, they mooch back up to the house.

'I'm stuffed,' his new friend says. 'I'm back on arvos from tomorrow, so I'll be right for doing something tonight if I can get a few hours now. You look pretty fucked yourself,' he adds, and then, 'Mum said you can stay at ours for a few days, if you want. Save driving you back into town, anyway. There's a spare bed in my room—you can have that, if you like.'

Mick is surprised by how easy it is here. How quickly sleep comes, how simple it is when he's someone else, just a boy running from his father, and not a boy who's running from himself. What bliss to lose consciousness. What luxury. For the first time since Angie's death, he's not thinking about her. For the first time since Angie's death, he's sleeping the deep, untroubled sleep of the young.

Late that afternoon, after another enormous meal has been wolfed down (a slab of rich cheesy lasagne that Shane retrieves from the fridge and reheats), the two boys head back down to the beach. They go out on the boards for a while but the surf is inconsistent and they quickly give up and lie in the sand, trading stories.

The conversation moves rapidly from waves to music, from music to cars, from cars to girls. Mick has had to improvise a little when it comes to cars—he's still months away from getting his learner's permit, and though he can tell the difference between a V8 and a rotary engine, he knows bugger all about Holley carbs, air shocks and Detroit locker diffs—but he's surprised to find himself sounding almost expert when they move on to the always vexed issue of girls.

Shane's romantic life is already startlingly complicated. His girlfriend Alison is a year older than him and a deadset spunk, tits out to here, an arse you could eat. It had been bloody hard work getting her to go out with him in the first place, and banging her had proven to be a feat of herculean proportions, but now he's got her, she's stuck on like a leech, won't let go. She's even hinting about getting engaged. But Shane isn't yet eighteen, he's ready to move on, he has his sights set elsewhere—in fact, having his sights set nowhere at all would be better than being so pathetically under the thumb, he confides gloomily.

'She's worse than my bloody mum, man. Somedays I think I should just piss off—like you. Escape.'

'Yeah. Well, I guess it's got its moments.'

'You got a girlfriend?'

'Yeah.'

'You banging her?'

'Yeah.' A girlfriend. He likes the way it sounds, the way it feels—like something from another life.

The other boy raises his eyebrows. 'Jeez. You don't waste time. What are you—sixteen?'

'She's a bit older'n me. She's nineteen.'

'Well, you better watch out, man. Older women like that—before you know it they want rings, houses, babies. You should go for someone more your age. Or younger. A fourteen-year-old. But then you wouldn't get any nooky, I guess. Always a trade off.'

'Nah. She's not like that. She's got her own plans. She's left school already, you know.'

'Yeah? What's she doing?'

Mick doesn't even have to think. 'She's at art school. She wants to be a painter.'

'Man, that's cool.'

'By the time she's done her course, I'll have finished school. We're going to travel together. Europe. America. Asia. Maybe even Africa. We've had it planned for years.'

Shane gives a slow nod of approval. 'Yep. That's the kinda woman I'm after, man. She got a sister?'

She changes her mind every second week about what it is she wants to do. For a while it's modelling, and she's prancing about the place in her best—or briefest—gear, her face made up, hair blow-dried and sprayed, striking poses, inviting his comments.

'So what do you think, Mick?' she asks. 'Should I send some photos in to *Dolly*? Or should I get an agent or something first? There's this girl at school and she makes something like a hundred a day and she's not even half as good-looking. She's a bit of a dog, really. Do you think I'm good enough?' She does a little shimmy, wiggles, pouts. 'Do ya think I'm sexy?'

He thinks she's more than sexy, imagines that her photos would be quite likely to blow anyone—any bloke—away, but he picks up a dirty sock and hurls it, hits her square in the face.

'Gross.' She picks it up, throws it back, hard, and all ideas about modelling are forgotten in the heat of battle.

Next it's music, she's going to give up piano and take up guitar. Who cares what her mother says?

'There's this girl in my year, she's into the drums, and if we can find someone else to play the other guitar, you know, the deep one—'

'Bass.'

'Yeah, that one. If we can find someone who plays that, it'd be unreal. Why don't you get one, Mick? You could be our bass boy.'

'Who's gonna sing?'

'Well, d'uh.' She frowns. 'Me, of course. The guitarist always sings. You know, like Suzi Quatro.'

'Suzie Quatro plays bass, you idiot.'

'Oh, so what. I'm still gonna sing.' She flicks her blonde mane, thrashes her air guitar, starts the first verse of 'Devil Gate Drive'. Mick covers his ears with his hands, falls to the ground, writhes on the carpet. *Nooooo* ... It's a joke, but only just. Even Mick can tell that Angie's musical talent might not get her very far.

The art idea comes up during that last week. The whole thing begins as an excuse to get away from Jane, whose hero-worshipping tendencies are beginning to bug Angie even more than they bugged Mick.

His mother remonstrates, if feebly, 'I don't see what difference Jane being around will make if you're only drawing, for God's sake, Mick. You're just being mean.'

But Mick is well prepared.

'We can't concentrate when Jane's there, Mum. She doesn't shut up. And we want to get these drawings done for that competition you clipped out for me. The one in the *Sun–Herald*.' He has her approval now, he knows. For some reason Mum's always been keen on Mick getting involved in anything arty— insisting he has his talent even when he knows that compared to the boys who can really draw or paint, his own skills are pretty unremarkable.

'Well. If you're really going to make an effort. The prize is pretty good—a hundred dollars and a term of classes at some place in the city ...' She shrugs and, as he knew she would, gives in.

At first they don't put much effort into the drawing—there are other things they're more interested in doing, after all. But when his mother asks to see the results, they start spending at least some of the time drawing and soon enough they're both right into it: sitting at either end of the bed, pencils and sketchbooks in hand. They sketch each other, they sketch clothes, furniture, carefully arrange objects for still lifes. Mick spends hours developing two little cartoon characters modelled on him and Angie, then illustrates their various adventures. Angie draws flowing pictures of long-haired girls riding dappled ponies, dancing, running through fields of flowers.

One afternoon, after a particularly intense session, Angie pauses in her drawing, holds up one of her sketches. This time it's a boy on a surfboard, riding a great wave, carefree, confident, while another, bigger wave looms tsunami-like above him. The picture isn't at all typical of her efforts, the lines are simple and definite, and Mick is honestly impressed.

'Wow. That's cool.'

But Angie's clearly not pleased—she frowns and tears it out of the sketchbook, stares at it some more.

'You know, Mick. I'm crap at this now, but I like doing it— and I think maybe I'm going to get better. I think that one day I might even be very good.' She gives the page another critical look, then screws it up, pitches it at the bin.

Later that night, Mick up-ends the basket and goes through the rubbish until he finds the picture, unscrews the paper, tries to smooth it out. The boy in the picture is vaguely familiar, but it takes him a few moments to realise that it's him she's drawn. He smooths it out some more, opens the biggest book he can find—his *Guinness Book of Records, 1976*—and lays her drawing down gently over an image of Robert Pershing Wadlow, the world's tallest man, closes the book and shoves it underneath his mattress.

Angie never gets to be very good at art. She never gets to start that band, or to send her photographs in to *Dolly.*

A few nights later she's dead. And the boy in the picture—carefree, confident, fearless—he's gone too. That giant wave knocked him off his board, sucked him under. He's never coming up.

When they get back to Shane's place, both boys hot and sweaty from the uphill walk, there's a man sitting in the kitchen with Shane's mum, drinking a beer. Shane's introduction is brief and to the point.

'This is Mick. This is my dad.'

Shane's father holds out his hand to be shaken. His grip is vice-like, his gaze considering.

'G'day, son. Lonnie here tells me you're getting away from some sort of trouble at home. That you're going to stay here for a few days.'

'Yes, sir. If that's okay with you.'

There's something scarily familiar about this man. It's not his looks—Mick's sure he's never met him before—but there's something about his bearing, his quiet authority, his frank regard.

'Now don't get me wrong, I'm not saying you should go back home right away, you're welcome to stay here while you need. My Lon's a good judge of character, and she reckons you're just a good lad who's having a spot of trouble. But it's important that you let someone know you're up here, that you're safe. I dunno how many times we've had missing kids turn up at a mate's house after days of searching. You could save us coppers a whole lot of time and energy if you'd just make a call. You give that old man of yours a ring now, son. Let him know you're alive.'

When he asks her out for coffee again, after their second interview, she says yes automatically. Despite herself. It's true that he's attractive, that he's somehow charming, but she's certain he's not her type, even though she's not so sure what that is any more, or if she's ever had one. The only thing Erin's men have ever had in common is the inevitability of *her* leaving—generally before they get too close. It's not wise to get too intimate, to let people in. It's not safe. And right now it's even less wise, less safe than usual. Still, she says yes.

They meet in a cafe in Manly, and this time he's there before her. The coffee is good, and the cake isn't too bad either. They exchange stories, laugh a little. Mick has a surprisingly good laugh: when he laughs he looks younger, less angry, looks the way he might have done when he was whole. At other times it's evident that, Humpty Dumpty-like, his outer shell is critically crazed, vital pieces are missing; that there's only the thinnest of membranes to contain it all. It's as if whatever he's holding inside could burst out, splattering anyone in the vicinity, at the slightest bump or jolt.

After their coffee, they go for a walk through Manly Corso and along the promenade. He walks like a police officer—his strides long and purposeful, attentive to everything that's around him. She always notices how people walk; it seems to say something about them. She has known men who step as if they are walking through a minefield, or through mud, carefully, unwillingly, dragged down and burdened. Others walk carelessly, as if they neither notice nor care where they're going. When he pauses he stands very upright, hands behind his back, legs slightly apart. The stance of a soldier at ease, but she knows he's not.

And when they walk they're talking. Though he doesn't say much that's significant, nothing that she's looking for, nothing that she wants to hear, still she's captivated. Can't resist. She finds that she wants to hear what he's saying. And finds that she wants him to hear what she's saying, too. But she knows she has to guard against this impulse—that there are some things she can say, and others that she never will. However much she wants to.

Still, she lets him have his say, and he tells her some things that are not about Angie, not about the family tragedy.

He tells her—of course he tells her, what did she expect?—all about his ex-wife: how hard he tried, how he should never have married her in the first place, how he was never truly hers, and how he'd hurt her. They'd tried an open marriage—her idea—as a way of getting around their unhappiness, but, of course, that was never going to work. And the kids, well, he hates to think what it's done to them, wonders if it's fucked them up—his behaviour, the PTSD, the disruption to their lives. How he wishes he could go back, they could all go back to the beginning and start again. He's willing to take responsibility for all their unhappiness. It's on his shoulders: it stemmed from his unhappiness, after all—with him not really knowing, after Angie, how to be happy. His wife said it to him so many times, and he always denied it, though he knew she was right: that he'll only know how to love, how to live, when he stops obsessing over Angie. Over the past.

And look—he's back there again. Obsessing. But Erin understands, she sympathises. She takes his hand, and he grips hers. He raises it to his face, presses it against his cheek, briefly, almost unconsciously, then lets it go.

'I'm sorry,' he says. 'It is some sort of madness, this obsession with Angie. I wish it—I wish she would leave me. She did for a few years, back in my thirties, but now, just lately, she won't let go. Or I won't let her go. I don't even know why any more—I can barely remember her. I barely remember whatever it was that was between us. And, really, it was nothing. We were kids. But I just can't forget about her. It'd be like ... abandoning her. Which I know is ridiculous—she's dead.'

'That's okay,' she tells him. 'I understand.' And she does.

His hand finds hers again. 'I would ask you back to my place,' he says, 'only I'm living at Mum's. It'd be ... awkward.'

'I would ask you back to *my* place, only I don't have one.' Her lie is automatic, necessary.

'Oh?'

'I'm just staying with some old schoolfriends at the moment. Couch surfing, you know.'

'Couch surfing. It sounds interesting.'

'It sounds uncomfortable.'

'Well, if it's comfort you're after, I know a good hotel. An old friend runs it. Not too far from here.' His voice is hopeful, there's a hint of laughter, of lightness. 'It's nothing flash, but it's clean.'

'Flatscreen? Cable? Minibar? Giant clam spa?'

'Well, maybe not the spa. But the rest. Mate's rates.'

'I'm in.'

She has no illusions about his state of mind, and no fantasies about helping him, or changing him, or about bringing a ray of light into his world. She knows that he's probably beyond repair, and that whatever she does he'll still be dark and sad and broken—that the golden boy he could have been, and that occasionally resurfaces, is long gone. She's never been one to believe in redemption—on earth or in heaven. He's suffering a dark night of the soul, she can feel that, she can see that—and there's nothing she can do to alleviate it.

She thinks she could probably really like him, under different circumstances. But this is one of those situations—no different to being a teacher, she supposes—where a real relationship is an ethical impossibility. An emotional relationship, she means. Sex—now that's a different kettle of fish completely. There's never any ethical impediment to that.

'So, tell me, Erin,' he says, his voice dreamy. He is lying on his back with his eyes closed, a half-smile on his lips. 'Tell me something about you.'

'What sort of something?' She hadn't expected this playful after-fuck chat from him. He had been straight to the point, there had been no softening up, no foreplay, no sweet nothings whispered; their coupling had been swift and almost business-like—a physical urge satisfied, an itch scratched, nothing more. No future, no promises. This was how she liked it, too. But now he has gone soggy, all soft and vulnerable and open. She had expected that he'd want to get out of there as fast as he could, but no, he wants to lie on the bed, all mellow and sated, and have a drowsy post-coital heart-to-heart. It's not how she imagined it, not how she imagined him, and maybe it's not really what she wants, either. But there's something she likes about him, this square, hard man; she feels more relaxed than she has in years, cosying up beside this virtual stranger. This man who she is manipulating, lying to. Using. She should be running, getting away from him as fast as she can, but somehow she can't. Somehow she doesn't even want to.

'Something I don't already know.'

'Well, there's quite a lot that could fit under that heading. You don't actually know anything about me.'

'Oh, I dunno. Feels like I know quite a bit about you already. You've got a little sticky-out mole under your left breast, for instance, and a red birthmark on the back of your neck. You bite your fingernails.'

'That doesn't tell you anything.' She doesn't quite manage the scornful tone she was attempting, instead she sounds playful, encouraging.

'Maybe not. But I also know that there are scars on your wrists. Old ones. Scars running the right way. Scars that say you knew what you were doing. Why don't you tell me about those?'

'You don't want to know, believe me.'

'I've told you about some of my scars. Maybe you could

reciprocate. He takes her hand and turns it over, runs a warm finger along the raised welt that bisects the soft skin of her forearm. She pulls her hand away, but he tightens his grip, raises her wrist to his lips. 'C'mon. They're not recent—they're ancient history. Tell me.'

She relents, tells the story as if it's about another person, another girl. That's the only way she can tell it. She only tells him some of it: the parts she can bear to tell. The parts she thinks he'll understand, the parts she understands herself.

There is a girl, a teenager. Call her Erin for convenience—although that may not have been her name then. She has just left her home in the middle of nowhere and moved to the city to get a job. She's not sure what sort of a job, she is likely to get—she's only sixteen and left school without any qualifications. She is a pretty girl, Erin, not so pretty that it will be a problem, but pretty enough, with the sort of looks that can be modified, augmented, non-descript in a way that is full of potential: her hair thick and shiny, her skin pale and clear, her features regular. Her eyes are her best feature—large, wide set, the colour reflective and endlessly changeable—ice blue one moment, then deepest ocean dark, steely grey the next. She is small, but her figure is trim, and she has curves in all the right places—bust, waist, hips—and with a bit of effort she could be sexy. But she's not aware of any of this; she hasn't yet learnt that she can use her body as a tool—or as a weapon.

What she wants right now is to work in an office. She doesn't mind what sort or where, but she can imagine herself sitting at a desk, in a file-lined room, answering the phone, a switchboard even, in her bright office-y voice. She can even imagine what she might wear in such a place: sees herself dressed in a grey pencil skirt that ends just below her knees, with a tucked-in shirt—pastel, with a Peter Pan collar—and she would wear seamed stockings, patent pumps with pointy toes, kitten heels. She would pile her hair up in a bun, carry a clipboard. She would have a typewriter on her desk—she'd have to learn to touch-type—and a timber tray for stationery. Her boss—she imagines a man in a dark suit, shiny shoes, handsome and clean-shaven—would be too old for her to regard in any sort of a romantic light, in his thirties at least. Instead he would be a sort of father figure, giving advice, looking out for her, making sure that her tyres have air in them, that her landlord is treating her right. She imagines the office would deal in something solid, respectable, the clients would be prosperous and pleasant—real estate, maybe, or an accountancy firm—and she would be efficient, competent. She would be admired and relied upon, make herself indispensable.

This was just her work life. Her other life—her real life, a life that no one at the office would really know about—would happen concurrently. In this other life there would be a boy. She would meet him somewhere unexpected—at a bus stop, or when she's out buying groceries. He would be the sort of boy she always wanted to meet. So different to the callow unambitious boys she'd gone to school with, focused only on sex, beer and football—though not always in that order—boys who have never once glanced her way, anyway. This boy would be a university student, he would be studying medicine or law, and he would play the piano or the guitar, would sing, read poetry, cook. She imagines his hair blond, long on top and short on the sides like Spandau Ballet. His teeth would be white and straight and he would be healthy and tall. He would come from some place that's very different to where she's come from: his parents would still be married, and they'd live close by in a suburb by the sea, or near the mountains, in a house surrounded by trees and flowers. And he would take her to meet them, and he'd take her other places, too—other countries, perhaps—and eventually she would move into a house with this boy, and they would make a home together, a home filled with love, and in time she would be able to forget the home she had grown up in.

The real story's different, of course. She gets a job, but it's not in the clean and organised office she'd dreamt of; it's a grimy little hole out the front of a dirty old tyre and mechanical repair service, and though she gets to answer the phone, she has to shout into the receiver because there's no soundproofing. She spends half her day filing and the other half trying to keep the black dust that settles over everything at an acceptable level and busily avoiding her boss. He is not the suited patrician of her fantasy, but a fat and greasy middle-aged fellow who finds a way to touch her every time she brings him coffee or a message. Though she does her best to keep covered up—those Peter Pan collars have become turtlenecks, skirts are almost to the ankle, baggy jeans are even more sensible—still his slippery fingers manage to find a way to breach elastic, buttons, ribbons, finding their way to her hot, resistant flesh. One Friday afternoon, when the men in the workshop leave early, he pushes her hard up against the desk and even her jeans and long-sleeved shirt prove no barrier—zips are unzipped, buttons unbuttoned, and this time it is more than his fingers that do the breaching.

There are other jobs, other offices, other bosses. But none is much of an improvement on the first—and some are worse.

There is no beautiful boyfriend either, but a series of boys, and later men, and no home lovingly put together, but dark corners, dirty bedrooms, car seats, the odd toilet cubicle. Her eyes are no longer bright and wide, but dull and distant. Her home is a room in a boarding house, a sheet strung across the window as a curtain, a shared bathroom, a kitchen that stinks of a hundred years of tinned soup and dirty dishes, of ground-in despair.

And the home she grew up in—that's not forgotten. Far from it. That home looms larger in her mind with every passing day. It seems there's no escape—how to choose between the tragic past and the hopeless present? There's no future, either. There's nothing but the logic of knife and skin. Nothing but the warm comfort of blood and the cool promise of oblivion.

'But you came back to the world.' He is still tracing the scar with his finger, absentmindedly now, watching her face closely. Too closely.

'Eventually. It took a long time. And there are still … things. There's still shit I need to get past.'

'Maybe some of us will always have shit we can't get past. Maybe we just have to accept it—treat it like some sort of disability. Like a paralysed leg or an amputated arm. Make allowances, find a way to live with it. Maybe it's just a … condition of our existence.'

She doesn't like making allowances for anything, and she doesn't like the way he uses the words *us, we*. It's her and it's the rest of the world: that's how it's always been, and that's the way she wants to keep it.

She pulls her arm away, his gentle touch suddenly irritating. Slides out of the bed.

'What're you doing?'

'I have to go.'

'What do you mean you have to go? It's only five. I thought we could have dinner, order pizza, stay over …'

'There are things I have to do.'

'What sort of things?'

'Work things.'

'What sort of work? More interviews? Connected to the doco?'

'You could say that.'

ERIN

'Evening, Mr G. Hope you've had a good day. It's been beautiful outside today. So warm and sunny—you can feel spring in the air, that's for sure. Well, you can feel the sunshine in here, even if you can't see it, so that's something. Nothing like a north-facing room. It's a pity to close your curtains, really—the ocean's an amazing colour—almost purple—like a bruise. Now, would you like me to do your hair? Such a good thick head of hair you have. Men half your age would be glad of it, I reckon.

'I was just looking at your photos there, Mr G. They're an odd thing for a blind man to have, aren't they? Did your wife bring them in, just in case? Like I'm talking to you, just in case? Anyway, they're lovely. Such a lovely family. It must be nice to be reminded. Of what life was like. Of your past. Anyway, I hope it is.

'I'm guessing this one's your family—the one in the gold frame? And that's your daughter and your son, there with your wife? They were sweet-looking kids, weren't they? Were they good friends? Here they are again, older now, with their own children. Must be lovely to see your family grow up, have children of their own. And little kids are always such a comfort. Or so they say. Though I've never wanted any myself—couldn't think of anything worse, really. But at your age they must give you hope. All those little bits of you, out in the world, going on into infinity. I guess you miss them.

'I like this one, too—of you and your wife when you were young. Back in the sixties? She was a stunner, wasn't she? You were a lucky fella. But then you weren't too bad yourself, really. Dark and brooding. The strong silent type. Your son's the dead spit of you, isn't he? It's those eyes. Gorgeous. Unforgettable. Man, I love those stovepipe pants. And the winklepickers.

They're all the rage again, you know. Who'd have thunk it. And your wife's dress—with that flared skirt, the fitted bodice—the girls can't get enough of them these days. They sell them for a fortune at second-hand places—or what do they call it? Retro? Vintage? We're all vintage eventually.

'Now, open wide, Mr G. Cook told me that it's something extra special tonight. Some sort of fish and mashed vegies. Open up, there's a dear. Now swallow it down. You don't want to keep it in your mouth like that—it's not good when it's cold. Good man. See, it's not so bad. And then I can put the telly on for you, you can listen before bed. You can listen while you're in bed if it comes to that. What would you like to watch? Sorry, I mean listen to? *Masterchef*? *The Voice*? Something like that? Oh, I know. How about a crime show? Being an ex-cop and all. I think there might be a new series of *Underbelly* starting tonight. You'd like that, wouldn't you, Mr G?'

Erin has slipped easily into her role at the nursing home. She can't say that she's a natural carer—she's too impatient, for one. All these old folk with their endless infirmities, most of them living half lives, if that. She can't help thinking that most of them would be better off put out of their misery—even a pillow over the face would be a better option than this sad lingering. Still, though she could do without the shit (of the literal not metaphorical sort), she finds herself almost enjoying the routine. And she really likes the old-fashioned uniform—the neat, white zip-up shift, the squeaky white shoes, her hair (a blonde wig, just in case, though she's only working outside visiting hours) pinned into a bun and tied up in a white silk scarf that management insists they wear. She has added a dash of pearlescent pink lipstick, and her reflection is pleasingly and unrecognisably old-fashioned. She could pass for a nursing sister from the fifties—tidy, efficient, self-effacing, keeping the place ship-shape, quietly saving lives.

The wards are almost silent during her shifts, all of the residents settled in their rooms for the evening, and once they're fed and in bed she's more or less a free agent. The nights are long and slow, but they suit her. Occasionally one of the inmates (as she thinks of them) has some issue that needs sorting—old Mrs Trafford has been having terrible night terrors, has been reliving the Blitz, night after night. But there's always an hour or two that she can spend listening to the interviews again, thinking about what she's been told, what she needs to ask, or to listen for.

When it comes to interviews, though, she *is* a natural. When she was a child—in that long-ago time when her future seemed to hold endless possibilities—she'd imagined herself in the kind of role that would require her to listen. A high school English teacher had once remarked on her report card that she had some kind of talent: *While she is not one to offer her own opinions, Kathy is a very empathetic child, with well-developed listening skills that are rare in someone her age.* She had asked her mother what sort of career might take advantage of such a rare talent, and her mother, for once giving Kathy her full attention, had told her that there were plenty of jobs that required good listening skills—in fact being able to listen was useful in nearly every job. But wasn't there some particular occupation that required listening *specifically*? Kathy had insisted.

'Well,' her mother's forehead wrinkling in that way it did when she concentrated, 'you could be a translator, I suppose, but you'd have to learn another language really well. And you're not studying any language now, so it's probably too late for that. You could be a psychologist, or a counsellor—they need to listen. But then,' she'd added, 'you'd have to spend your life having to listen to other people's troubles. People like me. God—*that'd* be depressing.'

But Kathy had held on to that idea, and for years when people asked her she'd tell them she was going to be a psychologist, even when it was clear that the possibility of a normal progression from school to university to career was moving further and further away. Though eventually she'd trained in film and radio production, she'd always been at the periphery, never behind a microphone. But now, running her own show, so to speak, for the first time, she's surprised to discover how satisfying it is, to be the one asking as well as listening, to be controlling the flow, setting the agenda.

She's especially intrigued by stories of other people's childhoods. Regardless of the tragedy they're discussing, as far as she can tell, Jane and Mick's childhood seems to have been relatively happy. Happy enough, anyway. Angie's murder was a terrible thing, they both agree—something that was difficult to recover from—but before that, their lives were good, and for Jane at least, things did get better eventually; life did return to normal.

She's not usually one to compare, but she wonders now whether there was some way her own family of two could have recovered, if there was something she and her mother could have done (a course, therapy, pills?) that would have let them go on to live a happy-enough existence. On reflection, she thinks probably not: after all, her own happy-enough childhood had ended before she'd even entered her teens. Their family life had come apart at the seams long before Kelly's death.

It's hard to pinpoint the moment when it all started to go downhill, but maybe it was the moment her parents separated. It seems too slight a moment to bear the burden of so much tragedy—such a clichéd and common trauma. How could that single event—an everyday calamity that was replicated in the lives of half the children she knew—possibly set her, set them, apart? Only it had. It hadn't seemed such a significant event at the time, not to her anyway. Looking back, she thinks a little guiltily that she really didn't mind that much when Dad moved out. She'd only been five, and it's true, children are resilient—and selfish—at that age. It's not like life was actually more fun when he was around. She remembers very little about her father—just that he was cranky and unapproachable, frequently creating impediments to her desires, diverting her mother's attention. His very presence seemed to generate tension. It was her sister, Kelly, older by five years, who had really been hurt by the split. Although it's not something she can actually recall, her mother had been insistent that it was only after their father left that Kelly's behaviour began to deteriorate—that the two events were connected, cause and effect. That before her father left, Kelly had been an easy child, a good child, a straight-A child. A more than ordinarily happy child. And she supposed that if her father had never left, that's what they'd have had too—a happy-enough childhood. Ordinary lives, with ordinary hardships, ordinary successes. Impossible to imagine, now.

Things had been tough all along—it had never been much of a life, she supposes, looking back. But the day her sister ran away from home—that's when any chance of Kathy having a mostly happy childhood really ended. After that there was no chance of getting back to normal. After that she could barely remember what normal meant.

JANE

I sip my wine, and watch from a stool at the breakfast bar as Rob prepares an omelette for the two of us. Jess has forgone the evening meal (having eaten two packs of highly nutritious Mi Goreng at four p.m.) and taken herself off to her bedroom with her laptop for the night. Her latest boyfriend, Jimmy, is travelling through Europe, and she's hoping she'll hear from him tonight—though in the months that he's been gone, communications have become increasingly infrequent. I've made the expected murmurings about not getting too serious at too young an age, about how there are an infinite number of fish swimming in the sea, about girls and men and fish and bicycles, and I've even, God help me, encouraged promiscuity—when the cat's away, et cetera, et cetera—preparing her for the brush-off that I fear is inevitable and imminent. But somehow she's managed to ignore every hint, explaining away Jimmy's increasing non-contact with an arsenal of excuses, generally a variation on the indisputable fact of his 'boyness'.

I held my tongue this evening, merely giving an encouraging smile as she distractedly said goodnight, then rushed down the hall the moment she heard the unmistakeable Skype buzz emanating from her bedroom.

'Oh, shit,' I murmur as her bedroom door closes firmly behind her, 'I wish she'd just get over him.'

'Eh?' Rob looks at me quickly, then back at his onion.

'Jess. I wish she wasn't still so keen. He's going to break her heart. I just know it.'

Rob gives a shrug. 'She's young, she'll survive. What's a broken heart in the scheme of things? It's all part of growing up. You need these hard things to happen. So you can build up strength to cope with all the difficulties coming your way. What's that term that's all the rage? Resilience. Isn't that the idea?'

I take another sip. 'So she can grow up to be just as well adjusted as her mother ...'

He says nothing, focused on his cooking.

Rob is a skilled cook—much more adventurous than me—and far more elegant. He doesn't look like a cook—he looks like the footballer he never was: not short but not tall, compact and nuggetty, his neck and shoulders powerful. He's still a good-looking man, his hair curling thickly—a little longer than is fashionable—the streaks of grey attractive, distinguished rather than a sign of deterioration. There's no bald spot, not even up the top—and maybe there never will be. His fingers are long and solid and strong; he's a magician with the knife, dexterous and efficient. I have always enjoyed watching him cook: wielding the cook's knife fearlessly, effortlessly dicing and slicing, making neat little piles of chopped foodstuff, eggs cracked and beaten with an easy flick of the wrist. Tonight, though, this very precision irritates me, seems old-man-like and fussy. I wish he'd crack the eggs on the bench, spill his neatly measured soy, toss the contents of the skillet into the air and miss the catch. The very familiarity of his every action, the way I can predict his next move, could probably do it myself, sets my teeth on edge.

'So, when were you going to tell me about this woman? The one making the documentary. Erin Whatsit.'

He doesn't look up when he asks—just flings the question at me casually, as he grates the cheese. I'm taken aback, don't quite know how to answer. I feel curiously panicked, try to formulate an answer.

'Oh, Rob. I didn't—'

'I just don't understand why you needed to keep it secret. What was the point of that?' He sounds hurt.

'To tell you the truth, I don't understand either. There wasn't any point, Rob. I just ...' my voice falters. I just—what? I couldn't explain it. Not even to myself.

Rob isn't waiting for my response. 'Jess told me, anyway. The woman wants to talk to me too, apparently.' He pauses in his grating, looks up, gives a slightly smug smile.

'Why? Why would she want to talk to you?' It's out before I have time to think, and I regret both the words and the tone immediately. Rob's mouth tightens, his eyes narrow. He goes back to grating.

'I guess because I actually knew Angie, too. I was around. Remember?'

'But the documentary's about the family. The effect on the *immediate* family. Or that's what I understood.' He can't miss my emphasis.

He shrugs. 'She's taking a wider view, I guess.'

'Well, you can't really say that you were involved. You'd only just started working for Pop, hadn't you? You would have only met her, what, half-a-dozen times. It's not like you really knew her.'

He pauses. Takes a gulp of wine.

'Well, maybe … But the police questioned me, you know. I *was* actually a suspect in the beginning. And I guess she wants to know about all the stuff since.'

'What do you mean? What stuff since?'

'Since she died. The effect on the family. On you, Mick, your parents. Our marriage, too, I suppose. Even Jess. I guess I do have a certain perspective on all that.'

'But this is so long after the fact. It's not like you had much to do with us back then.'

'It's not just back then, Janey.' He's speaking gently, patiently, as if to a child. 'She's interested in the long-term effects—how this has affected everyone. Over time.'

'What effects over time? We're all over it. Jesus, Rob. I can barely even remember it.'

He gives me a quizzical look. 'I don't get why this is upsetting you—me talking to this woman. It's not like we're discussing state secrets or anything. You're talking to her. Mick's talking to her …'

I don't know either. 'I just don't see the point.' Again I'm ashamed of the way I sound: petulant, childish.

'Well, maybe the point is getting a different perspective on her. On Angela. On you guys. On everything. And it'd probably be good to give this woman the opportunity to hear from someone who isn't wearing rose-coloured glasses when it comes to Angie.'

'What do you mean, rose-coloured glasses?'

'Oh, come on, Jane. You and Mick ... Angie wasn't—well, she wasn't the bloody angel you two make her out to be, that's for sure.' He halves a red capsicum in one clean slice as if to emphasise his point.

I've always secretly loved the fact that on the rare occasion that the subject comes up, Rob's attitude towards my cousin tends to be rather less admiring than my own, that he's sceptical about her, that he's not at all romantic. He barely knew her, after all, and could hardly be expected to see her as Mick and I did. And to be honest, his attitude still gives me a strange sense of satisfaction, of relief, just as it did when he'd told me that she had nothing on me, all those years ago. But right now this attitude—along with his presumption—makes me unreasonably angry. I'm baffled by this anger, can't work out what buttons are being pushed or why.

He sighs. 'Look. I don't have to talk to her. I haven't said anything definite. If you don't want me to I won't, Jane.'

I shrug. 'Do whatever you think you should, Rob. I just don't see what you'd be able to add. It's not like you really knew her, is it? You couldn't be expected to understand what happened.'

He pauses in his chopping, and looks at me a little bit sadly before he speaks. 'You know, Jane, maybe I know more than you realise. Maybe I understand things a little differently. Maybe I know things you don't know.'

ROB: I guess I didn't know her all that well. Or not like Jane or Mick did, obviously. Actually, I didn't really know any of them that well back then. I was a couple of years above Mick, and we went to different schools.

ERIN: So what was your link to the family?

ROB: Well, I knew Mick from cricket, originally. I mean, our lives probably connected in some other way—I think our mums knew each other from tennis or something—but the first time I actually remember meeting Mick was playing cricket. He was good. Really good. Much better than me, I was a footie head; cricket was just for summer fun. He played for the Manly Under-16s when he was young. I think he was only fourteen when he first played with us.

Anyway, I'd left school early—I left in Year Eleven. Mick's grandfather used to take him to the matches—don't think cricket was ever his old man's cup of tea. Anyway, somehow his pop ended up offering me a job. He just needed some brawn initially, someone to help with a bit of heavy lifting, deliveries. I was a big lug of a kid. Strong, y'know? It was a second-hand place then—mostly furniture, lots of big wardrobes, desks, bookshelves. Anyway, I helped him for a while, just casually, and then eventually he hired me full-time.

ERIN: So that's how you initially got involved with the family?

ROB: Funny how it works, isn't it? You meet a guy at cricket, get a job with his grandfather, and end up marrying his sister.

ERIN: And Angie ... you met Angie when? Where? How did that come about?

ROB: Yeah, I've been thinking about that. Trying to work it out. I know she'd probably been around. Maybe it was at the cricket, or at some cricket do? The three of them were always together. Apparently Angie virtually lived over at their place. She didn't like the furniture shop so much—but maybe it was there. Jane used to hang there a bit—I remember seeing her around a bit, but Angie hated it.

I don't really remember a particular event or anything, a first meeting. I just remember becoming conscious of her. You know in that way that you do. Girls are sort of at the periphery—and then all of a sudden they're there. Really there.

ERIN: From what everyone else has said, Angie doesn't seem to be the sort of girl who would ever be at the periphery of anything.

ROB: Well, if you're talking to Mick and Jane, that's all you're going to hear. The way they remember her, Angie was a combination of the Virgin Mary and Marilyn Monroe. But I think they've got it a bit out of proportion.

ERIN: From the pictures I've seen, she was a very pretty girl. Out of the ordinary.

ROB: Yeah, she was. It's true. But then so were a heap of other girls. Angie wasn't as ... remarkable, I guess, as they make her seem. It's just what happens when people die. When they die young, I mean. They're sort of transfigured or something. It's understandable. But I really don't think their perspective on Angie is necessarily the right one. Or the only one.

ERIN: I'm guessing you have a different picture, then? One that's more accurate?

ROB: I dunno about accurate. Like I said, I didn't really know her that well. And it's a long time ago. But there are a few things that they probably won't know about her. Or that they won't have seen. Or maybe, in Mick's case, that they didn't, don't want to, see …

ERIN: I'm intrigued. What do you mean?

ROB: Well, for starters, Angie was a bit of a tart. I mean, she was only fourteen when she died. But she wasn't a virgin.

ERIN: Yes, I think it was established at the inquest that she wasn't a virgin. But there was some suspicion, wasn't there, that she'd been raped?

ROB: No, I don't mean that.

Maybe it's not completely relevant to what you're doing here—the effect on the family and all that—but I imagine you're trying to build a picture of Angie as well. Maybe it's worth knowing that she wasn't just the sweet little innocent everyone makes her out to be. Look, this is pretty embarrassing, but she actually came on to me once.

ERIN: Oh?

ROB: Yeah. At her grandfather's shop. I was loading something into his truck, I was only new at the job, and pretty nervous. It was an old wardrobe, just a worthless piece of crap that he'd probably sold for five times what it was worth. I'd managed to get it stuck, halfway in the van. Anyway, I was panting and shoving and about to drop this bloody thing on the driveway, when Angie came out. She saved me—gave me a hand pushing it back in. It was a bit of fun in the end—we stood out the back laughing for a while. I lit a smoke and she asked if she could have a drag. So she had a puff, and instead of just passing it back to me, she moved really close—sort of teased me with the cigarette. It sounds silly, you know, but she made me follow her hand towards her face until we were kissing.

ERIN: And did you respond?

ROB: Maybe for a moment. It was just instinctive, you know. And she was pretty full on. But I ended it before it could go any further.

ERIN: What do you mean you ended it?

ROB: Well, I pushed her away. Said no, that we shouldn't, or something like that. I can't remember exactly what.

ERIN: And then …

ROB: And then nothing. I had a cupboard to deliver.

ERIN: Was Angie upset?

ROB: I don't really remember. I don't think she was too worried.

ERIN: Really? And that was it? There was never anything more?

ROB: Never. I saw her a few times, obviously, but nothing like that ever happened again. It was too risky. She was my boss's granddaughter. And I knew she was way too young for me— even though she didn't necessarily act it. But I do remember that kiss was amazingly … sexual for a girl that age. It wasn't just a sweet little schoolgirl kiss. She was definitely offering something more.

ERIN: I appreciate your telling me this, Rob. It changes the picture I have of the victim, shows her … other side, I guess. And it could be significant.

ROB: Well, it's all I have to offer, really. I guess it just seems important to set the record straight.

And actually, maybe it is significant. I mean, it could explain why it happened to Angie, and not someone else.

ERIN: What do you mean why it happened? It was a random murder.

ROB: Well, even randomness is relative, surely. There must have been an element of … choice. For the killer, I mean. It can't all be chance. It wouldn't have happened to Jane, for instance, because she wouldn't have done what Angie did. Jane wasn't the same sort of girl, she wouldn't have got herself mixed up with any sort of ... sicko. She was a good girl. Cautious. Followed the rules. Angie, on the other hand, was always looking for trouble.

ERIN: But if Angie was the first victim of a serial killing, then surely who she was, or how she behaved, didn't really matter. From what I've read these sorts of killers tend to be opportunistic—they take whatever's on offer. And there was no connection between Angie and the other victim.

ROB: But maybe they were both somehow vulnerable because of the types of girl they were, what they were doing. And I don't know—I've always thought that maybe Angie invited it somehow.

ERIN: I'm not sure I understand. According to witnesses, Angie left Ferber's at around 2:45 saying she was going home. The police thought that she must have been abducted—pulled or enticed into a car—during that short walk home. That sounds pretty random to me—not like someone who's inviting trouble.

ROB: Look. Before they found that other girl, the police were sniffing about all the boys she knew: Mick, Adam and the other boys who'd been at Ferber's that day, me as well. And there were rumours about some other blokes—older guys, maybe—who she hung out with. I didn't have a particularly tight alibi—I'd been into the city to meet a mate and just kind of mooched back, caught the ferry over, went into a game parlour at Manly. I didn't get home until after eight that night. It was nothing unusual, but no one could vouch for me once I got back from the city. And because of the reputation Angie had—because of those older boys, I guess—I was under suspicion too. The suspicion hung around all of us for months. Until that other girl was murdered, really.

ERIN: But were you under particular suspicion? More than the others? You hadn't actually been around that day.

ROB: I'd already had a bit of trouble with the cops, so it was more ... complicated. I've never told Jane this, but it all got a bit heavy. It was fucking scary, actually.

ERIN: What sort of prior trouble?

ROB: Yeah. Well, it's a bit of a long story. It was the reason I left school. There was this girl. She made a move on me at a party— it was her brother's eighteenth—and I said no. She wasn't my type. To be honest she probably wasn't anybody's type. She was a really nice girl, and smart as, but she was a bit of a dag—too tall, bad skin, overweight—and I was young and silly and that sort of stuff mattered. She was the sort of girl you wouldn't be caught dead with. Anyway, she made her move, and I didn't exactly behave well. In fact I laughed at her. She made a scene— said that I'd tried to force myself on her. She didn't cry rape exactly, and her parents must've had some sort of doubt because they didn't call the cops that night—they just kicked me out. But they made a report the next day, and made sure my parents knew what was going on, as well as the school. The police called over to talk to me, but it never went further than that. But it made my life at school pretty difficult—everyone had heard the rumours, and there was enough doubt to make things uncomfortable for me. So I left. I wasn't thinking of uni or anything so it didn't matter that much. Though I would've finished, done my final year. Anyway, Mick's grandfather gave me the job. Luckily he hadn't heard anything.

ERIN: I can see why you were so worried. But I still don't see what that has to do with Angie's reputation. What difference that really made to how you were treated.

ROB: Yeah. I know in the end it was just a random killer, a serial killer, whatever. But I reckon her reputation made things more complicated. That the cops suspected she'd gone with someone she knew, and that things had got out of hand. Because she was that kind of girl. You know. It could have gone really bad for me.

ERIN: You must've been relieved, then, when that other girl was found.

ROB: Oh, yeah. It probably sounds awful, but when they found that other girl's body, and linked the two crimes—and ruled me out—that was one of the best days of my life.

JANE

That night I dream about Angie again. I've had so many variations of this particular dream throughout my life that it's become an old familiar. It follows a well-worn pattern: usually in the dream I can't actually see my cousin, I just know that I'm chasing Angie, trying to catch up to her, that if I can catch her and stop her, everything will be okay. But something always prevents me. Sometimes I trip and fall, and am somehow both immobilised and muted—stuck and dumb—as if I've fallen face-first into wet concrete. In other versions, someone's physically holding me back, though I can never see who it is.

This time, though, Angie is visible—I'm viewing her from behind, dressed as she's described in the articles and posters: a girl with shiny, long blonde hair, straight out of a Pantene commercial, wearing a crocheted singlet top, shaggy cut-off jeans and a pretty silk scarf. Initially, she's walking ahead of me at a steady pace, but as I get closer, she moves faster, and then faster, and then I realise it's deliberate: that Angie's running away from me, and no matter how hard I try, I can't keep up, she just keeps getting faster. And as she moves away, she's changing: the colour leaching from her, her body changing shape, her clothes falling from her frame, then rotting and fraying, her hair darkening and disappearing until what I'm chasing is not a girl at all but an image of death, a skeletal figure from some appalling horror movie. Somehow the B-grade horror film effects don't stop this from being utterly terrifying. When I wake, I manage to stop myself from calling out, but I can't help clutching at Rob, who is sleeping soundly beside me. He stirs and murmurs 'yawright?', then rolls over and resumes his gentle snoring.

I'm not all right. I feel sick in my stomach and my heart is hurting. And I am sobbing—quietly, but desperately, and with no way to stop myself; I have to bury my head in the pillow to muffle the sound. I'm crying in a way that I haven't since I was a very small child. I sob as if my heart is breaking, sob myself back to sleep.

When I wake up the next morning my head is foggy. A strange lump—somewhere between heartburn and heartbreak—sits heavily on my chest. I look a wreck. I'm prone to bags under my eyes even when I sleep well, but tears and lack of sleep have swollen my eyelids, making me look as if I've been stung by bees. It isn't pretty. Rob does a double-take when I bring him his morning espresso.

'Jesus Christ, you look awful.'

I have to work hard to stop myself from pouring the coffee over his head.

'Thank you for pointing that out, my darling.'

'What happened? Are you okay?'

'I had a bad dream.'

'But your eyes?'

I shrug. 'I must've been crying in my sleep.'

'Haven't you had a few bad dreams lately? What was it?'

I shrug again, not wanting to discuss it. 'I don't know. I can't remember.'

'What's the time? Aren't you meeting the new tenant this morning? You can't go looking like that.'

'Oh, shit.' I'd forgotten all about it.

I reschedule the meeting for late afternoon. By that time, the swelling around my eyes has gone down, it's true, but nothing else about me is close to normal. I've been feeling oddly panicked all day, and when I'm not panicky I'm desperately tired. The shop, thank God, has been even quieter than usual, with only one customer to interrupt my desultory packing—an elderly woman who was happy to pay my rather optimistic price for a deco Shelley china rose vase.

'My best friend gave me a pair of these,' she tells me, 'as a wedding present. One of my granddaughters broke one last year—I didn't think I'd ever find a replacement. How amazing.'

Usually I'd want to know more about a woman like this, would be interested to know more about the friendship, perhaps, or about her marriage, or about how her life had panned out, but today I just want her to go. I wrap her vase in newspaper, and send her, mildly confounded by my unfriendliness, on her way. *We'll be gone in a few more weeks*, I think. *It's not like she'll be a returning customer, anyway.*

I've not met the new tenant; the rental has been arranged through an agent, and all I know is that he is planning to open a health food store. I feel a vague twinge of sadness, looking around at the carefully muted colours I'd painted the shop, all the work I'd done creating an atmosphere conducive to the sale of antiques—a trifle gloomy, almost sepia-tinted, the odd lamp casting a cosy pool of light in the dimmest corners. I imagine the clean laminated surfaces, bright paint, carefully arranged displays that will replace the carefully arranged clutter of my showroom, the chirpy vegans who will succeed my more subdued but eclectic customers.

When he arrives, a little earlier than I'd expected, he is not at all the sort of man I'd imagined. Although I hadn't spent too much time thinking about it, I'd expected someone a little alternative-looking—middle-aged, bearded and pale, wholesomely earnest, long and flexible from years of yoga, a long-shorts-and-Birkenstocks type of bloke who would arrive on a bicycle. Instead, the man who emerges from a sexy little Mercedes coupe is youngish, late thirties, tall and well built, dressed as if he's stepped straight out of a Hugo Boss advertisement, and so totally unlike the men (uncommon anyway) who frequent my shop that at first I assume he is stopping to ask directions. But he's not the kind of bloke who would ever get lost.

I watch him dubiously as he approaches my desk, his smile wide and outrageously white, totally assured of his welcome.

'G'day,' he says in an American accent, his beautiful brown and densely muscled forearm outstretched in greeting. 'Dustin

Macarthy.' Then, obviously mistaking my surprise for confusion: 'We have an appointment. I'm your new tenant.'

Dustin's handshake is a little too firm, and a little over-long. He's the sort of bloke that Rob would instinctively dislike, the sort of man who was once strictly Eastern Suburbs, or North Shore, but who's become increasingly common in the Northern Beaches over the last twenty years: smooth, oozing self-confidence, reeking of money. And though he's a picture of health, there's nothing of the health nut about him. He's the type of bloke that I would usually be a little sneery about, but for some reason, though my generosity had worn thin with my elderly customer, I'm feeling magnanimous towards my incoming tenant. After all, his rent will be supporting me for some time.

'Surely *you* don't run a health food store,' I blurt out.

He laughs. 'Is it so surprising?'

'I just—I don't know—really expected someone else, I guess. You don't really look like ...' I falter, embarrassed.

'Like what? Did you expect me to be wearing hemp?' He raises his well-kept eyebrows.

'Well, yes. Something like that.'

He shrugs. 'It's a chain. I own it. I employ people to work in it. I don't necessarily live it. Though I'm not exactly unhealthy.'

He smiles, and for the first time I notice the brilliant green of his eyes—impossible in nature, surely?

He's come in to inspect the building, take measurements for fittings, check out samples of flooring, paint colours and so forth, and to go over some minor details of the lease. I'd expected the visit to be brisk and businesslike, to have him in and out of the shop quickly, but instead he takes his time, wandering about the place looking at this and that. I take a phone call, and watch as he weaves his way through the furniture towards the back and is lost from sight momentarily. By the time I get off the phone he's reappeared, is making his way back to me, treading purposefully. When he reaches me, he gives a bemused, questioning look, presenting me with the same small timber object that Erin had previously found so amusing.

'It's a sock darner,' I explain before he can ask.

'A sock darner? Right. I remember my granny darning—though not with anything like this. That's surely a lost art. How does this darn a sock?'

I explain as best I can.

'I just assumed it was some bizarre sexual ... implement.' His smile is mischievous—and contagious. 'But I guess darning's a pretty bizarre thing, really, when you come to think of it.'

I offer the piece to him, too, expecting another rejection. But he turns it over thoughtfully.

'Thanks, I like it. Will you wrap it in something for me?' He hands the darner back to me and our fingers meet for a too-long moment. I pull my hand away, avoiding his eyes, and hurry over to my desk to find some tissue paper. He thrusts his hands in his pockets, and gives the room another considering look. 'So are you guys closing this outfit down or just moving elsewhere?'

I give him a brief rundown of the situation.

'Sounds like a sensible decision. But you must be sad. Your grandfather's shop. That's really something, isn't it? You don't hear of that kinda thing so much these days. Family businesses lasting for generations. Although you're living the dream, aren't you—don't we all want to retire early?'

'I am sad—and slightly frightened, actually. I know I'm going to miss the shop.'

He takes the wrapped darner from me. 'Maybe it'll be a good thing to be away from all this, anyway. It's quite a reminder, isn't it?'

'A reminder of what?'

'Our mortality. Give me health food any day. What could be more about the present? About denying mortality. Anyway, thank you for this—though I'm not sure what I'm going to do with it. I usually just buy new socks when I get holes.'

'I guess you'll just have to find an alternative use.' I blush.

He gives his long, lazy laugh. 'You know—I have a cure for

your sadness. How about you shut the shop and we go out for lunch? My shout.'

'Oh, I've got ...'

'What? Customers to serve?' His gaze is sceptical. 'Come on. Why not? I can finish what I need to do here relatively quickly. And we can sort out all that paperwork over a bottle of Veuve. Maybe you can even teach me to darn. There's no reason,' he adds, 'that we can't mix business with pleasure. I've taken that as my personal motto—and so far it's working.' He is almost a caricature of a forward-moving, positive-affirmation-spouting American, but I have no desire to mock, not with that warm smile directed at me, and not when that startling green gaze is so damned *appreciative*. Instead, I'm feeling lightheaded, dizzy. There's a pleasurable fluttering in the pit of my stomach that I haven't felt for a long, long time.

I think of all the reasons why I should stay, take a deep breath.

'Why not,' I say. And go.

The lunch ends up being a long one. He takes me to a wine bar in Collaroy that I've never noticed before. It's a strangely muted place, cavern-like. The clientele seem determinedly quiet, unobtrusive, and even the staff speak in hushed voices, the whole atmosphere weirdly clandestine. When I remark on this to Dustin, *call me Dusty*, he laughs. 'It's just the lunchtime crowd,' he says. 'Probably all feeling guilty because they should be at work.'

'Like me.'

'Like you. It livens up in the evenings. When the younger crowd turns up.'

'You're a regular, then?' I raise an eyebrow, assume an air of mock disapproval and an obviously flirty tone that vaguely appals me.

'I am. And if we stay late enough, you can be one too.'

I don't stay late enough, though I'm sorely tempted. I don't drink too much champagne, and I don't say too much, either. I listen well, though, and discover that he spends six months of the year in Avalon, and the other six on the French Riviera, that he's a divorcee with no children, that he's six years younger than me, that he does indeed ride a bike—though not in hemp shirts and sandals but in lycra. I learn that he likes to swim, but hates chlorine pools, likes fish but doesn't eat seafood, prefers cats to dogs, studied law at Yale, and that his father was a hellfire and brimstone Baptist minister on the weekends and a successful car salesman during the week. I give him my highly unremarkable life story then offer up odd titbits of information, anecdotes, gossip. Neither of us discusses what's happening, why we're here. We don't need to—there's an elephant in the room and it looks, sounds and smells a lot like lust.

When I arrive home in the early evening and Rob asks me where I've been; I'm deliberately vague. Just a bit of shopping, I say. And then I called over to see Mum. I don't elaborate, and Rob takes me at my word, doesn't give my dodgy account a second thought. He pours me a glass of wine, serves up the green chicken curry he's prepared. Jess is home tonight, and the three of us sit around the table together, a rare occurrence. I do my best to participate in what should be a jolly little family occasion, but I'm distracted, my mind won't be still, lurching back and forth between tingling anticipation and hideous guilt.

First secrets, now lies.

When I pick my mother up later in the week for shopping, I ask her how Mick is going. Is he drinking less, getting out more, finding a way to talk civilly to Sarah, seeing the kids regularly? She informs me, with a faintly smug smile, that he seems vastly improved. I'm driving along that maddeningly slow strip of Pittwater Road in Dee Why, somehow managing to hit every single red light.

'It's talking to that journalist,' my mother says. 'Erin. You know, I think it's been good for him.'

'Good for him? I'm surprised that discussing the events surrounding Angie's death could be good for Mick in his current state. He's been advised to keep clear of trauma, Mum. Bad memories, that sort of thing. Don't they just exacerbate his condition?'

'Oh, but she's a lovely woman, Erin, don't you think? I think it must almost be like talking to a doctor for him, poor love. I know it was for me—' She stops, realising what she's said, gives me an anxious look as I jam my foot down fiercely at an orange light, and glare at her.

'You're talking to her? I thought you said it was a bad idea. That it was only stirring up trouble.'

'*We-ell.*' She fiddles with the clasp on her handbag, refuses to meet my eyes. 'You were all talking to her—and then Mick seemed so cheerful afterwards. Anyway, I thought I should give her a call. She's quite a charming woman, isn't she? So smart and—forthright. And good-looking—very good for her age. Lovely skin. And such a lovely figure.'

I ignore her reflexively pointed comments and cut to the chase. 'So you've spoken to her, what? Once? Twice? And what does Mick think?'

'Oh, a couple of times, love. I'm meeting her again next week, I think. I haven't told your brother—and you're not to either. It'll only upset him.'

'So what made you change your mind? I thought you didn't want to stir up all the old troubles.' I take off fast, then pull up hard at the next set of lights, but Mum doesn't notice.

'I thought it was important that she got all sides of the story, Jane. I wanted to set the record straight.'

'What do you mean, set the record straight? There's no conflict, as far as I know.'

'To give my perspective. About what happened. *And* about Angie.'

'What about Angie, Mum? Angie was murdered; she was a little girl. It was a terrible, terrible tragedy. What other perspective can you provide?'

The smile my mother gives me is slightly pitying. 'Well, you have your memories, darling. And I have mine.'

ERIN: Thanks so much for meeting me, Mrs Griffin. It's really kind of you.

BARBARA: That's okay, love. But I would prefer it if you didn't mention it to Michael just yet. He's very sensitive about all this. He'd hate to think of me talking to you about Angie. About what happened. I'll let him know myself, when the time is right.

ERIN: That's fine. It's very generous of you to talk to me.

BARBARA: Yes, well, as I was saying over the phone, I thought it was important that you get a different perspective. Different to Michael and Jane's, I mean.

I'm not saying it wasn't an unimaginably dreadful thing—it was—it could hardly have been worse. And I've never ever forgiven myself for letting her go there on her own; I was responsible, after all. But the thing is, a young girl ought to be able to walk up to the shops and back alone by the time she's fourteen. She ought to be allowed out. And what happened didn't stop me with my Jane. I didn't become one of those mothers. Oh, I might have been a bit overprotective for a while, but it didn't last. Because it's giving in to them, isn't it? That's what they want. It's just like those terrorists: they want us to be afraid. Well, that's not the sort of person I am. I've never been like that.

ERIN: So are there things you remember differently?

BARBARA: Oh, it's not so much that I remember anything differently. I'm sure you've heard all the details of that terrible day, and you don't need me to go over them. It's more that I wanted to talk about Angie herself. The way those two tell it, Angela was some sort of ... I don't know ... a goddess. But that's just silly. In my opinion. Angie was just an ordinary little girl, who had extraordinarily bad luck.

ERIN: The worst.

BARBARA: I don't mean to appear cold, but Angie wasn't my daughter, and she wasn't Jane and Mick's sister. And I've always thought it was so unfortunate and unfair—the effect that Angie's death had on both of them.

Michael might've had a silly schoolboy crush on his cousin—and so might Jane, for that matter—but if you ask me, and they'd deny it, they've both let it take up too much space in their lives.

ERIN: How do you mean?

BARBARA: Jane could've gone off to uni, you know. She was a bright girl. Much brighter than Angie. Though Jane would never see it herself. She was always in Angie's shadow. I actually thought it was going to be a great thing—Angie moving away like that. Going to another school. I thought it might set Jane free—help her shine a bit. Let people really see her. Find the things she was good at, instead of trying so hard to be like her cousin. But when Angie was killed, it was almost as if Jane was paralysed. I don't think she ever found those things. It certainly wasn't my dream for her—that she would leave school to work in her grandfather's second-hand furniture shop. Don't get me wrong, she and Rob have made a good go of it—it's a very different sort of place, now. But she's never done anything else. Never lived anywhere else. Never even really been anywhere else. And I'm fond of Rob; you couldn't have asked for a better husband. But he was practically her first proper boyfriend. A girl should, you know, look around a bit more. I was pregnant at sixteen, so I know what I'm saying. I've never regretted marrying Doug, but sometimes I wonder ... And for my Janey to be in just the same position—oh, she wasn't pregnant, and she was a bit older, of course, but still she settled for the first boy who came along when she didn't have to. Ah, well. It's not all that important. They're happy enough. And at least Jess isn't in any hurry. She changes boyfriends like most people change their shoes ... She's probably one of those lesbians, knowing my luck. Oh, dear, you're not—

ERIN: No. That's okay. I'm not.

BARBARA: Not that I'd mind. But you know ... you just want the best for your kids. And then there's Mick. I know they think I don't realise how bad he is, but I do. He should never have joined the force in the first place. I know that's not Angie's fault, really, but he just never got over her. He goes to the cemetery every year, on the anniversary, leaves flowers. It's almost as if he won't let himself get over it. He stopped thinking for himself, stopped *wanting* for himself when she died. It was as if ... as if she took a part of his soul with her.

His father more or less forced him to go into the police force, but it was a bad decision. I knew that at the time. He was never that sort of boy. He was sensitive. Sweet. He was interested in other things—music, books, art. He was always drawing—little sketches, cartoons. I always imagined he'd go into teaching, something like that. And he should have. Look at him now, poor bugger. He's barely there. He blames work, of course, but it goes back further, back to Angie. The doctors say it doesn't, that there was no pre-existing trauma, but I can't believe that what happened to Angie didn't start it all—or at least make him more vulnerable. I know they're exposed to some terrible things in the force, but my Doug was all right, wasn't he? He survived tougher commands, and he stuck it out for forty years. His father hasn't ever said it, but I know he thinks that Mick is just ... weak. But I know it's not that. Angie's death has had such an effect on every part of his life. You just have to look at his wife—his ex-wife now—Sarah. She's so very similar to Angie to look at: blonde, tanned, gorgeous. But she led him such a dance. An open relationship, she wanted. Open! Even after they had the littlies. I don't know what possessed him. It's just not possible to have a marriage under those terms. Why bother? I don't like to think of the damage it's done to their poor kiddies. It's just been a nightmare for him. An absolute nightmare. There've been times when—anyway. This isn't what you want to hear about, is it?

ERIN: Actually, this *is* what I want to hear about. It's all important to my project.

BARBARA: Oh, yes. I see. So you don't just want to know about Angie?

ERIN: Building up a picture of the victim is important, of course—it's crucial—but it's how her death affected you—

BARBARA: That's the thing—everything always leads back to Angie. That's been the whole sorry disaster of our lives. Oh, dear …

ERIN: No, that's okay. Here. Have a tissue.

BARBARA: Can I just tell you a bit about her? I'd really like to do that, I think. To give you a fuller picture.

ERIN: Please. You just tell me what you like. I'll be editing all your stories, anyway. The more the merrier, so to speak.

BARBARA: Well, I don't know that I'd want this in it. But I'd really like to—get it off my chest. I don't know. I don't suppose you could perhaps turn off the recorder? Just for a minute. It's background, but it's probably not something I'd like anyone to hear.

ERIN: If it's something you don't want made public, I'm happy to not use it.

BARBARA: Oh. Okay. Just as long as it stays confidential.

ERIN: So what is it you wanted to tell me? Was it something about your niece?

BARBARA: I'm just wondering where I should begin. I don't want to talk ill of the dead—and I never thought Angie was a bad girl or anything. And, of course, I was very fond of her; she was my brother's child, after all. But …

ERIN: But?

BARBARA: Look. I don't want you to think I'm exaggerating, or that I'm looking for excuses, saying that she got what she deserved or anything, because that's not what I'm getting at. No one deserves to be murdered. And she was so young … a baby, really. She could have grown up to be any sort of a person. Kids change such a lot, don't they? You learn that when you watch your own grow up. They never turn out the way you imagined.

But I don't know about Angie. At that age she was manipulative. This isn't something that you'll hear from Jane or Michael. Those two could never see it. But that summer, she was so desperate to stay with us. And it wasn't for the pleasure of Janey's company— or even Michael's—though both of them see that very differently.

I don't know what Mick got up to with her—I don't want to know, if I'm honest—but I do know it didn't go both ways. Angie certainly didn't have a crush on poor Mick. She was always nice enough to his face, but I could see her sometimes—her expression. She'd be irritable, impatient even, when he wasn't looking. And Jane bored her senseless. I remember the poor little thing would be on at her half the day to play a game, or to watch TV. I felt that sorry for her. Oh, Angie'd give her a little bit of her time, most days—a couple of hours of TV in the morning, say, and Jane would be so grateful. It was sort of … pathetic. But I don't think Angie particularly liked either of them. There was a coldness about her. It's the sort of thing a mother senses, I guess.

I've always wondered what it was she stayed for, those holidays—if it wasn't to be with the kids. I thought maybe it was the Ferber boy, Adam, but I'm not so sure.

ERIN: And what happened to Adam Ferber? Is he still around?

BARBARA: No. He died in his early twenties, poor lad. A drug overdose. But he and Mick were never close after all this happened.

ERIN: So why do you think she wanted to stay so badly? Did she have something planned?

BARBARA: No, I don't think she had anything planned, exactly, but I think in the beginning she might have thought she'd be able to get back with that lot she'd been warned off earlier in the year. I honestly don't know. Maybe she thought I'd let them roam the streets all day. Carol was much stricter than me, but I wasn't that easygoing. I still had to know where they were.

ERIN: Who were this lot she'd been warned off? What had happened?

BARBARA: Well, I never knew the exact details—it wasn't the sort of thing Carol was likely to tell me—but we found out later that Angie had been hanging about some much older boys earlier that year. And fairly undesirable boys, as far I could make out. You know the type: unemployed, drugs, fast cars. That was the real reason Barry and Carol decided to move house and book her into that private school. And when they found that she wasn't a virgin, even though she was so young ... Well, it didn't take a genius to work out that it wasn't necessarily connected to her murder.

ERIN: Oh, I see.

BARBARA: I suppose it sounds terrible, discussing my own niece like this, but despite what everyone says, she wasn't really all that nice a child. She was always looking out for herself. She was probably a bit like her mother—like Carol—that way. Carol was a terrible snob, a real social climber. You always felt she was measuring you up, seeing how you could be useful to her. And Angie was a chip off the old block—though obviously she wasn't trying to climb *up* any social ladders.

All that stuff about her being the sweetest, kindest, most wonderful thing ever—it's just not true. She wasn't sugar and spice and everything nice.

ERIN: Well, I appreciate that, Mrs Griffin. It certainly adds to my sense of how the family, well, how you all fit together. The dynamics.

BARBARA: Yes, and I think it's important—if you're building up a picture of what happened after Angie died, you need the— what do you call it?—the context.

Now, what else is it that you want to know? I've been rattling on for so long I don't know where I'm up to. I'm glad I got that out of my system, though. It's been upsetting me, the idea of you only hearing about Angie from those two. There's no, no balance.

ERIN: Well, I've spoken to Rob, as well. Your son-in-law.

BARBARA: Rob? Whatever for? I know he was under suspicion too, poor lad, but he barely knew her. Anyway, what else would you like to know?

ERIN: If you could tell me a little about what happened in your family just after Angie died. How the kids dealt with the situation. And your husband. Your sister-in-law and your brother. Maybe if you could start with the day she disappeared. Just for continuity's sake.

BARBARA: I went over this so often, you know. Back then. It seems odd to tell it again after so many years. You know the kids were all mad over those pinball games back then—they were like the computer games now, I suppose, only you had to go out to play them, which was healthier, if you ask me. There were those awful pinball parlours, of course, and they'd all be off there given the opportunity. There were a couple in Manly, down at the old pier, and in Dee Why, I think. But they had a machine just up the road at Ferber's shop and Mick and his mates had taken to going up there during the holidays. Angie used to go up, too—they'd probably spend a few hours every day at the shop, I'd say. I wasn't keen on Janey going up there—she was just that little bit younger, and the boys didn't want her there either, but Angie was a different matter. They were all nice boys, Adam Ferber and Jason Dunne and Darren Stokes, and there were a few others I can't think of right now. I could see Angie'd had enough of Jane towards the end of that week. Jane was still just a baby—only twelve. I took them over to the mall a couple of times, but, really, it'd been a bit boring. I could see Angie was itching to be out with the older kids. The boys. If only I'd known how besotted Mick was, then, I would have done something to discourage it. I'd have sent her home.

Anyway, that particular day, Mick had been out since early and then just after lunch Angie asked if she could go up to Ferber's, meet him up there. I said yes. It's something I'll always regret, of course—if only I'd found something else for her to do. But how could I have known? And you can't turn back time, can you? However hard you wish.

ERIN: No.

BARBARA: The rest of that day ... that time—it's actually a bit of a blank for me. I probably sound pretty calm about it all these years later, but at the time I was utterly devastated. It's hard to describe how terrible it was. I really felt that it was all my fault—I'd let her go out, I'd been responsible—and it took me years to get over that feeling. And the feeling that everyone, every person I knew and plenty I didn't, blamed me. Even if they didn't—I blamed me. But I can look back now and think that letting her walk up to Ferber's—just half-a-dozen blocks of suburban street—really wasn't letting her take any terrible risks.

But that whole time is a blur. First Angie didn't come home and we had to tell Carol and Barry. It was a few days before they found her body. Such a terrible time that was ... We were all still hoping, you know? We were sick with worry, but still there was a possibility she was alive.

And then when they found her, Michael disappeared. It was as if the world was falling apart. I couldn't take it in. I just stayed locked in my room—swallowing Valium like it was aspirin. And there was the press outside, and constant phone calls. It was an absolute nightmare. Poor little Jane, she was pretty much left to look after herself for days.

And do you know what? All that time, and everything that was going on, nobody actually visited. Nobody. None of our friends. People kept away. There were no calls to see if we needed help, no one bringing meals. It was as if we had the plague.

I went off the rails completely for months. Until they found that other girl. Doug was amazing, he really was. He just took over the best he could. Didn't complain. Oh, we had a row every now and then, but he never once said it was my fault. No matter what anyone else said. And my dad too—he was there for me as well as Barry. That made Carol hate him—Dad, I mean. She'd never really been fond of Dad—he was a bit too common for her. He was a rough old bloke—always had a fag in the corner of his mouth, he swore a bit, liked a beer, the horses, followed the football. A bit of a man's man, I guess. But a good heart. After Angie died Dad said straight out to someone or other—at the wake, I think it was, I wasn't there, but someone told me later—that there was no need for me to shoulder the blame ... that it could have been any girl, that it was just bad luck and the only one who should be blamed was Angie's killer. Well, after that Carol didn't ever speak to any of us again.

But he was right, wasn't he? It could just as easily have been Jane, after all. She'd walked that same route, those same blocks, so many times. It could have been *my* daughter. I used to feel guilty that I felt so glad, but I couldn't help it, you know. I really was glad that it wasn't my baby, that whoever had done it had taken Angie and not Jane. That's awful, isn't it? But I suspect there were other mothers who felt the same way.

Those first months were just terrible. I couldn't work, I barely left the house, I couldn't think of anything else. I stopped working, lost most of my clients, all my friends. I neglected the kids. I really have no idea what they did—half the time there was no dinner. I didn't clean, or do the washing. Nothing. I just wasn't coping. There was all the worry over Mick, too. He was a suspect. The world had turned upside down. It was as if I was trapped in some terrible nightmare. And Doug—I guess he was having a bad time too, in his own way. He was transferred out of homicide when they found that other little girl's body, officially anyway, but I think unofficially he was still involved. I remember he went to her funeral. It was somewhere out west, out past the mountains. He took that sort of stuff very seriously.

It was hard for all of us, but I suspect it was the children who suffered most. I don't know what Mick did—he spent way too much time alone, in his room, wallowing in it all. And he disappeared every now and then. Not for days, like that first time, but overnight sometimes. I just turned a blind eye. And poor little Jane—that's when she started spending all her time at the shop with Dad. She'd just walk there from school, instead of coming home.

I decided when they found that other girl that I would push it all away. That I'd force myself to stop thinking about it, stop dwelling on it. What had happened had happened. It might sound callous, but I had to do it. For the kids. For my marriage. And even then I think I might have left it too late, in the end. For Michael, especially. I did everything I could—I sent him to counselling, talked to him, kept him busy, tried to stop him spending so much time alone, but by that time he was fifteen and it's too late for a mother by then. You don't have much influence any more. It was better for Jane—but still, I think it changed her life.

Jane should've had more kids, you know. One—well, it's not right. Not for the parents and not for the kid. I saw what happened when Angie died. Barry and Carol had nothing left to live for. And it killed them both.

The sisters-in-law are not allies. Far from it. Barbara and Carol dislike each other, cordially, but profoundly. They have their little wars—wars that are waged silently, without comment or overt disagreements. They are wars over trivialities—the efficacy of fabric softener, say, or the superiority of butter over margarine—but as always the trivial is just a stand-in for far bigger things, for opposed ways of living, of doing, of being. It's always been like that.

Barbara often wonders just what it is that attracted her older brother to a woman like Carol. He'd been something of a larrikin as a kid, always fun to be with, full of jokes and high spirits. He'd been a bit different to other fellas, she remembers, and though he'd joined the school football team, played cricket, as he'd been expected to do, he'd also joined the school choir, got parts in the school musicals, learnt the piano. He'd had a dream of a voice as a little fellow—an almost shockingly pure, sweet soprano—and unlike most boys he'd been only too willing to use it, never saying no when he was asked to sing at school events or occasionally by their mother to entertain company. He'd disappointed their dad, of course, when he turned up his nose at the furniture shop and went into accountancy, but that wasn't what changed him, distanced him from his family. Carol was to blame for that.

Now somehow Angie herself has become a weapon in this unacknowledged battle of wills. Barbara isn't all that attached to her niece, if truth be known. She's fond of her in a lacklustre sort of way—Angie's her only brother's child, her only niece—but there's something about Angela, some indefinable quality in her character, that Barbara just can't warm to. There's something too knowing about her, something calculating—or perhaps it's just that Barbara senses some sort of a challenge to her adult pre-eminence, there's a feeling that the child has summed her up and found her wanting. But it suits her to be on Angie's side this time—to support the girl's wishes—even if that means cooking for an extra child for a week or two. The addition of another child to the family has its benefits; benefits that more than repay any expense of upkeep. Angie will keep Jane occupied during the slow final weeks of the holidays, those last two weeks when time seems to drag and the return to school starts to become tantalising. Angie's company will stop her mooching around in front of the TV the whole time, bored, or ringing up school friends ceaselessly—trying to arrange complicated meet-ups or outings that somehow inevitably involve her mother. With Angie around, Barbara can just get on with the endless things she has to get on with.

She isn't so sure about Angie and Mick's relationship. They've been close ever since they were toddlers playing in the sandpit together, but as they've moved into their teenage years their friendship has become more rather than less intense. The two cousins are currently perhaps a little closer than she's strictly comfortable with, but that's not something she needs to worry about really, not yet. Angie's only just fourteen, after all, and she figures that Mick has other things—his friends, sport, school—to keep him occupied.

When the children suggest that Angie comes home with them, the three of them rushing up the slippery stairs from the pool together, excited, urgent, united—a force to be reckoned with—it's hard to deny them. The parents are settled on Barry and Carol's verandah, enjoying their pre-dinner drinks, nibbling on the hors d'oeuvres that Barbara has brought—Jatz and French onion dip, a bright array of tooth-picked appetisers—cubes of Coon cheese, cabanossi, red and green pickled onions. Barbara knows that Carol would have preferred something more sophisticated—camembert, caviar, Christ knows what.

She'd seen the disdain in her sister-in-law's expression when she'd handed over her offering—you'd think she'd given her a plate full of dog shit, not nibbles.

When the children rush over with their request that Angie come and stay—*she's bored, she doesn't know anyone here yet, there's nothing to do, please, Mum!*—Barbara's quick to intercede on Angela's behalf, pleased to be given the opportunity to provide a contrast to her sister-in-law's snobbishness, which Carol tries hard to dress up as normal maternal anxiety.

'Oh, Carol, she'll be fine. Really. The kids can just hang around at home when I'm with a customer. And Doug'll be around a bit—he's got a few arvo shifts, I think. Haven't you, Doug? Before your night shifts start? He can take the girls to the beach—and I'll take them down to the mall. Maybe we'll go in to Manly, go to the movies. You'd like that, wouldn't you?' The smile she gives is broad and warm, full of welcome, and she relishes her moment of power, knowing full well that Carol will be rapidly stockpiling an arsenal of obstacles.

'No. I don't think so, Angela.' Carol is looking at her daughter, but Barbara knows that her conversational aim is intended to be more scattergun than pistol. 'You know we have to do a whole lot of things before you start school. There's not that long to go. We have to get uniforms fitted. They've given us a list as long as your arm of things we need.' She sighs, gives a tight smile. 'I don't know what it is we're actually paying the school for.'

'Oh, come on, Mum.' Angie sounds slightly exasperated, but her smile is winning. It's obvious she's keeping a tight rein on her frustration. 'It's weeks until school starts. There's heaps of time for all that. And what am I meant to do here, anyway?'

'Darling.' Carol picks up a red onion delicately between two fingers, considers it briefly, drops it back on the plate. 'We've been through this. You've plenty to do. Doctor Prescott has given you that extra maths work, and then there's the English reading list to get started on. And you've done absolutely no piano practice since the end of last term. Mrs Varley will be appalled. You're in the third form now—it's time to get serious.'

'But it's the holidays, Mum. Who does homework in the holidays? Or piano practice? That's ridiculous.' Angela has lost her battle with calm; her voice is shrill with indignation, and her father wanders over inquiringly.

'What's going on, love?'

'Mum won't let me stay over at Aunty Barb's.'

He raises his eyebrows at his wife. 'What's the problem, Caz?'

Carol's mouth twists in irritation—she hates being called Caz.

'She's got such a lot to do, before she starts her new school. Private school standards are slightly higher, Barry. We don't want her falling behind.'

'Jesus, Carol. Don't be ridiculous.' Barry has drunk just enough beer to argue with his wife. 'She's only fourteen, for Christ's sake. Let the child enjoy her holidays. She's got the rest of her life to work hard.'

'But there's so much to do ... there's maths, reading, piano. And the uniforms have to be taken in and shortened.'

'I can help her with the maths, Aunty Carol. I did pretty well, last year. They're moving me up to the A class,' Mick offers eagerly. 'And we've got the organ for her to practise on if she brings her music.'

'An organ is not the same as a piano, I'm afraid, Michael. So that doesn't really help.'

Barbara has to stop herself from laughing at the look of resigned distaste on her sister-in-law's face.

'And Mum can hem her skirts, can't you, Mum?' Jane chips in helpfully.

'If you like, Carol. Though it is still a few weeks away.'

'Come on, Mum. Dad? Can you tell her it's okay?'

Barry looks at his wife, frowning. 'Come on, love. It's up to you, but I can't see how there can be any harm in it. And what will she do here all day?'

'She'll be bored shitless, Cazza.' Doug has joined the conversation, though he's usually eager to stay as far as possible from domestic rows. His voice is a lazy, beer-soaked drawl. He picks up a black olive from a bowl on the table, pops it in his mouth, then spits it out on the table.

'Jesus Ch-riiist. What are those things? I thought it was chocolate.'

His expression is comical, his lips pursed, squint-eyed, and the kids are giggling, relieved that the tension's been broken.

As always, Carol indulges her brother-in-law. 'You are revolting, Doug. I can see why you and Barb never go out anywhere decent. You're a disgrace.'

Barbara has to bite her tongue, but Doug accepts Carol's attempt at humour with a grin.

'So can I, Mum? Please.'

'We'll make sure she does her times tables,' Mick offers, sensing some softening in Carol's armour.

She addresses Barbara. 'I don't want her going to Dee Why, or meeting up with anyone else.'

'There won't be any trips to Dee Why unless it's with me.' Barbara keeps her voice light, though she's fuming.

'And she's not to go to the beach on her own.'

'We don't ever—'

'Without an adult, I mean.'

'Mick's only just allowed, Caz,' Doug's tone is reassuring, calming. 'We wouldn't let your little princess down there on her own. We wouldn't let our little princess down there on her own. You dunno what mischief they'd get up to. Probably talk the boys into giving them their boards. Get out the back. And that'd be the end of life as we know it ...' He gives an expectant grin. It's an old argument between the girls and Doug, but this isn't the time. They're not interested now that they've won.

'So, can I go?'

Her mother gives a defeated sigh. 'Go and pack your bag, then. Take your own toothpaste, and soap and shampoo. You know where the travel pack is. Plenty of underwear. And zinc cream ...'

The kids aren't listening, have raced off into the house.

'Can you dry off a bit more?' she shouts after them, but it's too late.

The men have drifted out onto the lawn, drawn back into discussing some new business deal, or golf, or some police scandal or whatever it is that men discuss when they're drunk and the women can't hear them. *Probably some young thing's tits*, Barbara thinks uncharitably, annoyed at being left alone with her sister-in-law.

'I'm sorry to harp on it, Barbara, but I really don't want Angela meeting up with any of her old friends. We're making a clean break. This is such an opportunity for her. A new leaf. I don't want her dragged down. I know it sounds severe, but there's so much at stake.'

'But her old friends aren't so bad, Carol. I know most of the families. I mean, they're not doctors or lawyers, but they're decent enough people. Did something happen?'

Carol ignores her question, goes on as if her sister-in-law hadn't spoken, 'Angela's a bright girl, and I don't want her chances ruined by no-hopers. Those girls will all be knocked up at sixteen.'

There's a sting in the tail here that Barbara can't fail to notice, having been knocked up at sixteen herself. She and Doug had married, but she'd lost the baby at twenty-five weeks. A stillbirth. She'd been more relieved than anything else. And Doug too—though there was nothing they could do in those days about the marriage vows. They'd been more careful after that. Mick hadn't come along until she was twenty-five, and Jane three years later—she'd been considered an older mum by that time.

'And can you just keep an eye on her? Don't let her go off by herself all day. If they go to the mall, I'd rather you dropped them off and picked them up.'

'I would anyway. But I do let them go up to the corner shop and back. It's only a few blocks. And there're no busy roads to cross.'

'That's fine. But just straight there and back. And not alone. You hear so much about all sorts of creeps about the place these days.'

She smiles agreeably. 'Of course, Carol. You shouldn't worry so much. We do know how to look after children, you know. We have two of our own—and we really are quite responsible people.'

Carol looks momentarily embarrassed, as if aware that she's gone too far. 'Of course you are. It's just—you know. It's nothing personal. It's just that other families have different ... ideas about what's okay. Especially at this age.'

'I suppose so.'

'And she is our only child. It's different. She's doubly precious.'

Barbara doesn't know that she agrees, but there's nothing she can say. She gives a vaguely patronising smile, sips her wine. She's won.

The victory is short-lived, however. A week later, Doug is on the phone to Carol, telling her that her daughter hasn't come home, that she hasn't been seen for hours, that they don't know where she is. That they've called the police.

It's something no parent should ever have to tell another.

There'd been a situation once, years ago, when Angie had been in first grade and Barbara had been in charge of the pick-up of both Angie and Mick. Angie was coming home for the afternoon. Barbara had lost track of time and had been late, only ten or so minutes, but Angie hadn't been at the designated pick-up zone and Mick had no idea where she was.

'She was here a minute ago, Mummy,' he said. 'She just disappeared.' The school emptied out quickly in those days, so most of the kids had left, the walkers heading every which way, the younger kids already collected. Barbara had done a quick search of the school grounds, asked a few teachers, but the child was nowhere to be seen. In the end she'd driven home in a state of panic, searching the few blocks for the little blonde girl, pausing to ask each cluster of homeward-bound children if they'd seen her. She'd left Mick and Jane in the car and had run inside and called Carol, who was at home, and told her that she couldn't find her daughter, that she'd meet her back at the school, that they could search together.

She and Carol had pulled up outside the school simultaneously, had found Angie almost immediately, sitting on her cardboard port outside the front gate, the picture of injured innocence. Barbara had been so relieved that she'd hugged the child, and then her surprised mother, who patted her awkwardly on the back before pulling away.

'Oh, God! I'm *so* sorry, Carol!'

Her sister-in-law said nothing, turned to the child. 'What a fright you've given us, Angela. Where on earth were you?'

Angie had turned to her mother and pouted, 'Aunty Barb was late, Mummy. I waited for ages, and then I had to go to the toilet. I was busting. I couldn't wait. And when I came out, everyone had gone.' Her little voice shook piteously, her eyes filled. 'And I was very scared.'

Carol had raised her fine eyebrows at this, given Barbara a quizzical stare.

'Well, sweetie, you should really have waited. Or told Mick what you were doing.'

'But I told you she was late.' The child pushed her face into her mother's skirt, working herself up to a wail.

'Sometimes grown-ups get held up, sweetie. Sometimes it can't be helped.' Carol gave Barbara a tight smile, prised the child from her legs.

'Pick up your port, Angela. It's time to go home.'

'Can't I go back with them?' She paused in her crying, gave an indignant squeal.

'Another time. We're all a bit shaky after this.'

Angie started to wail again, and both Mick and Jane, who had thus far remained wide-eyed and silent, joined in.

'Oh, let her come, Carol. They've all been looking forward to it. Jane and I even baked a cake especially, didn't we, sweetheart?'

'I think they've probably had enough excitement for one day. Angela certainly has. I might get her bathed and put to bed early—and she can probably do without any sugary treats.' Carol's smile was perfectly pleasant, but it was clear to Barbara that Carol was making a point, that this was *her* punishment—the children were just the meat in the sandwich.

'You're probably right. I'll send an extra piece of cake for Angie in Mick's lunchbox tomorrow.' She beamed at her sister-in-law. 'You make sure you remember to ask him, Angie.'

Barbara marched back to the car, swinging the children's hands, ignoring their tears. On the way home she stopped at Ferber's and bought them a big bag of licorice bullets, telling them to save some for their cousin.

She has never forgotten the sick terror of those minutes when Angie couldn't be located (ten, God, maybe only fifteen max—they'd seemed longer, seemed endless), the horror of ringing Carol, the gasping relief she'd felt seeing the child there, perched on her bag, waiting patiently. Her guilt over what had been at least partially her mistake—though God knows whether Angie had actually been telling the truth; she wouldn't have put it past the child to have been hiding somewhere all along, or off playing a game—was only slightly dissipated by her sister-in-law's civilised hostility.

The hideousness of those moments pales, however, in comparison to what she's feeling now—with the teenage Angie missing, her movements unaccounted for, missing more than five hours from what they can work out, the police called, the night dark. And this time there's no escaping her own culpability: she should have known where Angie was. Why hadn't she?

There's no way Barbara can make the phone call. She lets Doug, practised at delivering such unthinkable news, do the dirty work. She stands by his side, listening as he speaks to her brother, his voice so gentle, and more solemn than she has ever heard it. She is shaking violently now, one hand clutching her own hysterically weeping daughter, the other clasped over her own mouth—in an unconscious effort to silence the scream that's bubbling up, threatening to escape.

The house is crowded with police by the time Carol and Barry arrive—the lounge a frantic sea of blue uniforms, noisy with directives and the buzz of radios, the panic temporarily submerged beneath the routine chaos of official procedure. A female constable answers the door and ushers the terrified parents in, offers tea, comfort, a senior officer to speak to, and Barbara takes the opportunity to remove herself, dragging the still hysterical Jane with her, to leave the room before she's forced to meet her sister-in-law's accusing gaze.

But it can't be avoided all evening, and eventually, when she has Jane settled—asleep, though the sobs still burst out in agonised little hiccups—Barbara forces herself back up the hall, and into the lounge room.

All that focused energy has evaporated now that most of the police have gone. Two officers are sitting at the dining table, talking to Mick, who is slumped against his father, his face blank. Barry and Carol huddle together on the three-seater; the female officer crouches before them holding Carol's hand and murmuring reassurances. Barbara breathes in deeply and takes slow steady steps across the room. Her sister-in-law looks up as she approaches, pulls her hand away from the policewoman, stands and waits, swaying slightly. Her dazed look has disappeared; her face is set, stony, rigid with anger. Barbara's own momentum falters briefly, but she pushes herself forward, stops only when she's within touching distance of her sister-in-law. The two women look at one other for a long moment and Barbara reaches out, but her sister-in-law gasps, flinches.

'Don't you—'

Barbara looks away, looks back, tries to speak. 'Oh, Carol ... I'm so—' But she falters. She cannot find words—not for what is happening. And not for what might happen.

And not, God help her, for what she will owe the other woman. There will never be words for that.

ERIN: So did anything change when the second girl was murdered? When you found out your cousin had been the victim of a serial killer?

JANE: I know it seems horrendous, but when that other girl died everything got better for us. For Mum, especially. The fact that it was random was terrifying, but it meant it was less her fault, if you know what I mean. And, of course, it meant Mick was in the clear.

ERIN: What do you recall about what happened when the other girl died?

JANE: I remember there were all those headlines, warnings about the Sydney Strangler, the police telling women and girls to stay in. It was pretty scary, I guess.

ERIN: The police decided that the two murders were linked almost immediately, didn't they? I'd have thought it would've taken longer ... I mean, just from what I've been able to glean from the papers, there were some pretty stark differences between the two cases. There was no evidence that your cousin used drugs, and she'd been moved some distance from wherever it was she was killed, whereas the police believed that the other girl died where she was found.

JANE: It wasn't just the fact that they were both strangled; there was something else, too. Dad always said the police had kept something back—some key piece of evidence that they didn't reveal, that tied the two killings together pretty conclusively. I don't know that Dad even knew what it was.

ERIN: What other things happened? Did it change how you felt about Angie's murder? And did it change how other people regarded you?

JANE: It had really just started to die down in a way. People weren't avoiding us so much. Everyone'd got used to it, I guess. But when they found the second girl, the press went to town. It was sort of exciting, I suppose—a serial killer. The scarf murders they called them. I've got all the cuttings from the papers and I reread them every now and then. There was all that 'fear in the community' stuff that seemed to go on for ages. It was different to now, of course, when everyone knows everything about serial killings. These days people know about profiling, about the sort of people who become serial killers. But back then it was all new to the public—and it was big news.

And for a while *we* were big news again. The press were camped outside, and hanging around the area, trying to get us to comment, or people who knew us. I don't know how long it went on, though. It seemed to go on forever, though probably it was only a few days—until there was some other thing to get everyone's attention.

ERIN: And did your family try to find out anything about the other girl?

JANE: I don't think so. I guess I never thought much about her at all after the immediate shock. You don't, do you, when you're a kid? Life just kinda goes on, you get used to it, take even the bad things for granted.

I've thought about her since, though. That poor lost girl. What a sad short life; what a horrible end. I realised I didn't know anything about her background, her family, where she was from. She was homeless. A child prostitute. That's all I know. And they couldn't find any connection at all with Angie, apart from their deaths. I know they tried, I can remember being questioned again, and Mick too, the police asking what

I knew about Angie and her friends. But there really wasn't anything that could tie them together. No link. There weren't all that many ways they could have been connected in those days without somebody knowing something. It's different now, all the internet stuff, there are so many ways. But living in the suburbs then, we were really protected. Or ignorant, I guess. We wouldn't have even understood what a prostitute really did, let alone known one.

ERIN: What about your aunt and uncle? Did they ever try to contact the other girl's family, do you know?

JANE: I honestly don't know. Though I doubt it. Carol just never recovered. I don't think she'd have thought talking to another family would help. And she and Uncle Barry split up later that year. No one ever said anything, it wasn't ever official, I don't think, but he just went—got a job in Darwin. Carol became a recluse. Mum tried to go and see her once or twice in that first year, but she never got past the front door.

I think at one point Carol considered suing Mum and Dad or something. She sent a letter. I'm not sure on what grounds—breach of care or something, I suppose. But Uncle Barry talked her out of it. Nothing was going to bring back Angie. Nothing was going to make Carol feel better.

So, are you looking for information on the other girl? Are you going to interview her family too?

ERIN: No. I don't think so.

JANE: But it would be interesting, wouldn't it—for your show, I mean? To compare the two families—their reactions, how the various family members recovered, that sort of thing. And there's a whole other story there, too, isn't there? There's always another story.

DENNINGTON, 1978

It's front-page news for a few days, but the headlines eventually peter out, and the story moves to page three, then a month later is down to one small paragraph in the middle of the newspaper.

There are interviews with people who knew her family. Not her mother, obviously—after her sister's death her mother had found it difficult to speak coherently to anyone, let alone nosy journalists looking for a quick story. But there is no scarcity of people willing to talk in a small town—an endless supply of 'anonymous sources' (were they trusted family friends? neighbours? school teachers?) offering up their unique perspective on the tragedy—determined to enjoy their allotted fifteen minutes. One piece particularly distresses her mother—the information could only have come, she insists, from someone who knew the family well, from someone she trusted. It's in the *Daily Mirror*, page three, just below the bosomy bikini girl.

Community in shock after murder

Sixteen-year-old Kelly McIvor, who was recently found murdered in Kings Cross, the second victim of what police fear may be a serial killing, grew up in the close-knit township of Dennington, New South Wales. The girl's mother was unwilling to comment, but friends of the family told reporters that the girl's murder came as a great shock.

Sources reported that Kelly had been having difficulties, but it was a surprise when the girl ran away from home late last year.

'Her poor mum ... to find out that she'd been living on the streets, working as a prostitute, taking drugs. It's every mother's nightmare.'

Kelly, who was known as 'Little Kell' during her time in Kings Cross, struggled with the breakup of her parents' marriage, a Dennington resident told our reporter.

'Kelly's been in all sorts of trouble with the police in the past few years. She was expelled from school—her mother just couldn't cope. She was a sweet kid, though.'

The community of Dennington is rallying around the victim's mother, Diana McIvor, and Kelly's younger sister. Mrs Elaine Wardle, head of the local CWA, says that many families have provided food and other forms of support to the family. 'Something like this affects the entire community. It's the least we can do.'

She can see why her mother is so distressed by the article: all the guff about the community rallying around was lies. Other than the food—a half-dozen casseroles that her mother had discovered, already going off, on their doorstep one hot afternoon, as if whoever had delivered them had been too afraid to knock on the door, had dropped their containers and run—there has been no community support. There has been plenty of community gossip, though, and rumours, and plenty of public avoidance. Instead of ongoing support for the devastated family, her mother lost her cleaning jobs a few weeks after Kelly's funeral. Both of the ladies she cleaned for—no doubt desperate to avoid having to sympathise, to face her unbearable sadness—had suggested it would do her good to take a few months' break from working, to give herself time to heal, to sort things through in her head.

But it was becoming more and more obvious that even ten lifetimes wouldn't be long enough to heal her mother, to sort this thing through. Her mum was gone, and however hard she tried to find her, to pull her out, it seemed that she was just as lost as Kelly. Her mum was never coming back.

She wonders sometimes whether they're looking at the old man all wrong—his daughter, his wife, even the son, to some extent. They're blind to the real man—and the old man knows it. Depends on it. If they saw him clearly, if they really understood him, they'd lose their perspective, they'd lose their way to measure everything, understand everything. The past, the present. Themselves.

Every now and then she captures an expression passing across his face in a blink-and-you'll-miss-it moment. Sometimes it's when he's listening to the radio, other times when she's blathering away about the state of the world outside, her life, his family, passing on some gossip she's heard about the other residents, the nursing staff, the doctors. Once she catches a furtive grimace—there's a politician speaking on the radio, excusing himself over some broken promise.

'I can't stand him either,' she confides in a whisper, changing the channel.

He doesn't look at her, stares stonily ahead, but she knows that there's something going on in his mind—it might just be a fleeting, primitive comprehension, or perhaps he's faking the whole thing. But she's confident that her strategy will have some effect—if she just keeps at it, keeps at him, eventually she'll hit on a moment when he's lucid, when he's there. That he'll crack. He'll tell her something.

He doesn't respond, doesn't look at her, there's nothing she can put her finger on, but this is one of those days when he's less absent than others. Days when she can sense some sort of human presence, latent but enduring—a sort of seething, simmering force, a rage, that she can't quite put her finger on. But then she can't put her finger on her own attitude towards the old man, either, veering between pity, suspicion and sometimes, for no particular reason, strong dislike. Occasionally her conversations are edged with something cruel, something slightly savage. This viciousness surprises her, but she can't help it, isn't sure she wants to. And it extends to the entire family—in theory she likes them well enough, but sometimes a feeling creeps up, a bitter imp that whispers in her ear, wishing them ill. Perhaps it's only the fact of their survival, their intactness—occasionally it stings her, like salt in a wound. This dislike never extends to Mick, though—beyond the evident, undeniable lust, she feels only pity.

She has to open Mr G's mouth and put the pills right at the back of his tongue—but this evening his fury is almost tangible, and she does it quickly, afraid momentarily that he might bite her. But he doesn't bite, doesn't even retch or cough, takes the water agreeably enough, swallows them down. Dinner, though—tonight it's a puree of some sort, or maybe it's meant to be a thick soup—is a different matter. He clamps his lips down over his teeth like a recalcitrant toddler every time she goes to give him a spoonful. She doesn't blame him—the puree or soup or whatever they call it in the kitchen looks like nothing she's ever seen before: it's the consistency of vomit, the colour of shit and it smells of old shoes. The old man's expression is mulish—it's obvious that he isn't going to eat. Though any sort of expression is something of a breakthrough.

Eventually she gives up. Puts the spoon down. 'I'd give you a beer if they'd let me, Mr G.' She sighs. 'Unfortunately, it could interfere with your medication and even cause a severe reaction.' Her voice slips into an approximation of the nursing unit manager's officious tone and then quickly out again. 'Though why the fuck they think that no reaction is better beats me.'

The old man sits in his chair, staring at nothing, his gaze just a few degrees to the side of her, his face settled back into its characteristic vacancy. She leans in close and waves her hand in front of his eyes. He doesn't even blink. 'Come on, Mr G. I know you're in there.'

She picks up his hand, takes the clippers and prepares to cut his nails. Pauses, then goes over to the little handbasin, and fills a dish with warm water, a squirt of antibacterial soap. They've given her an aged tub of sorbolene—greying, gluggy and fragrance free—to use as hand cream. She digs in her handbag, finds her own lavender-scented lotion, her nail file and buffer. She lays out a towel on the narrow kitchen table, arranges her tools, manoeuvres the old man's chair so that he's as close to the table as possible. She sits directly across from him and pulls his hand towards her. He's so unresponsive he could be a mannequin, and she'd imagined his hands to be cold, but they are heavy and warm, the flesh firm and pliable. She moves his left hand into the dish of soapy water, holds it in place.

'Seeing as you're never going to tell me anything, Mr G, maybe I should tell you a story. You know that's what we're told to do—to read to you, or talk to you, to stimulate you in some way. I could read from a book, but I don't know what sort of stuff you like. I don't know if you want fiction or what sort of fiction you might like. You don't strike me as a fantasy man, or sci-fi. Maybe romance, secretly, or a bit of erotica—a little BDSM, though actually you seem like a vanilla sort of fella to me. And I figure that being an ex-policeman, you're not much into crime novels—you'd think they were all wrong, or just silly, light, escapist shit. That the made-up stories are never as big as the real ones.

'So, how about I tell you a story. A true story. It's about me—me and my family—my sister, and my dad, and my mum. They're all gone now—Mum and my sister are dead, and Christ knows what happened to Dad. And it's a true story, every bit of it. They're not people you've ever met, but I think you'll be familiar with our story—and if not this story exactly, you'll have heard something just like it.' She takes his hand from the dish and lays it gently on the towel, rubs it dry. She begins with his thumb, clips it carefully, slowly, trying hard not to cut into the thick ridges of dead skin that lie on either side of the nail.

She's enjoying herself—taking the opportunity to experience

what all her interviewees experience—the catharsis, the relief of telling, the unburdening, taking the opportunity to set the story straight—but without the constraint brought on by the recording, the interjections of the listener. She could be talking to a cat or a dog, or even a chair.

'So, this story I'm going to tell you, Mr G, it's about a family, a family pretty much like your own, with a mum and a dad and two kids, except that instead of a son and a daughter, there were two little girls. Once upon a time—I guess I should start out where all good stories start—these two little kids and their mum and dad are living in a small town in the country. The parents are young and happy. The dad, he's no one special, works for the government, on the railways, and the mum, she was a nurse once, but now she's happy at home being a mum. When our story starts, the older one, we'll call her Kelly, is ten and her little sister, Kathy, is only five. They're the most ordinary little girls, living their ordinary lives in their ordinary house in their ordinary country town. They're both okay at school, they don't mind the readin', writin' and 'rithmetic part, or their teachers, but they prefer playing with their friends. They both love animals, and at home they have two dogs, three cats, guinea pigs, a rabbit, chickens and an aviary full of finches. They have a little chestnut pony, Nugget, that they leave out at a friend's place. Their mum, she grew up on a farm, and it's important to her that her girls learn to ride, even though they're town girls. They have their friends and their animals, but most of all they love their mum and their dad and each other, and their mum and their dad love them back, and all four of them are the happiest of happy little Vegemites leading their ordinary happy lives.

Then one day, their dad, let's call him Pete, one day Pete decides that he's had enough of all this ordinary happiness. You see, it turns out that he's not at all happy. He's sick of his job, sick of his wife, sick of being responsible for bringing home the bacon to his hungry family, and he wants something else, something exciting, something new. And so he leaves. One day they wake up and he's gone, headed off to the city, without even saying a proper goodbye. He leaves a letter for the girls, though—telling them he loves them, that he's off to seek his fortune—their fortune—that he'll send for them when he's found whatever it is he's looking for.

'He'll be back, the girls' mother tells them, it's just a phase. It's not us, he still loves us, she says, it's him, and he'll be back when he's sorted himself out. But the girls don't believe her, and nor, it seems, does she. After he goes she's no longer an ordinary happy mum, and it's no longer an ordinary happy life that these girls are leading. Instead—you guessed it, Mr G—it's an ordinary unhappy life. They have to move out of their old, rambling house, with its big yard and its climbing trees and its chook yard and rabbit pen and aviary, into a much smaller place, a housing commission place, filthy and damp and with only a patch of weeds for a yard, in the roughest part of their small country town, and the pony and the rabbit and the chickens and the dogs and the birds all have to go. Their mum gets a job, cleaning the houses of the rich ladies in town—the doctors' and bank managers' wives—and the girls have to go home every afternoon to an empty house, and look after themselves. Instead of afternoons spent playing in their yard with their pets or on their bikes, taking trips out to ride their pony or to the shops or the library, or doing their homework at the kitchen table, or helping their mum get dinner ready, the two little girls are latchkey kids. They come home to an empty house and strict instructions to stay indoors until Mum gets home. Both girls are sad, sad as can be, as sad as ... Cinderella preparing her nasty stepsisters for the ball. But there's no fairy godmother in this story.

'The little one, she just sits on the couch, in the afternoon, watching telly and eating biscuits and waiting for Mum. Sometimes she draws pictures of houses, of happy families with dogs and rabbits and ponies and chooks. Happy families with mums and dads. But the older sister—she's twelve now—is angry as well as sad. She doesn't stay in and watch over her baby sister, instead she hangs out with the other kids in the street, wild kids, kids from bad families, kids her mum has told her to keep away from. And she's getting sadder and sadder and angrier and angrier every day that passes with no news from their dad. But the mother, who is so unhappy and so tired that by the end of each day she barely remembers to breathe, she doesn't know what's going on, and when little Kathy tries to tell her, she doesn't listen. Can't.

'And so little Kathy spends every long, long afternoon by herself, waiting for her mum to get home, while Kelly spends every afternoon with her new wild friends, and by the time their mother finds out it's all too late. Kelly's too far gone with that crowd, swallowed up by her anger, and she's not coming back.

'Soon Kathy can barely even recall that other life, with cut lunches and hot baths and ponies and picnics and pancake breakfasts on weekends, and rumbles in the bed with her dad and her mum and her big sister. Soon she thinks it must have been a dream, that other life—that it was never something real, anyway.

'By the time Kelly's sixteen she's gone for good. There've been a whole lot of things that have happened to that angry girl in that sad house by then: expulsion, arrest, time in a psychiatric hospital. An endless list of sad things for everyone.

'There've been one or two happy times—like when the dad came back one winter, to give it a go, give it a second chance, to see if they could turn things around for Kelly. And for a while it seemed like things were turning around for all of them. It was a miracle—Kelly became a different girl, happy and bubbly, she had friends over, helped with chores, and their mum had seemed better too. She'd started cooking properly again, cleaning, gardening. She'd taught the girls to knit and they'd both made beautiful winter scarves—blue and orange stripes. There'd even been a birthday party.

'But of course the reconciliation hadn't worked out. Their father had started to get edgy, started getting bored, over it, and one day he just up and left, without saying goodbye again, and they were back to where they started, only worse this time. This time Kelly runs away from home, to the city, so the sad mother and her sad little Kathy are left alone together.

'Their world gets even sadder—of course it does—when there's no trace of Kelly anywhere and no one wants to help them find her, not the police, not anyone. She went of her own accord, a runaway, she's sixteen, a big girl, legally independent, so there aren't any of those 'missing' posters up like other girls get, there's nothing on the telly. In the end there's no one left to ask, nothing they can do. She's lost to them. Lost to herself.

'And now the mum, who hasn't really been the same since her husband left, who hasn't been the same since her oldest daughter started on her downward spiral, but who has tried her best to keep them all afloat, now the mum is sinking too. Sinking fast. She's drinking, every night, from casks of white, she's falling asleep on the lounge, too weak, and too tired to do anything but weep over her missing daughter, and sometimes, even still, her missing husband.

'The little one, Kathy, she's given up, too; there's never going to be a fairy godmother, she's on her own now. She learns quickly how to look after herself and her mother. She learns how to cook her own meals, and to wash her own clothes, and to get herself to and from school, and to make it look as if humans inhabit the house. Soon she learns to clean the vomit from her unconscious mother's face, to make sure she doesn't choke to death, and how to ring her mother's work and make excuses. But the most important thing she learns is how to keep it all locked inside her, how to make sure nobody knows. How to keep it from everyone—including herself.

'And then one day the police come, and at first she's excited and pleased, thinking that they've come to give her good news about her missing sister, that they've come to tell her they're bringing her home, and that some of the sadness will be gone at long last. But instead they bring more sadness—and this time it's a sadness so big that it seems she will be swallowed up by it, like Jonah and the whale.

'The officers take off their hats and sit her mother down, and the policewoman offers to take Kathy outside—*Let's go get an ice-cream, we'll go to the park, you can play on the swings*, she says, *while the others talk to your mother*—but Kathy says no, she has a right to stay, she's ten now, not a little baby, she doesn't want to play on the swings, and they let her stay, because already this baby is starting to sound like someone who shouldn't be argued with. Then the police tell them gently, because they can see how sad her mother already is, and how sorry their lives have become, that they've got bad news, terrible news, the worst, that they think they've found her. There's a girl, Kelly's age, who's been found dead in the city. That they want Mum to go and look at her, because they think it might be her lost girl. Her wild and angry girl. Her Kelly.

'Have you worked it out, Mr G? You're a clever man, with a good memory, and I know you remember that murdered little girl in the city. That sad little girl they found in a warehouse with a needle in her arm and a scarf wrapped nice and tight around her throat—just like your niece, Angie. Little Kell, they called her. Well, she was my sister. And you know something? Her death, that's been the story, the sad story, of my life.

'And you know something else, Mr G? I have a feeling, a really strong feeling, that you know something about her death, something you've never told anyone.

'Did you want to say something, Mr G? To add some detail to my story? Because you can. Anytime you want, Mr G. Anytime you feel like talking about it, I'm here. And I'm good at listening. Ask anyone.

'Look at these nails.' She puts down the buffer and picks up his hand, looks at his fingers admiringly. Pats it down gently on the towel, and picks up the other.

'We've done a good job on these, Mr G. It's been time well spent. Now, do you want to try some of that delicious soup again?'

JANE

Though the shop was my grandfather's, it's the one place from my childhood that contains hardly any memories of Angie. She had none of the passion for the old bits of furniture that I developed at an early age. She visited the shop, of course, but Carol, whose relationship with my grandfather was frosty at best, rarely called in, and certainly never dumped Angie there for hours on end. But I spent long happy days hanging out in the shop—or the warehouse, as it was then—with my grandfather. I'd enjoyed learning how to polish and date the occasional piece of silver, to mix and apply shellac. Angie, though, had hated the place, found it creepy—she hated the big, dank, gloomy cavern of the shed, all the old stuff; the smell of dirt, of dust, of old people—she imagined it was the smell of death itself. But it's a smell I love. A smell that soothed and continues to soothe me.

Every once in a while, when her social life and study permit, Jess will spend the day in the shop with me. It's funny how things turn around: like Angie, Jess had hated the shop as a little girl, hated the forced confinement during her school holidays, the boredom, and the dust that made her sneeze. But over the last few years she's loved being here—has volunteered on occasion, eager to help sort and price the latest purchases, to talk to the customers, displaying her (reluctantly acquired) knowledge of eras and styles, willing even to help do the dull jobs, the endless dusting and polishing, and rearranging of the showroom.

But today Jess is reluctant to do any of the tasks I give her; she's out of sorts, glum and argumentative. Eventually, annoyed by my irritable requests that she keep on working, and having lost an argument about a Bakelite tray that she insisted is art deco, she screws up a piece of newspaper and throws it at me.

The source of her misery is revealed.

'Oh, this sucks, Mum. Isn't there something else you can do?'

I sigh. We've been over this a hundred times. 'There's nothing, Jess. Nobody's buying antiques. It's costing us money to keep the shop open.'

'Can't you just wait it out? Things might change. What goes around comes around or something?'

'And sometimes it doesn't. There's virtually no one coming in off the street—you may have noticed. Even the people we've been selling to for years have disappeared. Antiques are passé—and we could be broke before that trend changes.'

Her look speaks volumes. There's no convincing her.

'Well, I can't bear doing this any more. I'll go and get coffee. Cake? Or is it a carb-free day for you?'

She pokes at my stomach rudely, skips away before I can swat her.

I watch as Jess swings through the door, admire her straight shoulders, her confident stride, the way her face is set towards the world with such exuberance, ready to take on the future, whatever life might throw at her.

I sigh and go back to my packing. I enjoy having Jess's company in the shop—glad to have someone to chat to, to share a coffee with, to discuss the possible histories of each beloved, or not so beloved, object, even the odd inevitable disagreement doesn't detract from the pleasure of having my daughter take an interest in my work. I understand, all of a sudden, how pleased my grandfather must have been to share his passion with me—how pleased and surprised, and oddly humbled too. It seems so unlikely that my Jess, with all her potential and possibilities, and the absolute and intractable certainty of youth, would gain pleasure from the same things as her middle-aged mother. And there's joy in the continuity, too. On the odd occasion, I've even fantasised about offering her permanent work, imagined the two of us working together at some unspecified time in the future. Closing down the shop has put an abrupt end to these as yet unspoken fantasies.

Having an only child wasn't something I'd ever considered before I had Jess. Even when I was pregnant, I still imagined I'd have more, three or maybe four. The idea of a large noisy family was appealing—a solitary spoiled brat, not so.

I'd had Jess when I was young, relative to most of my peers. I was twenty-two, Rob twenty-seven. We'd been married for two years by then, and the shop had started doing well. Very well. Rob had had the brilliant idea of using just the front section of Pop's shed, turning it into a proper shopfront, with plate glass doors, plenty of windows, a reasonable ceiling height. Pop had always used the whole shed and crammed it willy-nilly with furniture. Rob envisioned a respectable, but not over-large, space, with proper antiques—furniture, art, jewellery and bric-a-brac—artfully displayed. He had done most of the work himself, back in the days when you could. He had converted the rear of the shed into two small factory units, suitable for small manufacturing businesses, carpentry, upholstery, that sort of thing. One we used for ourselves, fitting it out for simple furniture restorations, spraying and French polishing. We'd received rent from the factory, and gradually built up a name for selling reasonably priced, reasonable-quality antiques. We weren't the high end of the market; we didn't offer European pieces that only the very wealthy could afford. We sought out the more homey colonial pieces—the scrubbed pine tables with turned legs, refractory tables, old pews, oak dressers, cedar side tables, marble-topped washstands, old lamps—the sort of things everyone was mad to furnish their houses with before new furniture became so cheap and desirable.

By the time we had Jess we were pretty comfortable, financially speaking. We'd bought a house, nothing special, just a little weatherboard cottage in Bellevue Parade in need of some 'refreshing', as the real estate agent put it. But we knew we were lucky being able to buy at all and unlike most of our peers, who were caught by the Sydney housing spike, we were able to buy where we wanted, to stay close to family, and we were on our way to having a large portion of it paid off. So, even though we were young, we had a house, our very own house, to bring our baby home to.

We were lucky, too, that our occupation was relatively baby-friendly. It was difficult to take time off, but running our own business did mean that we could be flexible with our 'workforce' of two. When we both had to work, there was always Mum, who was usually willing to spend time with her first grandchild, and when all else failed and I had to take Jess to work with me, there were no complaints from bosses or co-workers.

And she was an easy baby, Jess. A dream baby really; she had no problems taking to the breast and she even slept through at six weeks, the way the books said babies were meant to. She slept, she didn't grizzle inexplicably, she was healthy. I couldn't have asked for more. And if it'd been up to Rob she'd have been the first of many—he'd have liked two at least, maybe even three.

But I couldn't.

I never for one moment wished Jess away, but as soon as I'd given birth I knew that, given my life over again, I wouldn't have children at all. I wasn't unhappy being a mother, in fact I was ecstatic, and the practicalities of new motherhood came to me easily. But. Having Jess—loving Jess—made me understand just what it would mean to lose a child. I felt vulnerable, exposed and, some days, panic-stricken. I knew that children died—and I knew what happened to their parents. It had never occurred to me before, the horror of Angie's death from her mother's perspective. I'd only ever thought of it from my own. But now, I understood that my survival hinged on another's in a way I'd never imagined.

Some people say that having more kids helps if you lose one—there's something else to focus on, something to keep you alive. They might be right. But there was no way I could get past that all-pervading fear of losing the one I already had. It didn't matter what Rob or Mum said, I couldn't bring myself to do it again. Couldn't bring myself to open myself up further to that sort of risk. So that was my Jess. Jessica Angela Tait. I'd deliberately put all my eggs in one basket—figuring that if I had only one basket to carry there was less chance I'd drop it.

I carefully wrap an ornate Edwardian silver teapot that I bought in a job lot from a deceased estate a few years ago. The sale had been at a house in Avalon, an unusual old sandstone place, a Burley Griffin design, built as a holiday house in the 1930s, that had only ever belonged to the one family. The middle-aged daughter of the owners was at the auction, had been happy to see the items go.

'God, I suppose I should keep some of this stuff,' she'd said, picking up the teapot. 'This was a wedding present to my grandmother, I think. Some sort of an heirloom. But I'd never use it—and none of my girls would either. You know what?' she'd added, laughing, 'Mum never used it either, but she'd still be horrified to see me sell it. I'm not sure why she kept it, why it seemed so important. All this holding on to the past that people do. I can't think of anything of mine that I want my kids to keep. I don't want them to forget me, but I don't see how holding on to things is going to help. Photos, maybe ... they're different.'

I'd known the age and provenance of the teapot almost immediately, hadn't needed to check the marks. I could tell just by looking that it was Bristol silver, made around 1910. This skill would once have made me proud, but now what I felt was closer to despair. What, after all, was the point of such knowledge? It was all just unwanted junk when you came down to it.

And when you came down to it, perhaps this really wasn't the life I wanted for my daughter, amongst these old things, breathing in the dust of the past, the dead. In fact, maybe I don't really think that this is a proper life for any young person. Jess's life will follow its own complex web of possibilities, and this is how it should be. I don't want my daughter settling for the past, for stability, for stasis. I want my daughter to live in the present, to move and keep on moving. There's time enough for settling. And time enough, when what's ahead of you is shorter than what's behind, to contemplate the past.

The music of harps interrupts my gloomy reverie and signals not the arrival of an angel but that other emissary of the gods: a text message.

Before I can even read the first one, a second arrives and then a third. All in a matter of seconds. They're abrupt, each no more than a single sentence, but they speak volumes.

That was fun.

When can we do it again?

I want to see you.

They're from an unknown number, but I know. Just reading them I can feel a slow flush rising from my chest, up my neck, until my cheeks feel warm. Other parts of me are warm, too. Deliciously. At first I resist. Delete. Delete. Delete. But then the fourth one arrives. *I want you.* Nobody has said that to me for some time. For years. It's just not something that gets said all that frequently in a marriage spanning more than two decades. And suddenly those twenty-odd years of happy monogamy are disregarded in a moment of wanton recklessness. *I want you too.* I press send. Then, *More Later.* His answer comes immediately: *Hurry.*

I look about the empty store, my face flaming now, heart thumping in my chest, worrying that somehow my message, only syllables, but swollen with betrayal, will be burnt into the air, hologrammed, for any stray visitor (or, God help me, Jess) to see. Delete. Delete. Delete. I turn off the phone.

By the time Jess comes back with the coffee, I have taken many deep breaths, my complexion has recovered, and though my heart is still whumping away loud enough to wake the dead, my hands have stopped shaking. I give my daughter what I imagine is a beatific smile as I accept the cup, although she barely registers it, is busily texting away. I even manage to greet Rob with some degree of normality when he walks in the door only seconds later.

'Hello, family.' Rob is as cheerful as always. Also unsuspecting. 'So, where's my coffee?'

'Actually, Dada, you can have mine. Alex has just texted to

say they're all meeting down at Groovers at twelve. It's already ten to.'

Neither Rob nor I have any idea who Alex is, or they, or whether Groover is a person or a place, but we ask no questions, just offer the standard imperatives to drive carefully and leave the mobile alone. She rushes off to her next engagement, all promises to help out for the day entirely forgotten.

Rob's smile is indulgent. 'She's a whirlwind, that girl.'

'Not your genes.'

'No? Well, I hope there's not something you're keeping from me …'

'What?' It takes me a long panic-stricken moment to get the old joke, to recover enough to give a weak laugh.

'Bit slow on the uptake, there, old girl. Too much on your mind?'

I stash the phone in a desk drawer, leaving it switched off until Rob leaves. He's loaded up the truck with cartons and odds and ends of furniture to be taken to Vinnies, and I manage to wave them away without a second glance, without a pang, too consumed by my own immediate future to be even mildly concerned about the fate of any inanimate object.

When he's gone I switch the phone back on. The harpist's divine solo heralds the arrival of a single message from on high. *BragBar 2night at 9.* I sink breathless and jelly-legged onto the nearest seat. I couldn't feel more overcome had it announced an imminent visit from the Holy Spirit. My return messages are equally brief, but my hands are shaking so much I have to type each word twice. *Can't.* Send. Then: *Not tonight.* Send. Delete. Delete. Delete.

TRANSCRIPT OF INTERVIEW: ERIN FURY

She sets it up just as she would a real interview. Puts the recorder in the middle of the table, gets a bottle of water, a glass. She even lays out her notebook, sets the pen beside it. But instead of two chairs, she lugs the hanging mirror out of her bedroom, leans it against the wall. She clicks the recorder on, waits for the red light.

Asks herself the first question in her coolly polite interviewer voice.

ERIN: What I want to know is, what exactly are you hoping to achieve by asking yourself these questions? You do know this is completely mad, don't you?

ERIN: I guess. But not when you think of other things I've done. There's been far madder. Honestly. Talking to myself? That's nothing. And this interview—it might be helpful. It might help me to 'move forward', as they say. And, you never know, if I ask myself the right questions, I might even come up with some answers.

ERIN: Well. I thought I might start by asking you what you think you're doing—I mean, why are you interviewing this family?

ERIN: I'm just doing some digging. Seeing what comes up.

ERIN: And if something ... *useful* comes up—and you have to acknowledge that it's pretty unlikely after all this time—how is that going to change things for you?

ERIN: It's not about changing. It's all about closure. Isn't that what they call it?

And, hey, at the very least I'll have a bunch of interviews—enough for a radio documentary.

ERIN: So is it actually getting you anywhere? Any closer to the truth? It's beginning to seem a little like some retrospective police investigation. Isn't that a bit … pointless? It's not like you'll ever be able to find the killer. Everyone agrees that it was some psycho nut job. You're not going to find him here, so what's the point?

ERIN: Oh, I dunno. Who knows what I'll find out? Anyway, the more I dig, the more it doesn't quite add up.

ERIN: But that's the same with any story—time passes, facts get lost, memories blur. No one ever has the same story, the same perspective. You've always known that. It doesn't necessarily mean anything.

ERIN: But maybe it does mean something. Someone's telling lies. Maybe more than one person. Someone knows more than they're saying. It's all far more complicated than it should be.

ERIN: And what about Mick? What's going on between you two? Now *that's* mad. Actually, it's a bit scary.

ERIN: I know. It scares me, too. But … I can't help it. I like him. And maybe when it's all over, it could turn into something … real.

ERIN: But how can that happen? What you're doing isn't real. *You're* not real. Erin Fury doesn't exist.

ERIN: Maybe she does. Maybe she's just as real as everyone else. We've all got some kind of a front, all got a cover. Anyone who says they haven't, well, they're lying to themselves.

Anyway, who knows what'll happen when it's all over.

ERIN: When it's over? What do you mean by over? When will it be over?

ERIN: I guess—I guess when I find out the truth.

ERIN: The truth? Aren't you being a little bit naive, now?

ERIN: Maybe.

ERIN: And what will you do with it when you find it? The truth.

ERIN: I don't know.

ERIN: Then why does it matter? Why are you doing this?

ERIN: You know why I'm doing it. I'm doing it for Kelly. I promised.

When she is fourteen, in the brief period of relative calm just before her mother begins her final irreversible descent, a travelling medium visits the town. Her mother buys tickets for them to see her at the local RSL club. She doesn't ask her daughter if she wants to go and, though Kathy can think of a thousand things she'd rather do, she doesn't demur. There's no question that she will accompany her mother to such a public event—if only to keep her away from the bar beforehand.

The medium—she calls herself a clairaudient medium, though what that means is anybody's guess—is visiting from America. She's only a small fish in the psychic ocean, not famous like Doris Stokes, and nobody in town has ever heard of her, but the event is sold out.

Although none of her classmates are at the show, it's a small enough town that Kathy knows most of the audience, but their various reasons for attending aren't immediately apparent. She suspects that most are merely curious, a few true believers, some sceptics and many hopefuls. A few, and she can count them on her fingers, she recognises as her fellow bereaved, desperately in search of comfort.

The seating isn't numbered—it's just the RSL auditorium, after all—and by some miracle they manage to arrive early and lay claim to seats in the second row. Kathy isn't nervous or anxious, though she had expected to be, and for once her mother is sober—or sober enough—so that Kathy's not feeling the usual defensive shame. She doesn't know what she feels, certainly not excited, or hopeful or nervous, or any of the things that she'd expected she'd feel. She is really far too young to be attending such an event, and she notices a few of the more respectable members of the town eyeing her mother disapprovingly, or perhaps pityingly—but they know, as does everyone, that her mother is above censure, beyond caring.

Kathy's not sure whether she believes in any of this medium stuff or not. Other than a persistent belief in the future, in the possibilities of elsewhere, Kathy doesn't believe in anything much these days. Her mother, though, has real faith. She's certain that there is another dimension, what we call heaven, perhaps, that her murdered daughter exists within it, and that this medium—who the promotional leaflet claims is a 'Supreme Spiritual Seer', who has been given the gift of communicating with desperate departed souls—will have access to it and to Kelly.

Her mother has already had several sessions with locals known for their psychic abilities. None have brought her peace of mind, or any sort of comfort. There have been no meaningful messages, no expressions of hope or love, no assurances of Kelly's contentment in the afterlife—they have brought nothing but guilt and despair.

Her mother has told her what it is she is hoping for from this medium: she isn't seeking information about the murder, she doesn't want to know who the perpetrator was, she doesn't even want to know if her daughter died in fear or pain—what's the point? All she's after is a sign that her Kelly is free of pain now, that she knows her mother loves her, and an assurance that they will be reunited in some not too distant future. When her mother says this Kathy feels vaguely sick; though she has always been aware that in the years since her sister's death, her mother's one consolation has been the possibility of reunion with her murdered child, it's still painful to be reminded that her mother's love for her remaining daughter isn't strong enough to tether her to the world.

Kathy had, at first, seen the murder as being uniquely her sister's tragedy; she was the one who lost her life, after all. And Kathy had, at first, been inclined to hate both her mother and father, seeing them as being equally to blame for her sister's withdrawal, her running away, her unimaginably terrible end. If her father had never left; if her mother had only coped. But now she knows that it is just as much her tragedy too. What sort of a childhood is this? She has spent what feels like her entire life witnessing her mother's decline, the terrifying prospect of being utterly alone looming constantly. And she has no one else. Her father's long silence has made it clear that it is all too painful for him, that he wants no reminders of his former life, his former responsibilities. He could be dead for all she knows. Or cares.

Unlike her mother, Kathy is interested in finding out the details of her sister's death. She'd like to know who, know why. And if it is really possible to contact her sister, that's what she'd ask.

The medium, when she finally comes on stage, is a disappointment. The poster had shown a glamorous dark-haired beauty dressed in long, flowing robes—an alluring witch-like creature in a landscape of fire and mist. An artist's vision of the other world, Kathy supposes. In reality she is grey-haired and dumpy, dressed in an unfortunately clingy black dress, with a hooded red satin cape—a little too short, faded, the hem straggling—hanging over her shoulders. Her shoes are scuffed old-lady moccasins with unfashionably pointy toes. The medium's shabbiness is apparent even to a country-bred teenager: communications with the spirit world are clearly not a profitable enterprise.

The woman—whose name is Joan Miller—has a flat and rather nasally voice. Her plump face is fine-featured and apple-cheeked, and a pair of pink-framed reading glasses perch on the tip of her nose. She looks more like a school librarian than Kathy's idea of a medium. She is seated on a sagging velvet armchair that someone has dragged into the middle of the stage, and a carefully angled standard lamp casts a pool of yellow light around her.

She is introduced by a handsome silver-haired man dressed smartly in funereal black, his accent deeply southern, his words smooth as honey. He is her husband, apparently, though they seem an unlikely couple. The woman's opening patter involves a brief and clichéd address on love and comfort and loss that provokes a general murmur of appreciation from the audience. She tells some long and convoluted tale about how she came to find her gift, as she calls it. It's a story of tragedy and redemption that involves a serious illness and voices and intimations of madness before a life-altering visitation in a shopping centre car park, and it leaves many in the audience, Kathy's mother included, sighing and wiping their eyes.

Her description of the spirit world, which appears to be made up of a lower plain connected by many paths and bridges, along with upper levels accessed by metaphorical lifts and the odd moving staircase, is muddled and bewildering. Even as a fantasy landscape, what she describes is utterly incomprehensible. It makes no sense either physically or emotionally so far as Kathy can see, and a large number of the audience appear to be equally unimpressed—there's an increase in throat clearing and shuffling from the rows behind her. Time is running out, the bereaved are becoming restless, so the woman moves on to the serious business of the evening, what they've all been waiting for: the summoning of spirits, communing with the dead.

The summoning is surprisingly banal—there is no fog or ectoplasm, no sparkling lights, no visual stage effects whatsoever. The woman doesn't go into a trance but continues to sit primly in her lounge chair, smiling benignly, her expression oddly distant as if she's gazing inward, nattering away disjointedly to a busy mass of people that no one else can see. It's a little like a reversal of watching Miss Angela on *Romper Room* looking through the magic mirror—'I can see Jimmy and Sandra, oh, and there's Stephen, and yes, is that you, Margaret?'—but without the sweet anticipation of hearing your own name called out.

'Ooh, yes, my dear, I can see you. Now, if you could just wait your turn, there—you're a bit of a barger, aren't you, my darling one? Were you always so pushy? Yes, I can see you, but you're going to have to ... Oh, no, no, no—that was last time. I shouldn't think you'd be needed here again ...'

Eventually she turns her attention to the audience, who wait expectantly, their collective breath held. She scans the crowd slowly, gazing vaguely along each row, and then pauses and leans forward, her eyes keen and sparkling under their gaudy plastic frames. She waves out into the audience, her focus somewhere towards the back of the auditorium.

'Oh, yes. You. In the back row. The young lady in the blue jumper. Yes, you with the pretty pink scarf.' She waves again and the crowd turns around to look. A young woman who Kathy recognises from the local greengrocers gives an uncertain smile and waves back nervously. The medium's husband, who has been waiting at the stairs for instructions, strides down the hall to the young woman, leans forward and whispers in her ear. She stands up and he accompanies her as she walks self-consciously, her face pink, eyes lowered, to the foot of the stage. The man hands her a microphone, then moves to the side.

'Hello, my sweetheart. Now, there's no need for you to look so worried. You're here for a purpose, aren't you?' Her tone is sugary and yet somehow faintly sinister. 'You're hoping to hear from someone, aren't you?'

The girl's shoulders are hunched, she murmurs something unintelligible into the microphone, there's a shriek, feedback, and she winces, holds the microphone at arm's length. Kathy is finding the whole thing excruciating at this point, would be happy to leave if it wasn't for her mother, and the matter of their being seated so close to the stage.

'Just speak into it properly. Hold it back a little. That's it. Now, I can sense that you're here for someone. Someone who's passed recently?'

The girl's voice comes through this time, tremulous, but shockingly clear. Slightly defiant.

'No. No, I'm not, actually. I just came for the show.'

'Oh, now, I don't think that's quite true, is it? Sometimes we don't even know when we're looking for someone; sometimes it comes as a surprise. You see, there's someone here for you, and she's telling me—now what's that?'

The medium's expression loses focus, is directed inwards again.

'Yes. Yes, my darling one. That's just fine and dandy. I'll tell her, don't you worry. Just you hush now.' She turns back to the girl. 'Now, I've just been given an interesting piece of information. You're adopted, aren't you?'

The girl looks stunned.

'I ... Yes. Yes, I am. How could you ...? I've only just found out myself.'

Kathy leans forward, intrigued now.

'You don't know who your mum and dad are, do you? Your real parents, that is. You're not in contact at all.'

'No. All I know is that my mother was a Catholic girl from Queensland—that's all they told them. My adopted parents. Is she—is she dead then?' The girl's voice sounds pinched, fearful.

'Now, don't be afraid. It's not that, it's not your mum or your dad I'm with, don't worry. But I've got someone else here, someone telling me you're her granddaughter. It's your grandma I'm talking to. Your ma's ma.'

'Oh ...' The girl's sigh of relief is audible; there's a collective exhalation from the audience.

'Now your grandma—and she's a dear little lady who passed away a few years back. Elsie her name is, or maybe Elizabeth. Something beginning with E, I think. Or maybe A. Agnes, is it? Anyway, she wants you to know that she's with you. That she's always with you. She's keeping a special eye out for you now that she can, because she never got the opportunity to do it when she was here.'

The girl swallows, her jaw works, but no sound emerges.

'She always felt so sad that your mum couldn't keep you, she tells me. She feels like she was to blame, but the situation was too hard. What's that, darling one? I'm not quite reading you ...?

'Oh, yes. She wants me to tell you that your mum—your real mum—loves you too. That she thinks of you each and every day. Every day of your life she misses you. And that one day you'll be reunited. And she also wants me to tell you that you're lucky—that you're with a good family, that you've had wonderful opportunities that your birth mum couldn't ever have given you. That you should be grateful.'

'Oh, thank you.' The girl's voice is a sob. 'Thank you, so much. You can't know what it means.' She almost curtsies in her gratitude. Kathy can hardly bear to watch her as she moves back to her seat, her face red, puffy with tears, but her expression joyful, almost triumphant.

Kathy's mother, who is quietly sobbing, turns to Kathy, clutches her hand. She whispers something, but Kathy doesn't hear, doesn't want to.

The next subject is an elderly man, thin and unkempt, his eyes rheumy, who shuffles to the front of the room, his head bobbing with excitement. Kathy has seen him around town, too, and knows he's slightly odd. He walks a little hairless dog, hangs around the park. He's the sort of man that mothers warn their children to keep away from.

He takes the microphone, leans into the stage, breathing heavily.

The woman smiles down at him kindly. 'If you could just—if you could just move your face away, slightly. That's it.

'Now, it seems there's someone here for you. It's a woman. Your wife, is it? You've lost your wife quite recently, haven't you?'

The man looks confused. 'No. No. Never been married.' His voice is a slightly indignant squeak. 'Don't have a wife. Never wanted one.'

There are muffled titters from the audience.

The woman is not the slightest bit put out. She returns to her otherworldly companions. 'Mmmm. Yes, yes, I see.'

'My mistake. It's your mother,' she says, her voice calm, unruffled.

'Yes, that's it.' He nods, gives a relieved smile. 'Poor old mum.'

The medium beams down, gracious, magisterial. 'I misheard—it happens from time to time, you understand. I don't speak to them quite the same as I talk to you—not what you would call a normal conversation—it's more like codes, signs that need translating.' She speaks directly to the man, but it's obvious to Kathy that this last is directed at the audience—specifically to the sceptics amongst them.

When he's finally shuffled back to his seat, satisfied, the medium flops back in her chair, sits completely still for a lengthy moment. She closes her eyes, nods every now and then as if agreeing with some silent statement. Finally, she opens her eyes, looks about the room. At first her gaze passes straight over them, but quickly returns, focusing directly on Kathy and her mother. There's no mistaking it. Her mother grips her arm again, her fingers painful, and leans closer to Kathy, as if fearful. The medium's husband awaits her directions, ready to escort them to the stage, but the woman waves him away.

'She doesn't need to come out. She's only a child. You shouldn't even be here, should you? This is no place for children. There's too much sadness. You've already had enough sadness.' Her face is stern. Distant.

'I have a girl here. She's looking for someone. A friend? A sister? It's something like Helen, or Ellen—or maybe Erin? Is that you?' The woman is looking directly at Kathy. She waits for her response, but Kathy can't speak, can't bring herself to correct the woman. She swallows, bobs her head around, and the woman smiles and continues. 'She was taken when she was around your age, wasn't she? She was someone you loved, someone close. Something awful happened. When she died. It was something terrible, wasn't it? I'm getting the sense of a lot of sadness. She was a long way from home when she died, poor wee thing. And there's anger. I'm getting a sense that there was a lot of anger even before. Oh,' she gasps, sits up straighter. 'Oh—it was a—a bad death. A terrible death. Violent. There are ... there were police involved, weren't there? This is what I'm hearing. Is that right?'

Her mother calls out, her voice hoarse, her words stark, 'She was murdered.'

'Ahhh. Yes. That's always difficult.' The woman's voice is quiet, calming. 'On the earthly plane as well as the other. She seems so restless—but she always was, wasn't she? I'm getting that feeling. That things were hard for her. Life was hard for her. Always. She isn't easy ... You're not easy to talk to, are you, my darling one? But she wants me to tell you that she loves you. I can sense that. That she's looking out for you. She doesn't want—she doesn't want to stay long, she's getting ready to go ...'

Her mother begins weeping noisily. Kathy hangs her head in embarrassment.

'But there's one other thing, sweetheart. I think this is what she's saying—she's looking out for you.' The woman hesitates, frowns. 'No. She's telling me something else. There's something *she* wants, too: she says that she wants you to find out something, it's something about her passing. She's saying trust, maybe? Oh, I think it's *truth*, that's what she's saying. She wants you to find the truth.'

Her mother's sobs have become a desperate wail, and Kathy can't bear it any longer. She pulls her to her feet, and then guides her, stumbling in her haste, half-blind with the shame of it, along the aisles to the exit. Most of the audience keep their faces turned away, their attention on the medium, but a few twist to watch their frantic escape.

Outside in the car park, her mother sinks down onto the hot bitumen, still sobbing, overwhelmed. Kathy squats, tries to comfort her.

'But Mum, Kelly came through. It's what you wanted, isn't it?'

Her mother pushes her away, inconsolable. 'But the message was for you, Kathy. Not for me. She hasn't forgiven me. That's the truth. She's still blaming me. For her father. For putting her in that hospital. For letting her die. For everything. Even now. She won't forgive me.'

Kathy is relieved to be able to reveal her scepticism. 'Oh, Mum. It's not real anyway. Truly. The whole thing was a set up. That woman probably already knew about us. It's bogus.

Anyone in town could've pointed us out to her. And we made it so easy, sitting down the front, like that—right where she could see us. It was crap, Mum. Just crap.' Kathy strokes her mother's arm tentatively, but her mother pulls away, covers her face, will not take the comfort of her daughter's words or touch.

A few years later her mother drove out to the old reservoir, a dank and dangerous pool that had provided the town with its drinking water before the dam was built. She'd dosed herself up with a mixture of Valium and gin, weighted herself and jumped in.

She left Kathy a letter.

My darling Kathy,

You are sixteen now, almost a year older than your sister was when she died. I want you to know how sorry I am that things have turned out like this. I wanted the best for both of you, my darling girls. If only you could know how much I love both of you. I have tried to stay strong after everything that's happened. I can't. But you are strong, Kathy, and you're smart too and I know you can look after yourself. There is no use in my staying—life is nothing but pain for me now. Remember that I love you.

Mum xx

Mick has come down to the shop to help Rob with a truckload of furniture—the final one—that he's delivering to a dealer in the western suburbs. The shop is almost empty now, there's only the furniture to go to the auctioneer, some cartons that will be sent to Vinnies, and a few odds and ends I haven't quite made my mind up about. Mick heads over to the cafe, brings back coffee, sits on one of the last remaining chairs (a rickety rush-seated bentwood whose fate is still undecided) and watches as I potter about ineffectually.

'This is killing you, isn't it, Jane? Getting rid of this. Closing down.'

It's been a long time since Mick has shown interest in anyone's troubles but his own, and I'm so surprised that it takes me a moment to process the question.

'I think it's more like I'm in shock, Mick. I've been doing it for so long, I almost can't believe that it's over. I don't really know what I feel. Maybe it's a bit like when someone dies.'

Mick raises his eyebrows. 'Hardly that bad, mate.'

I put down the broom I've been waving about for the last half hour, sit down beside him on my worn office chair (definitely heading to Vinnies) and take a sip of lukewarm coffee.

'I've been thinking about Angie a lot, you know—about what happened to us all, after she died. Well, it'd be hard not to, with Erin and all her questions.'

'It's been … interesting, to put it mildly.'

'It's that feeling that I had back then—I have it again. A feeling of something ending—of life as we know it being over. It's hard to describe.'

'But it's a beginning too, isn't it? You're young enough—you guys could do anything. And you've got enough money, Jess's grown up. The world's your oyster, Jane.'

'It doesn't feel like a beginning. I feel like I'm at the edge of a … a precipice or something. Like I need to do something drastic, or I'm going to fall off.'

'Tell me about it.'

We sit in gloomy silence for a moment.

'So, what do you think of her? Of Erin?' Mick asks.

The question seems casual enough, and my reply is just as offhand. 'I don't think anything, really. She's okay. Why?'

'No reason.'

'I'm not sure that I'll ever want to listen to the bloody documentary if it gets made.'

'It could be interesting. And I've found it kinda … cathartic, to be honest.'

'A bit of extra therapy? I was worried about you talking to her—thought it might blow things up a bit, things you don't want to be reminded about. I blasted Jess when she told me she'd given her your number.'

'Maybe. But then again, maybe it's *not* talking about things that blows them out of proportion.'

'I've enjoyed it, too, in a weird way. And Rob spoke to her as well. Did you know that? I've no idea what about, do you?' I throw the question out casually, secretly hoping that Mick will know something that I don't.

'No idea. But she's talked to him a couple of times now.'

'Right.' I keep the surprise out of my expression.

'He must've had something interesting to say if she requested a return visit. She's not one to waste her breath.'

I change the subject. When I finish my coffee, I pick up the broom and raise some dust.

Erin listens to the recordings, over and over, downloads them onto her computer and her iPod, listens when she's in the car, when she's walking. She goes to sleep with the family's stories in her ears. Jane's especially, and sometimes Barbara's. Mick's she doesn't listen to as frequently—she doesn't need to.

It's fascinating, listening to their lives spilling out so uninhibitedly. So intemperately. All the stories people manufacture so they can live with themselves. The mythological worlds—past, present and future—they create just so they don't have to face the mess they've made of their lives. So much of it isn't quite the truth, sometimes conscious lies, but mostly it's not deliberate dishonesty, they're just telling half truths, telling the parts they can bear to remember. But occasionally, just occasionally, something honest slips out. Something real. Something true.

What is it that she's listening for? It's not just for some sort of slip-up, or admission, some confirmation of her feeling that something's being hidden. Although it's that too.

She'd like to say she's searching for the truth, waiting to hear the truth, but it's not that simple.

Perhaps she's waiting for recognition, some acknowledgement of her own predicament, her own pain. But she knows that can never happen. How can it when they don't even know who she is? Or why she's there.

At first she just wanted to meet them, to hear their story—stories—to find out if there was anything, some clue, some connection, between the two girls, something vital that everyone else had missed.

And now she's begun to worry that she'll end up knowing more than she's anticipated, more than she needs. And maybe even more than she wants.

ERIN: I know we've spoken about this before, but I just wanted to get a clearer picture of the time just before Angie died—a picture of what you all did.

JANE: Well, nothing really. You know, we just watched telly. Rode our bikes. Hung around. Went up to Ferber's. Nothing more than what I've already told you. There wasn't anything else. Oh, we went to the mall once or twice. Mum dropped us up there. We had a bit of pocket money to burn, I guess, or maybe Christmas money.

ERIN: And did all three of you go, or was it just you and Angie?

JANE: Oh, it would've been Mick too. He wouldn't have wanted to miss out.

ERIN: On a trip to the mall? He doesn't seem like he'd be into shopping.

JANE: No. On an outing with Angie. There's no way he'd have let us go without him.

ERIN: So, they did spend a lot of time together, those holidays. More than with you?

JANE: I don't know about more. I'm sure Angie made a real effort to hang out with me—but I can still remember being peed off when they went off together. I remember teasing them about being in love … That wouldn't have gone down well with either of them.

ERIN: And did you really think they were in love?

JANE: God, I dunno what I thought then. I know I said it, but I don't know that I really thought it. I probably just said it to stir them up, or get them into trouble, you know? I just remember being jealous. Feeling left out. I mean, one minute Angie was my best friend, and the next she'd be locked in the bedroom with Mick, ignoring me. I can remember standing outside Mick's bedroom door and kicking it, when Mum wasn't around. They'd just turn the music up louder.

ERIN: What about looking back? What's your take on it now?

JANE: Looking back? Well, yeah, I guess it's possible. I can remember them looking weird, red-faced, embarrassed. I thought they were just mad at me. But then maybe they were taking something. Smoking dope? Although that wasn't likely—not at our place, not with Dad around. Yeah. Or maybe they were fooling around. Having sex ... but even if they were, it didn't matter, did it? They were only kids. It didn't mean anything.

They know all there is to know about one another, the two girls. Or that's how it seems to Jane. In reality it is Angie who knows all about Jane, and not the other way around. Jane tells her cousin everything: about how her so-called best friend Fiona hasn't invited her to her birthday because Jane accidentally bought the same outfit to wear to the end of Primary School social—a little brown velvet vest worn with a red-checked shirt, a flared brown skirt. They'd seen it together at Grace Brothers, enthused over it, and Fiona insists she told Jane that she was going to get it, but Jane knows she didn't. Tells her about the boy she has a crush on, Mark Nailor, another friend's slightly older brother, blond and blue eyed and tanned and so cool he doesn't even know she's alive. Tells her about the spin-the-bottle game she played in a cave at Narrabeen beach, about the boy she'd had to kiss, shoving his tongue down her throat, the humiliating laughter of the other kids as she pulled away, gagging in fright and disgust. Tells her how scared she is about starting high school next year—especially now Angie won't be there. She's heard that the First Formers have their heads flushed down the toilets; that there are no curtains or doors in the school change rooms, and the older girls snap the younger girls' bra straps, or pull down their bloomers given the opportunity; that the school canteen is a front for drug distribution. Angie is reassuring: none of it is true, and she will make sure her old friends look out for Jane. She laughs away Jane's fears. She laughs about the boy thing too. *Boys aren't worth worrying about. You'll learn how to kiss soon enough, don't worry, and, anyway, older boys don't worry about things like that.*

Older boys. Jane asks the question shyly, while they're watching television, not sure whether it is something she should ask, whether her confidences will be reciprocated. Lately Angie has seemed more mysterious, more contained. Jane senses that there are things going on in her cousin's life that she doesn't know about, that she might not even really understand.

'Do you have a boyfriend, Ange?'

Her cousin gives her a brief quizzical look, shrugs, turns back to the screen before answering. 'Nah. Not really,' her voice is determinedly casual. 'There's this boy I kinda like. But it's not going to happen. It can't.'

'What do you mean?' Jane can't disguise her interest. No one has really said as much, but she has a vague idea that Angie's had some problems to do with boys, that this is one of the reasons her aunt is sending Angie off to a new school. She can imagine her cousin being at the centre of a doomed romance, being involved with some wild youth, a tragically misunderstood genius, a hero in the mould of Patrick Pennington in the *Beethoven Medal* books she is currently reading.

'Is he too old for you? Too wild? Has he already got a girlfriend? Is he going out with one of your friends?' Even at this age Jane knows that stealing a good friend's boyfriend is absolutely prohibited, would signal the end of even the closest friendship.

'Oh, something like that. It's just sort of complicated. I can't explain. But boys are pains anyway, don't you think? Who needs 'em. I'm sick of TV. Do you want to do something else? Why don't we find Mick, and see if he wants to do something? Didn't Aunty Barb say she'd drop us at the mall if we wanted to go today?'

Jane doesn't really want to go to the mall, even the prospect of wandering around the shops unchaperoned for a few hours doesn't appeal as much as it ordinarily would. Her time alone with Angie is precious; she'd rather not have to share her with Mick. But she agrees reluctantly, sensing Angie's determination, turns the television off, tries to locate her mother. It's Jane's job to talk her into giving them a lift, a few extra dollars to spend.

'But don't hassle her,' Angie warns. 'Don't give her the pip.

See if she can take us in half an hour or so—it'll take ages to get Mick up.' Angie goes up the hall to rouse Mick out of his post-lunch stupor. Jane hears the bedroom door close after her, muffled laughter, the key turning in the lock.

They go to the mall several times during Angie's visit. It's only a twenty-minute walk, but Barbara always drives them anyway, keeping her promise to Aunt Carol with good grace. Their mum always presents them with a small list of chores to do, things to buy—half a pound of DJ's jelly babies, a bag of special blend tobacco for Pop, shoes to Mr Minit for reheeling—as well as a couple of dollars each to spend.

She drops them off and arranges to pick them up two hours later. They always ask for more time, but their money never lasts very long anyway. Even augmented by the couple of bucks she's managed to cadge over the holidays, Jane usually only has enough for a bag of hot chips, a Coke, and a caramel cream doughnut from Donut Dan.

After the money's spent there really isn't that much to do. Well, there's probably plenty to do, but there's nothing they all want to do together. Mick is always keen on the music shop, while Angie wants to look at clothes. Jane loves the pet shop, where there is always a kitten or puppy in a cage that needs patting. Even the goldfish can provide a few minutes' entertainment—in particular the giant carp that swims right up to the glass and glares when you knock on the wall of the tank. And though she'd never admit it, Jane still loves to wander through the David Jones toy section. She loves it, but just lately she's found herself surveying the toys with sad bewilderment: somehow the dolls and stuffed animals and trinkets have lost some of their magic, but she has nothing to replace them with yet. It's difficult to imagine how Christmas could ever be exciting again, impossible to imagine what might bring her as much joy as hearing the crunch and rustle of her filled-to-the-brim Santa sack. And yet what on these shelves does she really desire? She gazes with embarrassed longing at the new blue-pantsuit-clad

Bionic Woman doll, with peel-back rubber on her bionic fore-arm, a modified ear and a bold red mission purse, filled with intriguing bits and pieces essential to a life of heroism. But who would she share this doll with? Her friends would laugh at her, and who could blame them? At twelve she is really far too old to be playing with dolls. Still, the Jaime Sommers doll is far more appealing than the magazines and clothes and music that seem to be the focus of most teenage girls' lives. She can't see the fun in that.

This particular visit, with the day of Angie's departure getting closer, Jane is loath to leave her cousin's side, unwilling to let Angie and Mick head off on their own, and so the three of them stay together.

As always, Angie is the only one who really buys anything substantial. She has a wallet full of unspent Christmas money, along with the cash her mother has given her for the stay. After each of their three visits to the mall, Angie has come home with a handful of new records. Some have been bought at Mick's urging, like The Clash, Blondie, Sex Pistols. And then the ones Angie wanted herself—Shaun Cassidy, Little River band, Abba, Hits of Summer.

Angie has bought a couple of scarves too—long strips of colourful silk and Indian cotton—which she has lately taken to wearing. It is an unusual look for a girl her age and not exactly the rage during the heat of summer. Still, she puts time and thought into her selection, and even Mick gets to put in his ten cents' worth about colours and patterns, length and strength.

During this last visit, Angie chooses one that Jane thinks is especially glamorous from the mall's token hippy shop—extra long and fringed, striped in multiple shades of blue and with a glittering silver thread running through the fabric. She tries it on down the back of the dim patchouli-scented shop, wrapping it around her throat several times before tying a loose knot at the front. It shouldn't really have gone with her otherwise entirely conventional outfit, but somehow it works.

She stands in front of them, hands on her hips, a model's pout on her lips. 'So, what do you think? Is it me?'

Jane nods. 'It's beautiful.'

Mick agrees, then grabs the ends and tugs. 'And it's tough stuff. You could probably lift an elephant with this.' He grins. 'Not that you'll ever need to do that.'

The two older cousins look at each other oddly, as if holding back their laughter. Jane feels a sudden spurt of jealousy, shoves her brother in the back.

'C'mon. This is boring. It's my turn now.'

Mick groans. 'Now what? Not the pet shop again. Can't we just ring Mum and get her to pick us up early?'

But Jane is determined. 'It's my turn. I've been waiting all morning.'

The other two sigh, but follow Jane as she marches through the maze of shops, not pausing until they reach the cage of mewing kittens.

Back home, Mick and Angie hurry to Mick's bedroom with their goodies, lock her out.

There were times, plenty of times, more than she'd care to count, when it was just Mick and Angie in Mick's room, the door locked against Jane, who would be left stranded on her own, kicking at the door, her sense of outrage and injustice overwhelming her.

Her mother would tell her to scoot, to scram, to go and play outside, or watch television. *They're older, lovey*, she'd say. *They can't always be playing with you.*

But what are they doing? Jane would wail at the unfairness of it. *And why can't I do it too?*

Jane, her mother would say, impatient now. *Go and occupy yourself for a while—or I'll find something to occupy you.*

Even Dad, who could usually be relied on to take her side, told her that she should be glad that her cousin is happy to spend so much time with her. *There aren't too many big girls who'd take notice of a baby like you, Miss Jane*, he'd said. *So give her a bit of a break now and then.* He'd give Angie a friendly wink, which she would gratefully accept before scuttling off with Mick. Jane would pout and mutter and stamp away to her bedroom or the lounge, feeling the hot tears welling, feeling like the baby they all kept insisting she was, but would be back out as soon as she heard them emerge from the bedroom.

We've only been drawing, they'd say, dismissing her whinging accusations, or sometimes, *We've just been listening to records.*

They'd offer up their drawings as proof. But they would giggle and look at one other for no apparent reason, their faces flushed, and their eyes ever so slightly bloodshot.

ERIN: Did you ever have sex with your cousin?

MICK: Fuck me. What sort of question is that?

ERIN: Were you lovers?

MICK: No. Jesus. We bloody well weren't. What gave you that idea?

ERIN: According to the autopsy your cousin wasn't a virgin. There were rumours that she'd been raped, but that wasn't true, was it? There was no evidence of violence, no contusions, no swelling or bruising. And no semen. So if she was having sex, it must have been consensual.

MICK: Yeah. I already knew all that. But thanks for the reminder, Erin.

ERIN: And your sister told me that she'd had suspicions, not at the time, but later when she thought back. She remembers you spent a lot of time alone together in your bedroom that summer, and that when you came out, sometimes you had red faces, behaved weirdly. She thought it might've been drugs, that you might've been smoking dope, only there was no smell. So then she thought maybe it was sex.

MICK: Fuck. I thought she'd got over that. Jane was always so fucking jealous.

ERIN: Anyway, it made me wonder, too. If she wasn't raped she must've been having sex with someone. Was that someone you, Mick?

MICK: Jesus.

ERIN: Mick?

MICK: No. You know, for years after she died, I used to think about it and wish that we had—more than anything. But we didn't. It was a mad thing, with Angie. In the beginning, it was cool, the fact that she was staying, but it was really just a kids' thing. I mean, we got on, we always had, and it was fun having her there. Having someone to talk to. Sometimes the holidays started to drag by the end—but having Angie meant there'd be … you know, company.

Anyway, we got close and I guess I … I guess I kinda fell in love with her. Which was so weird because she was my cousin; it wasn't something that was meant to happen. But it felt right. Being with Angie felt more right than anything ever has since. I mean, she knew me. She really knew me. Even with Sarah, even after ten years of marriage, two kids, I never felt like that with her.

But that's not what you're interested in, is it? You want to know what happened.

ERIN: I'm interested in hearing everything, Mick. Whatever you want to tell me. Did Angie feel the same about you?

MICK: That's the thing, isn't it? Nah, I don't think so. She—she didn't lead me on or anything, though, not really. I mean we got a bit hot and heavy once or twice, but she stopped it pretty quickly.

When I found out about the sex, I drove myself crazy wondering who she'd been sleeping with. It was pretty clear, in those last few weeks, that she had someone else on her mind. I always thought it was Adam, though he swore not, and to be honest, I could never figure out when they would have had time—not while she was at our place anyway. There's no way she was with him alone—either the three of us were together or she was with Jane. Unless she was sneaking out at night, but I don't think even Angie would've been that game. Then again, what did I know? I thought I knew her. I thought I knew her better than anyone. But I didn't, did I?

I don't know what hurt more: the fact that it wasn't me or the fact that I didn't have a clue. And for years this was all I could focus on when I thought about Angie—the fact that she'd had sex with someone else. I couldn't get it out of my head. I had this image of her doing it, with everyone I knew, basically. It was sick.

ERIN: That's a terrible image—an awful way to think of her.

MICK: There was a worse one though: Angie lying dead, with that scarf wound around her neck, then tied across her eyes. That's a shit way to remember someone you loved, let me tell you.

ERIN: Thanks for talking to me again. I know you're busy, but if I'm going to do justice to this story, I really need to get it right. All the facts, you know.

ROB: That's okay. Although I'm not quite sure what more I can tell you. I was really just very peripherally involved …

ERIN: No, that's okay. It's something quite specific, actually. I just wanted to ask some more about something you mentioned.

ROB: Oh. Right. Okay. Fire away.

ERIN: You told me, in our last interview, that Angie had made a move, a move you thought was highly charged sexually …

ROB: Oh, well, it seemed that way. Maybe I was having myself on—maybe I'd misinterpreted it or something.

ERIN: You told me that you thought she was coming on to you. And you resisted her, you said you pushed her away, said no. That's a hard one to misinterpret, I'd have thought.

ROB: Yeah. I suppose—

ERIN: I've been thinking about it … about how you described it. Rejecting her. Being worried about her being too young, your boss's granddaughter. All that. And, you know what—somehow I don't think you were telling me the truth. You were, what? Seventeen? And this girl, who might've only been a minor, who might've only been fourteen, comes on to you. But she doesn't look fourteen. Everyone says that. And she doesn't act like she's only fourteen. And she doesn't kiss like she's only fourteen, you've admitted that. And she seems to be offering something that most boys of seventeen would be only too willing to take—you could tell that straight away, apparently. What boy of that age—what ordinary, desperately randy teenage boy is going to say no to that? Come on.

ROB: Well, I did. It might sound unlikely, but—

ERIN: No. I don't believe you. You can say she was only fourteen, that you were scared of being caught and that you worried about the consequences, you can tell me that until you're blue in the face, but I won't believe you. I can't believe that you didn't take her up on that offer.

ROB: I told you—

ERIN: It doesn't matter, you know. It was a long time ago. You were a kid. You're not going to go to prison or anything.

ROB: I don't see why—

ERIN: Did you sleep with her, Rob?

ROB: No.

ERIN: Oh, come on.

ROB: Jesus.

ERIN: Rob?

ROB: Okay. Yeah. So I slept with her. I was young and I was fucking stupid, and she was—she was eager. It felt all wrong—believe me—but not because she was only fourteen. Or not just. It felt wrong because she was my boss's granddaughter, and I was going to lose my job if I was caught. To tell you the truth, the legal stuff never even occurred to me at the time. It was only later, after she died.

But I'll tell you something. She might've only been fourteen—she might've been a kid—but I wasn't the first.

It's not that he hasn't had sex before. He's done it a few times—gone the whole way with a girl who was older, more experienced, on the pill.

She was the older sister of one of his schoolmates, and she'd initiated the whole thing one Sunday afternoon when he'd rocked up unannounced, planning to hang out with his mate, play some records. His friend's sister had answered the door, said hi, told him to come in. Peter would be home with her parents in half an hour or so, she'd said, eyeing him curiously, as if noticing him for the first time, he may as well wait. They'd sat together in the rumpus room watching TV—he couldn't remember what—and the whole time there'd been a distracting kind of sizzle between them. He'd fidgeted nervously until she'd moved close enough to him to make the first move, and then the second. And then he'd let her have her way with him, right there on the rumpus room floor. His arse and then his knees had been grazed by the shag pile carpet, but he regarded the minor discomfort as a trophy, had enjoyed every moment of it—who wouldn't? They had repeated the act on another two occasions—it was all spontaneous, there had been no premeditation, no planning—and while ultimately satisfying, each time they'd fucked had been hasty, a one-off. It was clearly a no-strings-attached, and don't-tell-your-friends kind of affair.

He didn't tell his friends, well, no more than the bragging about the fact that he was no longer a virgin.

And then Angela makes her move, latching onto his lips like a thirsty leech late one afternoon out the back of her grandfather's warehouse. Though he pulls away nervously when she makes her initial advance, he doesn't seriously consider not responding. He isn't worried by her age. Instead he motions to her to wait, makes it clear that he is more than keen to resume, makes promises to sort out a time, a place. He's been more than happy to take the lead this time, to co-ordinate the finer details so to speak—the original impetus may have been Angie's, but he's had experience with an older woman, after all.

So he makes it seem like a favour, tells old Mr Buchanan that he is happy to drop her home after his last delivery of the day, and the old man agrees, telling Rob he can take the van home overnight—pleased to avoid the trip through peak hour traffic at the end of his long day.

Angie hops up into the van, and wriggles her way beside him on the bench seat, her legs straddling the gearbox. She wears the centre seatbelt loosely, his attempts to tighten it a failure, his fingers tremulous and slippery with sweat.

Rob manages to get them safely to his carefully chosen destination, Manly Dam Reserve, which is close enough to her home in case things go wrong and he needs to get her back fast. His driving is erratic, his gear changes even jerkier than usual, and in an embarrassing display of ineptitude, he twice stalls the old van at the lights. It isn't simply nerves: Angie keeps running her hand up and down his thigh, and although it is less a full-blooded sensual act than a childish tease, there is no way to tell his body this—his blood still leaps, his breath comes in shallow bursts, his concentration lapses.

He is relieved in more ways than one, when, after a bumpy drive along the dam road, he is able to turn off and park behind a dense clump of trees. The moment he pulls up the handbrake it is on: their lips smack together and limbs entwine, neither of them suffering in the slightest from angsty self-consciousness. They almost fall over the seats in their rush to move into the back of the van, eagerly tugging at each other's clothes, giggling in between long dripping kisses. The act itself is sweet, neither of them doubtful, each of them experienced, and each of them knowing which part goes where—and when. There are no

condoms involved, and no questions asked about contracep-
tion—that's strictly girl's business.

When they finish—and it is no time at all, less than half an
hour—they zip and tuck and button. Rob gets Angie home well
before dark—her face slightly flushed, but not suspiciously so,
hair neatly brushed. They grin at each other before she saunters down her drive; they make no plans to meet again. But it is
easy enough to arrange the odd meeting—and they've discovered the perfect place.

There is no possibility of any public relationship, and Rob
isn't all that interested in continuing a dangerously clandestine one for too long—it isn't worth it. He knows what people
would think—that she is far too young for him, that he is taking
advantage of her. He knows better, of course: Angie may only
be fourteen, but it is clear that she knows exactly what she is
doing—and that she's done it all before.

I contain myself—wait until we're in bed, lights out, Rob drowsy and ready to sleep, before asking.

'Mick tells me that you've spoken to Erin a few times. Not just the once. You didn't tell me. How come?' I try to keep my voice level, but fail.

'It wasn't like it was a secret or anything, I just—'

'So what did you tell her? I don't understand why you needed to talk to her the first time. You barely even knew Angie, Rob. You didn't even like her much. Rob?' I nudge him in the side with my elbow. 'What was it you wanted to talk to her about? Why did she want to talk to you again? What was so important?'

'I just told her she came on to me once. Not long before she was killed. Just after I started work for your grandfather.'

I'm wide awake, now. 'She did not. You must have misunderstood. Angie was way too young. And she'd have thought you were an old man. I know I did. You're having yourself on.'

'She was only two years younger than me, you know, Jane. I'm really not making it up—there's no doubt she was coming on to me. You don't want details, but to be honest, she was pretty good at it. Too good at it for someone that age. Angie knew what she was doing.'

I turn my face away, holding back tears.

'It was a long time ago, Jane. It shouldn't matter. It doesn't matter.

'But.' I can barely speak. 'Why have you never told me this before? Why keep it a secret? That does make it matter, Rob. If Angie came on to you, if you kept it secret from me all these years—well, that means something. It changes things.'

'It doesn't change anything. That's ridiculous.'

I turn back to look at him. 'So that was all that happened? She came on to you—and you what? You rejected her? Said "thanks but no thanks" and left it at that?'

I can see the whites of his eyes as they flicker, slide away from my gaze. He brushes the hair away from my face, pushing it back behind my ears.

'It's all silvery, Jane.' He sounds surprised, as if he's never noticed.

I catch his hand, move it away from my face, clamp it down beneath my own on the bed.

'It was nothing, Jane.'

'Rob?' I can hear the fear in my voice. The sudden realisation. He closes his eyes, turns away.

'Were you having a thing with her? With Angie? Were you *sleeping* with her?' I sit up and switch on the bedside light. 'Rob. Look at me.' I pull at his shoulder, force him to turn back to me.

This time he doesn't look away. And he doesn't need to say anything, his expression tells me everything I need to know.

What she had never expected was that she would like them. The family. It was, she had to admit, a bit of an impediment to her enquiries, to the *purity* of her investigation. Jane, for instance. Even though their relationship is one circumscribed entirely by the purpose of the interviews, still she's friendly, warm, funny, and then there's her appealing honesty, her openness, her willingness to look at her past, as well as her present. She doesn't seem to skirt around the more difficult issues, even if they point out her own vulnerabilities, her weaknesses. Honesty, openness—they're not traits that Erin has ever cultivated. In fact, she'd have to say that her life has been a pursuit of just the opposite. She's tried hard to get rid of any weakness, and those she can't she disguises. It's been a life of hiding, as much as possible, from her past. And no one, but no one, would ever call her warm or friendly. She's aware of that, and she's never ever cared. Before.

The husband, Rob, seems to be a nice guy, too—amiable and laid-back—despite the magnitude of his revelation. Even Barbara, with her bitchy passive aggression, her dislike of Angie that she can't disguise, Erin thinks she might even like her—the flashes of sharp humour, the tartness.

And then there's Mick. There's something there—oh, there's the fact that she's sure he's hiding something, but it's more than that. Something that makes her heart beat fast when she remembers the warm strength in his fingers, something about the way his eyes—those eyes, fathomless, guarded, distant—lighten when he gives her one of his rare, rare smiles. Him, she's trying hard not to think of.

She likes them all, she only wishes—futile thought, this—that they'd met under different circumstances. For some other reason. In some other life. She's amazed at just how much this family have to say, how much they want to say, need to say, about what happened after Angie was murdered.

Her own life following her sister's death can be so easily summed up with just a single three-letter word. There are other words, longer, crueller words, expletives that would express her experience more pungently, but she likes the crude eloquence of those three letters, the brutal simplicity. Her life reduced to a single cold hard syllable: BAD.

They're all convinced, this family, that what happened actually changed their lives. But the mother's right: she was just a cousin. They still had their cosy little home, their cosy little family, their cosy little life. They talk about guilt and sorrow, but they don't know anything.

And they don't really care. It's obvious. What have any of them ever done to find out what happened? Or why it happened. Or the crucial thing: who did it and why. That's something she's pondered every day and every night since it happened. And more than pondered. They might think they're obsessed, but they're rank amateurs, this lot. They know nothing about obsession.

JANE

Rob has taken the last load and the shop is empty, all the furniture and cartons gone, all the shelving, all the bits and pieces. All that's left is the kettle I've been using, an old porcelain one from my grandfather's days, miraculously still working, a box of Twinings tea bags and a couple of mugs. There's a used bar of soap in the bathroom, and half-a-dozen rolls of toilet paper. I suspect that Dusty will have very particular ideas about these essentials. No doubt he'll bring his own organic handwash and thrice-recycled toilet paper, environmentally sound cups and a five-star-rated kettle, not to mention organically grown, hand-picked, fair trade tea in bags made by free-range silkworms. But still it seems mean not to leave something for those first chaotic days.

The day's efforts have been conducted in an atmosphere of frigid near silence. The long night had been spent apart, me on the couch, unable to sleep. Rob's desperate attempts to explain himself this morning were met with a resistant fury that surprised me no less than him. Nothing he said in his defence made any impact whatsoever: *I was a fool, a dickhead, yes, sure, agreed, but I was only a kid. And it meant nothing, it never did. It was a long time ago, I can barely even remember.* I said nothing, could think of nothing to say, every justification only fuelling my anger, and my despair. When he told me that he wasn't the only one, that Angie wasn't a virgin anyway, only then did my voice return momentarily, as if shocked into service.

'As if that makes it any better. She was a kid, Rob. She wasn't even fucking legal. She was fourteen. Imagine ... Imagine if she had been our daughter. Your daughter. It was wrong. Just wrong. There's no excuse.'

It was natural to couch my anger in such a way—it was all about right and wrong, it was all about a vulnerable young girl being taken advantage of knowingly by an older boy. It was all about Angie. It was much easier than to try to express the other, darker source of my rage—the thoughts that had kept me awake all night, and that were still making my head spin now—the fact that Rob had lied, not about sleeping with my cousin, but about *liking* her. That this wasn't just about his betrayal of Angie, but about his betrayal of me.

Alone now, the place empty, I give in to a creeping exhaustion. Sink down on the concrete floor and stare at the wall, trying hard to think about nothing. When my mobile sounds the arrival of a message I can't even summon the energy to cross to the other side of the room to my handbag. I ignore the sound of a second text and even the third, dreading a sweetly penitent dispatch from Rob that will somehow defuse my (righteous, surely?) anger. When the fourth, fifth and sixth messages come through, then a seventh and eighth, my curiosity wins out.

BragBar tonight 9pm.

The same message has been sent and resent and resent, and has just announced its tenth arrival when I finally manage to key in a response and hit send.

Okay.

Just four letters, but already I'm feeling immeasurably better. My heart is still beating hard, only now it's not with anger, but with anticipation. I'm not sure, though, whether it's the prospect of seeing Dustin again that's so exciting. Or whether it's the prospect of revenge.

I have made up my mind to leave the house without any explanation, but relent at the last minute, pausing outside the kitchen door as I head down the hallway.

'I'm meeting Shaz, Rob. I'll sleep on the couch again. Don't wait up.' These are the first words I've spoken to him all evening. I went to see Dad after work, arriving home as late as possible.

I had refused the mushroom risotto Rob had prepared, and declined his pleas that we talk about it, sort things out. Luckily, Jess is spending the night away, so there's been no need to answer the inevitable questions about what's going on, why we're not speaking, whether we're getting a divorce. Instead, I spent the early evening locked in bedroom and bathroom, getting ready for the night ahead of me.

Rob is sitting at the kitchen table, a glass of red wine and a half-empty bottle in front of him, his bowl of risotto pushed aside, congealing.

'Another girl's night out, eh?' He looks me up and down, gives a low whistle. 'You scrub up all right for an old chook.' His smile is cautious, uncertain. 'No kiss goodbye?' he holds out his hand, pleading.

As I hesitate, a horn blares outside and I give a wave, relieved. I rush out the door to the waiting taxi, feeling vaguely nauseated, either from shame or excitement, or maybe a gut-churning mixture of both.

BragBar is a local nightclub of dubious reputation, notorious for violent drug- and drink-fuelled brawls and public fornication—a hole, my daughter and her friends would call it, and they'd be right. It's a weeknight, so there are no queues and the solitary bouncer waves me through without a second glance. I feel highly self-conscious as I make my way down the red carpeted steps and into the bar—my skirt too long, my heels too low, my cleavage too restrained, my hair not long enough or blonde enough, and, most conspicuously, my age too advanced. I am old enough to have parented a large portion of the bar's clientele, and no doubt they see 'cougar' written all over me, that's if they notice me at all.

I have been nervous all day about coming here, wondering why on earth he's chosen this venue, but all of a sudden I understand. The incessant noise, the flickering lights, the crowd: this is a place not to be seen, but a place to lose yourself. A place not to think, but to be. Once my eyes grow accustomed to the light, I home in on Dustin's face, his eyes gleaming green, almost luminous, from a dim corner. And then I don't think of anything much at all. For the next few hours I don't think of Rob or of Angie. I don't think of the past or the future.

I am as fierce and unthinking and wild as any untamed feline, nothing but instinct, all hunger.

Call it payback.

ERIN

She likes the fact that Mick wants her to talk about herself.
They're not usually like that, men, not in her experience, anyway. They don't really want her to share; they don't need to
know who she is.

But Mick—he's different. Perhaps it's the illness—the PTSD—
perhaps that's the thing that's shattered him, left him hollow,
empty of everything but an echoing anger. But she thinks perhaps the illness has also opened him up, the way sadness has
opened her up, made her hungry for other stories, other lives.
Sometimes, listening to them, it's as if she's filling herself up, as
if their noise will muffle her own sadness.

He's always wanting to know what she's done, where she's
been. It's obvious, he says, that she's not that fucked-up and
fucked-over kid she once was, it's obvious that she's moved on
since then. There must've been quite a bit of water flowing under her bridge—so where's she been floating?

'Just about,' she tells him. 'Nowhere in particular.'

'But look at you—you're a professional woman, obviously
well heeled, set up; you're making a radio documentary, for
Christ's sake. How did you get here?'

'Sometimes you just ... arrive.'

'Tell me something. Anything. Where do you live? I don't
even know that. What's with all the mystery?'

'There's no mystery. There's just ... there's nothing to tell.'

'What, nothing happened from twenty to thirty? The last ten
years have been just a blank?'

'Not ten,' she laughs. 'More like twenty.'

'How old are you? I thought you were only in your early
thirties.'

'I'm not that much younger than you—just well preserved.'

'Jesus. Really?'

'Really. Thought you'd lucked out, did you, getting a younger woman?'

'Had to be too good to be true ... But about those twenty years. They've been what, good years? Easy years? Tough years? Have you married? Had kids? No—you haven't had kids, have you? I'd be able to tell that. Come on. You know all about me—I want to know more about you. About who you really are.'

Who she really is—she'd tell him if only she knew. Instead she keeps it light, tells him she's done this and done that, been here and there. She tells him a little—some truth, some fabrication—enough to keep him satisfied. She's not so sure that he really needs to hear the truth, anyway. He needs happy stories, she can sense that, not stories like hers. He just doesn't know this yet.

She wonders herself where those twenty years have gone, wonders at the speed of them, wonders that she's got nothing to show. She's spent twenty years being busy, but doing nothing. Going everywhere and getting nowhere. Twenty long, fast years of doing everything she can to move on, to escape, but still never quite managing to leave herself behind.

If things had been different, if things had been normal, would she still be such a mystery to herself? Or is everyone ultimately opaque? Their motive and intent clearer to others than to themselves, the patterns evident only to those who look on, a comfortable distance from the hot confusion of the life that's being lived.

She wishes she knew the answers, or at the very least had someone to ask. If things were different, she'd like to ask him, ask Mick. He wouldn't know the answers, but she's pretty sure he'd understand the question.

This morning before she leaves, he asks her where she's heading, where she lives. Other side of the bridge, she tells him, waving a hand in a westerly direction. He captures her hand between his own, long fingered, strong, pulls her back down beside him on the bed.

'Yeah. But that's most of Sydney. Where exactly? And who do you live with? What sort of place is it? A house? A unit? You know all about me. Come on, Fury. Tell.'

She pulls away and he releases her hand, reluctantly. 'Would it change anything, if I told you all that stuff?'

'No. Why would it change anything? I'm just curious.'

She walks through the door, blows a kiss from the hallway.

'Then you don't need to know.'

JANE

I hobble up the still-dewy garden path, my feet bare, shoes and tights abandoned during some lost moment last night. I look a mess. My skirt—a sweet black pencil skirt I'd bought only the week before—is smeared and grimy, the fabric caught and tugged and laddered somehow. My hair is a disaster, my eyes smudged with mascara. I stink of cigarettes and booze, and my mouth is more furry than it has been since I was eighteen. My mind is worse than furry. My mind is a complete blank.

There are some worrying gaps in my memory of the previous night. I can recall leaving home and that moment of anticipated abandon some hours later, but other than that there's nothing. I'd woken early this morning quite alone, in a strange bed, in a strange flat, somewhere in Manly. I managed to get a taxi, to arrive home more or less decently clothed, and basically conscious. I'm desperate to get inside, desperate to get cleaned up, desperate to crawl into bed, but I'm not so desperate to face Rob. The thing is, I have no idea what I've actually done—no idea just how many vows I've broken, or how badly.

'Jesus Christ.' Rob flings open the door before my shaking fingers have even made it to the doorbell (*my keys? Where are my keys?*). 'Where the fuck have you been? Why didn't you answer your phone? I've been up all night, waiting for you. I've just been on the phone to the cops, for Christ's sake.'

His eyes are red, his hair is all over the place, his face shockingly old-looking, haggard. I push past him, anxious to get inside and out of public view. I head down the hallway, saying nothing, and Rob follows me, shouting now.

'Jane. What the hell is going on? I know you weren't with Shaz. I rang her—she didn't have a clue what I was on about.

She's not even in Sydney. This is crazy. I thought something happened to you. I've been worried sick. What the hell's going on, Jane? Is this some sort of revenge because of Angie? Talk to me.'

But I can't talk. He's been worried sick, but right now I'm just sick. Too sick to think, let alone speak. I don't quite make it to the toilet bowl. But at least I'm over the threshold of the bathroom before I throw up. Really, there's nothing worse than cleaning vomit off carpet.

Small mercies. I'm praying for more of them.

My memory comes back in fits and starts during a miserable day spent fighting waves of nausea in between fitful bouts of sleep. Both Jess and Rob tiptoe into the bedroom every now and then. Jess comes bearing cups of peppermint tea and her equally scalding opinion of my behaviour; I feign sleep whenever Rob looks in, avoiding his reproachful, and anxious, eyes.

I still can't recall everything about the night before, but what I do remember is important: though the entire evening had moved pleasurably and inexorably towards it, the longed for, planned for climax had never arrived. Instead, when we finally reached Dusty's apartment, ready to take the hot and heavy session we'd begun in the taxi to its inevitable conclusion, my head had begun to spin, my stomach to heave. I had been too sick to be embarrassed, too wiped out to even feel bad for Dustin, who had been calmly philosophical about the turn of events. He had led me into his bedroom, helped me out of my shoes and stockings, had covered me with his doona as I huddled wretchedly on his beautiful big bed. He had even provided a glass of water and a basin. I have no idea where he slept, or where he was when I came to, but there had been no happy ending the night before, I was certain of that.

And now, back at home, back to the reality of my life, I am glad of it. Whatever madness possessed me has just as quickly burnt away, leaving me tired, sick and sorry. It seems my desire has disappeared, along with my desire for revenge. This morning my behaviour—from my reaction to Rob's confession right through to the events of the previous night—looks like nothing more than a spoiled brat's tantrum.

I am ashamed of yesterday's anger, ashamed of my lack of understanding, ashamed of my too-easy decision to destroy what has been, up until now, a good marriage. And relieved. Glad that I haven't done anything I'll regret forever, that one moment's stupidity hasn't ruined the rest of my life. I'll have some explaining to do, apologies to make, but somehow I think things will be okay. Not such a small mercy, really.

Late in the afternoon, I force myself out of bed, shower, then go searching for Rob. My head is still foggy, and there's a weight on my chest, which is not just to do with the cigarettes I smoked. The house is dark and quiet, but the doors and windows are open, and there are empty longnecks on the kitchen bench.

I find him eventually, lying in the hammock on the verandah, his eyes closed, a bottle of beer perched on his chest.

'Ah, Sir Rob,' I make my voice as cheerful as possible, give the hammock a playful swing. 'You look like one of those—what do you call them, effigies?—at Westminster Abbey. A beer bottle for a sword. Or a bible or whatever. Though I guess the bottle is more appropriate.' He doesn't open his eyes or smile.

'Rob, I ... We need to talk. I need to explain what happened. What's been happening ...'

'I'm not interested in your explanations, Jane. Just like you weren't interested in mine. I. Don't. Give. A. Fuck.'

He pushes himself out of the other side of the hammock, and stalks back into the house without looking at me. I hear him open the fridge, the soft *pffft* as he opens another bottle.

'We're meant to be at your mother's place in an hour. Sunday dinner, remember. With your *family*.' His words are thick, his voice dark. 'Though maybe you're not interested in being a part of a family any more.'

'Are we going, or should I ring Mum, tell her I'm sick?' It's hard to say which option is least appealing: a family dinner in my hung-over state, with all the unresolved tension between me and Rob, or facing my mother's reaction to my crying off her slaved-over dinner.

'We're going. Jess is meeting us there. You'll have to drive. I'll wait for you in the car.'

ERIN

They are lying in bed in their usual and by now very familiar hotel room. The TV is on, some reality show—dancing, singing, cooking. She hasn't even bothered to look at it; the sound is down, anyway, so it's just a flickering light at the periphery of her vision. Mick is lying back against the pillow smoking a cigarette. It's something he can't get away with at his mother's, he says, but it's okay here—no one takes any notice of the no-smoking signs, no one takes notice of any of the signs here. And he's right—there's even an ashtray provided, precariously balanced on top of the television. For once she's not in a hurry, she's finished her shifts at the home for the week, is feeling pleasantly sleepy, content, is even considering staying overnight if Mick makes the suggestion again.

'You know,' he says, 'it's fucking weird being back home.'

'I can imagine,' Erin murmurs, though in truth she can't.

'It's almost as if the last thirty-five years haven't happened. I could be fifteen again. Or ten. I mean, things have changed, obviously—Dad's not there, or Jane—but it's all so the same. Jesus, my room's *exactly* the same. Same sheets, same bedspread. I lie on my back and trace the same damp stains on the ceiling, count the same red circles in the wallpaper ...'

'Is that a good thing?' She takes the cigarette from his lips, draws on it, hands it back.

'I dunno. I guess it takes away some of the ... urgency of what's going on. It gives me space to think, it's not all so in my face. Work, home, the kids, Sarah. All the shit. And it's given me space to think about old stuff too. About Angie. Not that I've really ever stopped thinking about her.'

She remembers what he told her about his memories, about

the image of Angie dead, is about to ask whether he has ever spoken to a shrink about it, when she realises. She doesn't stop to think, asks the question as it occurs to her.

'You know what you told me about that picture you have of Angie, dead, with the scarf wound around her neck—and then tied around her eyes. Is that how she was found, or just how you imagined it?'

'How she was found.'

'But I've never read anything about that. About the scarf being tied around her eyes, I mean. It wasn't in any newspaper reports that I remember. Nobody else has mentioned it.'

'No.' His voice is slow, thoughtful. 'No, you wouldn't have heard about it.'

'What do you mean? Is it something your father told you?'

He watches her, his face impassive, draws back on his cigarette.

'Mick? How could you know that?'

He speaks, but he doesn't answer her question. He's talking to himself. 'I've really got nothing to lose any more, have I? I've fucked everything. Career. Family. My head. It's not like it was when I was fifteen. When I had everything in front of me, when it looked like I might've had some sort of a future. I've got nothing now. What does Jess call it? An epic fail. That's me. But maybe I had nothing then, either. Maybe it was always an illusion. Some sort of sick fantasy. It's not like I deserved anything after Angie.'

'Mick? What are you talking about?' She is sitting up now, watching him anxiously.

He sits up too, not in response to her, but to some internal compulsion.

'I want to tell you something.'

'Oh. But maybe this isn't such a—' She pauses. All of a sudden she's afraid.

'*Shhh.*' Mick presses a finger gently against her lips. 'It's okay.' He tucks the blankets around her naked torso, then gets out of the bed, pours two glasses of wine, passes one to Erin. 'Have you got your little recorder?'

'I think so. In my handbag. But—' For once she's reluctant, fears she's not going to like what he's about to tell her, and isn't sure that she wants to listen.

'Good. I've got something to say. I'm going to tell you first ... and then I want everyone to hear it.'

He gives her the machine, climbs back into the bed. He takes a sip from the glass, then downs the rest in one swallow.

'Okay.' He nods. 'Turn it on.' He takes her free hand and holds it tight, leans against her and closes his eyes. Speaks.

It's as if what he says comes from every part of him. He's so desperate to tell her, to tell anyone, or everyone, that it's as if he's sick with it, the words spurting like vomit: involuntarily, bodily, in a gush that can't be stopped.

This was not what she expected, not what she had ever imagined. And, even though it explains so much—oh, God—it's not what she wanted.

JANE

It's apparent from the moment we walk in that Mum is in a bad mood. We're much later than expected and Mick is God knows where, and the dinner—a roast leg of lamb, vegetables, gravy, some sort of packet-mix pudding for dessert—is already spoiling. Jess rings on my mobile just as we arrive; she's running late too.

'I just got held up at work, Mum,' she explains huffily, when I scold her. 'We had a heap of customers at the last minute. Anyway, you've got no right to say anything, have you? Not after your behaviour. I won't be long. Just say sorry for me. Can you ask Nana to save me some, if it's not too much trouble?'

I can hear noise—chatting, laughter, music—she's not at work, I'd guarantee it. But I don't say anything more, just pass the message along to my quietly seething mother.

Mum decides she's over waiting, and serves up anyway. Rob and I hover nervously in the kitchen as she slaps the food on three of the waiting plates, slops on the gravy, pushes our plates towards us unceremoniously. I scrabble in the drawer for knives and forks, while Rob pours each of us a drink. He offers Mum a nice long glass of the chardonnay he's brought with him, ignoring her request for tap water. The three of us eat almost silently—bar my mother's frequent sighs—at the kitchen bench at Mum's request: 'There's no point in setting the table and doing it all properly if no one even bothers to turn up.'

When Jess arrives, she is obviously pissed—inappropriately giggly, stumbling, slurry—and Mum turns away from her proffered hug with a snort. There are times when even Jess's charms are no match for Mum's martyrdom, and Jess soon gives up trying to bring her around, instead begging her father to carve her a few slices of meat, while she downs a glass of the white. She avoids both my and her grandmother's glares and rolls her eyes when she thinks no one can see.

Mum and I adjourn to the lounge, where we sit in the gloom, pretending to watch some painfully slow BBC police drama, while Rob and Jess clean the kitchen. We don't look up when we finally hear Mick's key in the lock, though Mum calls out in her most politely frozen tones: 'Well, I'm afraid you missed out, Michael. It was roast lamb, too. There might be a few scraps in the fridge, if Rob hasn't given them to Toto.'

Mick doesn't bother to respond. He flicks on all the lounge-room lights, and we turn, blinking.

'I need to talk to you.'

He isn't alone. Erin is standing beside him. She has lost her seemingly impenetrable composure; she looks anxious, maybe even afraid. Her hair is rumpled, her clothes slightly dishevelled, her eyes are red-rimmed, her face pale. Mick has a firm hold of her arm, and she's clutching her little recorder to her chest as if someone's threatening to take it from her. At first glance it looks as if she has been dragged here unwillingly, under duress.

'What's going on, mate?' Rob has walked in from the kitchen, tea towel in hand, wary. 'Is everything all right?' He looks point-edly at Erin, who gives a weak smile, nods.

'Oh, no. It's okay. It's just—' She pauses, swallows convulsive-ly. She pulls away from Mick, takes a deep breath. 'You all need to listen to this.'

Rob and I look at each other, uncertain about what's go-ing on, what we should do, our own worries forgotten for the moment.

'Oh, Michael. What is it now?' Mum, momentarily diverted from her sulk, pushes herself out of her chair. 'Surely there's been enough drama? If you've been drinking, just go to bed, and sleep it off.'

He ignores her. 'I want you all to sit down and listen. This concerns everyone—the entire family. It's important.' There's a strength, a certainty in Mick's voice that I haven't heard for a long time. If he's been drinking it hasn't been excessive—his voice and his bearing seem calm and controlled. We all do as he says, even Mum, without questioning. Erin and Mick sit close together on the long lounge, and Erin puts her little recorder in the middle of the coffee table. Jess, who wanders in from the kitchen, gives her uncle an easy hug, throws Erin an unsurprised *Hey!* and flops down on the floor.

'I want you all to listen,' Mick says again. 'I want you to hear this.' He gives Erin a quick nod.

She presses play.

ERIN: You said you had something important to tell me.

MICK: Yes.

ERIN: Is it something to do with your cousin's death?

MICK: Yes.

ERIN: Do you want me to record this? I can turn it off if you'd rather. Really.

MICK: No. Leave it on. I want it recorded. I want—I want everyone to know.

ERIN: If you're sure. But if you change your mind you can just say and I'll turn it off.

MICK: Okay. Here goes.

It was a game that Adam and I played. We started years back, when we were kids—twelve or so. We were at my place, playing some idiotic game, just the two of us, the sort of thing you play at that age. It was some variation on playing armies. We called it the hostage game. You know the sort of thing …

ERIN: No, not really.

MICK: We had these guns that fired some sort of paper pellet. They weren't meant to do much damage if they hit you. We built forts, just basic barricades, using whatever we could find outside—bins, boxes, outdoor tables, any old crap that we could move. The game really just involved us taking each other hostage. The captured soldier would be tied up somewhere while the enemy interrogated him. We were probably a bit old to be doing this, but I guess it was our last opportunity to be kids. You know, before high school.

So it started out innocent enough—actually it was always innocent, really. Just dumb. Just really fucking dumb. We'd chase each other with the guns, and the loser would be tied up to an old ghost gum out the back and interrogated. We'd use a pair of Mum's tights that we'd found somewhere—nicked off the clothesline probably.

Eventually, the interrogation became the point of the game, and it was getting a bit embarrassing doing it where everyone could see us, so we ended up in Dad's shed. We'd tie each other to something in there—usually a chair or the legs of the old billiard table Dad had stored out there, and we'd got hold of a few more pairs of stockings by then, some old scarves and some sheets that Mum let us tear up. And then we'd do the interrogation.

ERIN: What do you mean by interrogation?

MICK: Oh, it was just nonsense. Total fantasy stuff. You know, like in 24—the kind of thing cops dream of doing but never do. We'd tie each other up and ask questions about troop movements, enemy plans and all that—and we'd threaten to torture one another, or kill entire families, we'd tighten the ropes, put the guns to each other's heads. Just crap like that. It was just a dumb kids' game.

Anyway, this one time I'd tied Adam's arms and legs to a chair and the knots were too loose and he was wriggling out, and I got this brilliant idea to tie him up by his neck. You know, we'd been told a million times not to ever put anything around anyone's neck, but I'd made it pretty loose and the stockings were stretchy ... Anyway, the bloody chair tipped over when we were wrestling, and the bonds were all tangled by that stage, and the stocking around his throat tightened enough to strangle him. He wasn't in any real danger, I guess, but he'd just about passed out by the time I managed to get him loose. I had to cut the stocking with a pair of gardening shears. It was all a bit crazy—Adam was coughing and spluttering and writhing around for a bit, and I was in a panic.

Once he was free, I wanted to go and get Mum, but Adam stopped me. He stopped coughing, and I calmed down, and then he told me. He said it was actually really cool. That the whole time he was being strangled it was pretty amazing, that he'd had a sort of head spin, better than with cigarettes, and he thought it was probably like getting high. He said that I needed to try it.

I was a bit sceptical, scared probably, but he laughed. Then he told me that he'd done it before—once at his cousin's place. It wasn't accidental, though; apparently his cousins did it all the time. Deliberately. And nobody ever got hurt. And if you did it right, there wouldn't be all the coughing and spluttering. It just felt good. His cousins called it the choking game.

And so I tried it. I was scared—but I did it. Adam tied the stocking around my neck and looped a pen at the end to tighten it like a ratchet until I passed out. And he was right—it did feel good. We did it a few more times that afternoon. Experimented a bit with ways of doing it. In the end we worked out that the scarves worked best—they were even better than the stockings. You only needed to sling them around your neck in the same way you'd wear a woollen scarf, and then pull down on either side. You'd pass out relatively fast—and it was easy to loosen quickly. Not that we ever came close to choking—at least we never thought we did. It didn't seem dangerous.

ERIN: But you never told anyone about it, either, did you? So I guess you knew it wasn't really a normal game? That there was something wrong with it?

MICK: Yeah. I guess. It was the high more than anything that made it seem like there was something off about it.

ERIN: So were you playing it all that time? There's a bit of a gap—you were fifteen the summer …

MICK: We played it for a while and then kinda forgot about it—it just sort of petered out. But that summer we'd started smoking a bit of weed, and so we began experimenting with the game again. It's the sort of thing that appeals to stupid teenage boys. A free high. It makes you euphoric. A bit like autoerotic asphyxiation, but without the sex. And it leaves no signs—there's no smell, you don't act drunk or stoned. You don't get sick or hungover. It was something your parents wouldn't find out about. Not until you died. Or killed someone else.

ERIN: And then Angie got involved?

MICK: Yeah. She caught us. And when she found out she wanted to join in. She was that sort of girl. She wanted to try everything. And of course when she got involved it got bigger, more elaborate. She bought special scarves. Made special arrangements. She wanted to turn it into a sort of party—so Adam'd nick stuff from the shop. Nothing much, just drinks, chips, ice-creams. The occasional packet of smokes. We'd do it at my place, sometimes, just the two of us, but it was too risky. Mostly we'd do it upstairs at Ferber's. No one was ever around at Adam's place. His mum was always in the shop. Nobody ever thought it was weird, me and Adam going up to his room. Angie'd come up, but usually later.

You can do it alone—kids do, and sometimes they die, and their parents, everyone, just think it's suicide. We always did it together, though. Not for protection, it never occurred to us that it could be fatal. You always stopped, you see—there was always a point where you knew when to stop.

But this time … this afternoon with Angie, me and Adam had already had our turn, and she was eager, excited, kinda wriggly or something. I've tried to think what it was, all this time. I know we didn't do anything different. We stopped when we always did, just before she lost consciousness, but something must have happened. She must have twisted, or the scarf must've been in a different position. Or we pulled too hard. Anyway ... we tried everything, but she didn't come to. We'd strangled her. She was dead.

ERIN: And then what? What did you do next?

MICK: I rang Dad. He came and got her. There was no one around at that time of day—no one to see him. He took her ... You know what happened next.

ERIN: What about the other girl, then? What about the Sydney Strangler?

MICK: I don't know anything about that. Dad told me he'd sort it all out, and I guess he did. I never asked.

CURL CURL, JANUARY 1978

She catches them at it. When Mick and Adam clatter their way up the shop stairs to Adam's room that afternoon, Angie is still downstairs, engrossed in the pinball game. Usually they would wait until later in the afternoon, when most of the boys have wandered off elsewhere, but today Mick has insisted that he's bored, that he's over pinball, that they should clear off and leave the rest of them to it. What Mick is really over is watching Angie with the other boys. He'd intercepted a look that passed between Angie and Darren as she took her turn at the machine, then couldn't help noticing the way she pushed back into the boy's body whenever she could, the way Darren had responded, so casual, but so clearly aware. He had felt his heart shrivel; his throat had clogged with tears. He couldn't bear to stay another minute.

They lie on Adam's bed for a while, arguing over which tracks to play—Adam's evolving interest in the local punk scene baffling the more conservative Mick. They smoke a couple of stolen (payment for services rendered, as Adam justifies it) cigarettes, the window open wide to let out the smoke and some of the smell.

The game proceeds as a matter of course. Adam pulls his Manly footy scarf out of a drawer and slings it around Mick's neck, then kneels in front of him on the bed and pulls up hard. Angie enters the room noisily, just at the moment when Mick starts to feel the rush that proceeds what they refer to as 'liftoff'—the moment when the world recedes and begins to float away. It only ever lasts a few seconds, though it seems longer, and every time Mick thumps back into consciousness, he wishes it could be an eternity. But this time he misses entering that blissful state entirely, Adam dropping the scarf when his cousin walks through the door. Mick sits up, coughing irritably.

Oh my God. Angie stands as if rooted to the spot, her eyes wide, mouth open.

'Oh. My. God,' she repeats, grinning now, her voice full of laughter. 'I thought for a moment that you guys were having it off,' she gestures at the rumpled bed, the boys' awkward positions. 'Sick.'

The boys look back at her, their faces bright red.

'So come on.' She is impatient now. 'Tell me what you're up to.'

Of course she wants to join in. Mick tries to dissuade her, not so much worried about what might happen—the possibility that they're endangering their lives has never occurred to him—but because he doesn't want it getting out, getting around. What they're doing might not be illegal, but it's something that has to be done in secret, away from prying eyes, to be kept from parents and friends alike. The thought of any of his mates knowing is horrifying: unlike smoking, drug taking, drinking, reading dirty magazines or even having sex, the game isn't cool—just weird. Angie promises complete discretion, so long as they show her how it's done, just as long as they let her join in. And what Angie wants, Angie gets.

After that Angie and Mick play the game nearly every day, at home in Mick's bedroom, stereo blaring, door locked, the keyhole stuffed with a piece of scrunched up alfoil to block Jane's resentful curiosity. When Angie suggests that they invite his sister into the game, Mick vetoes the idea immediately and vehemently.

'No way,' he'd said. 'She'll dob. We'll get busted.'

So he got these hours of Angie to himself. They play the game for a bit, then do some drawing to keep his mother happy. Angie always goes first. She bears back against the mattress with all her weight, while he pulls upwards with the scarf ends. It's like some bizarre reversal of the sex act. He loves to watch her expression change: at first she strains, grimaces, but finally, when she falls into her moment of unconsciousness her eyes roll back and her vivid features relax. Her face is pale, still, beautiful. Perfect. He loves even more her moment of coming to—the way her eyelids flicker, open and then close again, the way her lips curve into a serene Mona Lisa smile, the way she lies there for a moment, just breathing. She gives a little sigh and a tiny shudder makes its way all through her body, before she opens her eyes and slowly sits up. Mick always feels an answering tremor; he hardens, has to resist the urge to touch her, restrain himself from pressing up against her loose, unresisting, semi-conscious flesh. When Angie is involved it isn't just a game for him, isn't entirely innocent.

Even when they play the game with Adam, the pleasure of watching his cousin's sensual return to consciousness still gives him more pleasure than the game itself.

On that last day, when she doesn't come back, everything's the same as always. Angie doesn't gasp for breath, she doesn't struggle against the tightening. She looks as beautiful, as graceful as always, her body thrusting ever so slightly upwards towards the boys before slowly sinking back, her face pale and tranquil, that half-smile playing on her lips.

It takes them an age—a deadly length of time—before they realise that something has gone badly wrong. To understand that this time she isn't coming back.

When he thinks about it later, it's as if everything that has ever happened in his life was always moving towards that moment, as if it had been set in motion years before, had moved step by inexorable step towards that terrible end. Like a film with an ending that might come as a surprise but still makes perfect sense. As if it was always meant to be.

ERIN

They think it's the end if it all.

How she would like it to be. How she would like to be the person she has told them she is—just a journo making a documentary, not involved, with no interest of her own, no ulterior motive. She could have sat back and observed, watched as the family wept over the prodigal son and brother's revelation, his spiritual return, vicariously enjoyed the resolution, documented their sense of closure. She could have joined in the hand-wringing: been wholehearted in her contemplation of whether or not Mick should hand himself in; been genuinely conflicted when she promised that she wouldn't disclose the information to anyone, police or otherwise, until Mick had decided what he should do with the information.

She says nothing at all that might remind them of the one thing they have forgotten—the death of that other, homeless, nameless girl. She wonders whether they're all in some kind of strange denial. There is not one thought spared, not one question asked, not one of them appears to notice the discrepancy: the huge gaping hole that has been left by Mick's confession. Then again, it's always the things people don't say that are the most potent. Perhaps they have their own suspicions. Perhaps they always have.

Erin stays with Mick that night—drives him back to their dingy Dee Why hotel room. She holds him as he sobs—his sorrow, his guilt, his relief. Her pity is genuine, her sorrow answers his own. They make love: the most real sex he has ever had, he tells her later. It sounds trite, but she can tell that he means it. She doesn't quite understand her own feelings, and doesn't really want to. All she knows is that Mick is someone she can be with, that in Mick she has found someone whose emptiness echoes her own, has recognised him almost immediately as a fellow traveller in the land of the lost.

When he tells her, a decision finally made, that he will go to the police tomorrow, that he needs to end it, close it, take whatever punishment is coming his way, she tells him to wait.

'What does it matter, now? There's no one left whose life this can change. Only yours. Your family? Your kids? Why make things harder for them. You've paid for what you've done. Why can't you think of it as closed? Over.'

She has surprised herself, saying this. She may even mean it.

And perhaps it doesn't matter, maybe they can all go on with this secret kept close to them. After all, it's true: there *is* no one left. Angie is dead and her parents long gone. The only people left to care are Mick and his sister. And now her. She does care. She has no loyalty to the dead girl—though her story is tragic—but Mick is another matter. For the first time since her mother's death, or before that, since her sister's death, she has found that she can care—can feel.

Perhaps one day soon something—she doesn't quite know what, doesn't dare to imagine it, name it—will be possible between her and Mick. But first there's one more thing she needs to do, a question she needs to ask. There's only one person who can give her the answer.

And once she knows the truth, anything's possible. Anything.

She leaves Mr G until last this evening. The other patients are all glad to see her, as always. They eat—or are fed—their dinner happily, take their meds. The time passes slowly, but she feels strangely patient, happy to wait, now that the moment's arrived. She doesn't interrupt old Mrs Penney's rambling memories, even flicks through the photograph albums with her, oohing and aaahing at all the right moments, exclaiming over pictures of this person and that, for once not resentful, pleased to provide an audience, to enjoy this evidence of others' happy family lives.

Mr G is sitting in the dark. As usual he is facing the window as if gazing out across the ocean. His evening meal is particularly unappealing tonight—even more unappealing than usual. It looks like it could be pumpkin soup—what else could be so violently orange?—but it smells vaguely fishy, and is far too runny, more like a broth. She butters the flaccid toast heavily, cutting the bread into triangles, then guides his unresisting hand, gently presses his fingers into the bread, keeping them out of the grease.

She makes the most of the dinner, as she always does, talking it up in an attempt to persuade him that it's worth eating—though she knows that her efforts are futile, wasted breath.

'Now, Mr G, there's some delicious soup for tea tonight—and it looks like it's homemade, so it should be good and filling. And warming. Now,' she dips the spoon in, 'here comes a spoonful, so open up ...'

He opens his lips tentatively, and she slips the spoon in and out. He swallows the mouthful and then closes his lips determinedly. Turns his face away.

'I know it isn't what you're used to, but you should try to eat some. It's good for you. And there's pudding tonight—let's see—it's—well, it could be trifle, I think.'

The small plastic cup contains some sort of unidentifiable cake at the bottom of the cup, and a glob of thick yellow custard wobbles on top. But Mr G can't be persuaded. He is determined not to take in any more of the soup, and she desists without too much angst. She has a packet of chips in her bag that she'll leave on the table, and she knows these will be eaten after she leaves. She wonders whether it is only her offerings that have kept him alive these last months. Wonders whether it's a good thing.

She buzzes around his room, tidying things, chat-chat-chatting as she always does, about Angie, about her death, about her own sister's murder, about what it has meant to her, what it has meant to them all. She is like a wasp, incessant, intense, but he has no way to swat her words away; he is helpless against them.

Every evening her buzzing has been getting progressive-ly more dangerous, the information she lets slip is becoming more intimate, closer and closer she moves, with her angry knowledge—*buzz, buzz, buzz*—and then away again, and she's moved onto something banal, some athlete's new steroid scandal, some celebrity divorce. She'll blather on and on, as irritatingly vacuous as it's possible to be.

But tonight she is ready to cross that line, she has reached the point of no return, she is circling her victim, round and round, there is no way to divert her, to smoke her out, she's readying herself for the attack—for the kill.

She sets her little red machine in the centre of his dinner table.

'I've got something for you, Mr G. Now, I know you can hear me. You reckon you can't see. And you won't speak. But there's nothing wrong with your ears as far as I can tell. This is your son speaking, Mr G. Your son, Mick. He has something important to tell you.

'I want you to listen.'

The old man turns his chair away from her. She leans back against the table and closes her eyes. When the recording has finished she moves his chair around so he's facing her and looks him in the eye. And he looks back at her, the gaze from those lion eyes direct, unflinching. This time she knows he's seeing her. And she knows he's heard.

'So, we all know, Mr G. We all know what happened to your niece, to Angie. And now Mick—now Mick can try to get over it. Get past it. Though I think it might be too late for him. But there's something else, isn't there, Mr G? There's still a piece missing. A piece that no one in your family seems to remember. That no one cares about. But I care. And you know that I care, don't you, Mr G? You know that I'm not likely to forget.

'It's sad thinking that we're the only ones left to remember her. I guess that's what happens to us all in the end. We all get forgotten eventually. But I thought maybe you'd like to share your memories. To give me that final piece before you're gone, too.'

His voice is croaky and hoarse with lack of use, as if it's rusted. The words come out slowly at first, hesitantly, but eventually they come faster and faster, an unstoppable flow, a flood. She doesn't bother to record him, knows she'll remember every word.

'It wasn't planned. None of it was ever planned. Not what I did for Mick—that was just pure instinct. I was just protecting my boy. What happened to Angela was an accident, but it would never have looked that way, would it? Who'd have believed them? They'd have been charged with manslaughter at the very least. And Mick, he was the son of a copper—he wouldn't have survived. I loved Angie, you know. She was ... well, she was my niece, wasn't she? She was family. But she was gone, and there was no way to bring her back—and there was no point ruining the boys' lives. They were stupid, yes. But they'd meant no harm.'

He pauses, trying to catch his breath, she supposes. Or perhaps he's thinking what she's thinking: that Mick's life was ruined anyway, that he hadn't been able to save his son from that.

He takes a deep breath. 'And maybe, maybe it *was* the wrong decision—maybe I should have taken the boys in, tried to get them through it the right way. But you see, I knew, better than most people, what happens once you're in the system. There's no getting out.

'So when Mick rang me, I told the boys to lock the door. To wait for me in the room. I told them at home I was going to the tip, and I left and went straight to Ferber's. It was four o'clock or so by that time, and I knew the shop would be closed. They always shut early on Sundays—it was their club day, bingo or something, and they were religious about it, so I knew Adam's parents wouldn't be there. And all the other shops on that strip were shut. It was pretty deserted on a Sunday. There was a back entrance to the shop, a laneway for the deliverymen. And so I came and got her—wrapped her in a blanket and drove around for a bit, headed up to Palm Beach. I knew of a reserve out there that was pretty isolated—there were some trails that didn't get used other than by the rangers every couple of months. No one saw me.

'That was that. I wrapped the scarf around her throat, then brought it back across her eyes like a blindfold, tied it behind her head. As if the killer had tried to hide her eyes.

'I left her there ... That was the worst. Just leaving her there. But what else could I do? She was gone.'

He pauses again. Wheels himself to the sideboard, opens the drawer and pulls out a bottle of Mylanta. Opens it and takes a long sip. He wipes his mouth. Coughs. Screws the lid on and puts the bottle back. He wheels back to face her. She can smell a sour tang—not the chalky medicine, but his breath.

'So ... the other little girl. That's really what you want to know about, isn't it?' He looks at her without pity; the beauty of those tawny eyes, so like Mick's, suddenly sinister. 'I was working. I got a call out. There'd been a sighting of this dealer we were after in a lane in the Cross. I went down there and he took off. I chased him into some filthy squat, but he disappeared. The girl just happened to be there, bombed out in one of the upstairs rooms. It was pretty clear that she'd OD'd—that she was on the way out. It was nothing, they were everywhere, the Cross was riddled with them—fucking junkies. Anyway, I shook her, but nothing happened. Then I noticed the scarf around her neck. It was winter, she had hardly enough on to keep her warm; she'd have died of exposure, eventually, if she hadn't died of an OD, but she had this bloody scarf.'

Erin interrupts for a moment, can't help herself.

'Was it a woollen scarf? With blue and orange stripes?' She makes no attempt to keep the eagerness out of her voice.

The old man looks back at her, face stony. 'How would I know? It was dark, and the scarf was filthy. Everything she had on was just ... black with filth. With disease. You wouldn't let your dog touch it.

'The rest was easy, really. I thought of Mick, thought of what was hanging over him. They were still investigating Angie's death, and though there had only been dead ends, they were still suspicious. I'd have been the same if it had been my case. That's the thing—I could understand it. And I knew Mick was always going to be under suspicion. Even if it wasn't the police, it'd be other people. Anyone who remembered. It'd follow him the rest of his life.

'It happened without me even thinking about it. I was checking to see if she was breathing, and I took the scarf in my hand. I just pulled on it, tightened it. It took less than a minute.'

'Did she regain consciousness?' Erin isn't sure that she really wants to know, but she has to ask.

It takes him a moment. 'I don't know. I doubt it. She was halfway to being dead when I got there. But just for a moment, I thought ... I thought I saw her eyes flicker briefly. And then she was gone. I arranged the scarf in the same way I had with Angie. Wound it around her throat and then back across her eyes like a blindfold. I knew I needed to leave something—a signature—to connect the two deaths. Then I left. No one had seen me. No one even knew I'd been up there—I'd never called in the job. It wasn't like today—no one kept tabs. We did what we had to.

'I went back to the city. I had an unmarked car, and I wasn't in uniform, so even if any law-abiding citizen did happen to see me, I wouldn't have registered.

'It was called in a day later—some old warb found her. It worked. They made the link to Angie straight away. There was no connection to me. And the heat was off Mick.'

His eyes—hard, cold, defiant—fix on hers.

'She would have died anyway, you know, if I hadn't found her. And if not then, later. That's what happens to girls like that. My son's life was worth more than ten like her. Junkies. Oxygen thieves. That's all they are.' His voice is a gasp now, barely audible.

There's only one more thing she needs to know.

'Kelly's funeral. I saw you there. Why did you go? What was the point?'

The man shrugs. 'I don't know. I thought—I thought it would look good, I suppose. Victim solidarity in the face of the Sydney Strangler. I was going to speak to your mother, make sure the press noticed that I'd attended. But in the end I didn't. Couldn't.'

She knows what she needs to do next. She's imagined it so clearly that she can almost taste the sweetness on her tongue. The old man's face is impassive again, a mask, but he's watching her as if he knows exactly what she's thinking, as if he's waiting for her to do what she came to do, what she needs to do, almost as if he's willing it, wishing it. As if he's ready.

She thinks of those two lost girls, of Angie and of her sister, Kelly, thinks of the other lives this man has shattered, without hesitation, without pity or even compunction—hers, her mother's. What he's done to those he loves—unwittingly, perhaps, in the hope of saving them. There's no way to balance it all out, to tease action from motive, consequences from intentions. His rationalisations are no defence.

Oxygen thief.

She can give him what he wants. Or she can make him wait. She knows that eventually, and in the not too distant future, perhaps, death will come for him. He'll get what he wants anyway. He might be ready now, willing, but she isn't taking his wishes into account.

She pulls away from his hungry gaze, turns her back. She leaves the room quickly, before she changes her mind.

JANE

Dad's wake is surprisingly well attended.

He had died only days after Mick's revelation, during the night, suffering a massive stroke. The nursing staff reported that when they'd looked in on him during the night, he'd appeared to be sleeping peacefully. By the next morning he was gone.

The doctor at the nursing home seemed to think that all the symptoms he'd been experiencing may have been leading up to it, though he assured us there would have been nothing they could have done, had they known. Anyway, he'd added, it would have been quick and painless. Not a bad way to go.

I look around the room. There's my mother, seated on the lounge, handkerchief at the ready. Jess, dressed for the funeral in all her brightest clothes, her only concession to mourning her newly dyed black mop, is squeezed in beside her grandmother, an arm slung around her shoulder. Mum is a bit dazed—the last few days have been hard for her—but right now she's laughing at something, some story one of Dad's old police mates is telling her, filling her in on the top-secret details of some ancient (and no doubt shady) escapade. Though clearly exhausted, she's looking younger, somehow, and lighter, as if some terrible burden has been lifted from her shoulders. I wonder, not for the first time, whether she'd known, or guessed. I might ask her one day. Or maybe I won't. Maybe I don't really need to know.

Mick's in the kitchen, pouring small glasses of lemonade for his two little girls who stand waiting quietly, patiently beside him. His ex, Sarah, is leaning against the doorjamb, her arms folded, observing the fetching domestic scene with a wry smile. He hands the glasses to his girls, watches as they make their way back into the crowded lounge room, carrying their glasses with two hands, careful lest they spill their drinks on Nanny's good carpet. Once they've arrived at their destination, and settled in front of the muted TV, Mick looks back at Sarah, gives a shrug, returns her smile. They stand there for a long moment, saying nothing, watch as their little girls take cautious sips, blinking when the bubbles burst. I'm glad to see that Mick and Sarah are being civil, although there's no possibility, according to Mick, of reconciliation. Sarah's already found a temporary replacement, another cop, oddly enough, and Mick has taken it in his stride.

'Mum was right,' he'd admitted during a late night of drink and confidences, reminiscences, in the days following Dad's death. 'She was never my type. Not really. I think it was just her physical resemblance to Angie that attracted me in the first place.'

'So what is your type, Mick? I didn't know you had one.'

'Oh. I'm kinda partial to short, dark-haired women these days.'

'Oh. Right. That type.' I'd laughed at my own naivety. 'Is that going anywhere?'

'I'd like it to. But she seems to have disappeared.'

'She'll turn up.'

He shrugged, looking worried. 'I haven't seen her since ... you know.'

'I guess it was a big thing to find out.' I leave it at that, just as we've all left it since his confession. Nobody knows what to say, or what to do. And because of Dad's death so soon after, the entire family cast into a further state of shock, we've been able to avoid facing all of the ramifications of that knowledge.

But now, with all the formalities of the funeral got through, and any inhibitions overridden by drink and grief, I don't even need to steel myself. 'And have you decided, Mick? What you're going to do? What you should do? About Angie.'

'I don't know.'

'But you're not going to, you know, turn yourself in, are you? After all this time. Who would it help? You'd still be charged, wouldn't you?'

'I would.'

'Then you can't, Mick. Think of the girls.'

'I am.'

'What about—what about Erin? Will she ... say anything? What about the documentary?'

'I don't know.'

'You need to find her.'

'I do.'

'There's another thing, Mick. Something I don't understand. That other little girl—the junkie. What happened—?'

He puts his hand up. 'I don't know, mate. It's something I've always wondered about. Always hoped was just a coincidence.'

'But it couldn't be, could it? Do you think Dad—?' I can't finish the thought, let alone the question.

Mick shrugs, but doesn't reply. He fills my wineglass, tops up his whisky. We drink in silence, lost in our own thoughts.

'So, what about you and Rob?'

I look up at him, surprised.

'What do you mean?'

'He told me about it, you know. About what happened with Angie.'

I can't hide my shock. 'He told you that? What did you—?' Again I'm having trouble finding words, But Mick knows exactly where I'm heading.

'I dunno. I'd always wondered who, but it had never occurred to me that it was Rob. I felt a bit sick at first. And then I felt like hitting him.' He gives a brief bitter smile. 'But ... Christ. It's so long ago. It shouldn't matter any more. It can't.'

'Did he tell you what I did?'

He snorts. 'Revenge, was it?'

'Something like that. Stupid, anyway. And pointless.'

'Maybe it's time we both got over it, Jane.' His voice decisive.

'Over what?'

'Over her. Over Angie. It's time to get on with it.'

'With what?'

'With the rest of our lives.'

I stare across the room at Rob. Look closely, try to view him as a stranger would, my husband of more than twenty years. Our future is entirely uncertain. We still haven't discussed what's happened. I've been staying with Mum since Mick's revelation, and we've barely spoken, full stop. He's standing in the background, well away from the subdued hubbub of the crowd, leaning against a wall in Mum's dining room, eyes half closed, beer in hand. Suddenly I'm overwhelmed by an unexpected feeling of tenderness, of understanding. I see not the Rob I usually see—still young, strong, full of certainty, good cheer—but a middle-aged man, hair greying, a little paunchy, his face lined, eyes sad, shoulders slightly hunched. He looks weary, uncertain. He looks like he doesn't know where he's heading, as if he's worried about what might happen next. He looks just the way I feel.

Rob glances up and over at me as if he can feel me watching him. He doesn't give me his usual easy smile, but gazes back at me with an expression that's unfamiliar—cool, appraising, distant. I don't know what he's thinking, and with a sudden surge of joy, I know that I'd really like to find out. I move towards him, hold out my hand, and hope that it's not too late.

EPILOGUE

She knows that he will come on this particular day—the anniversary of his cousin's death. She waits, out of sight, in the shadow of a large headstone. He arrives with his sister, each of them bearing flowers. Jane's bunch is big and bright, full of yellows and oranges and reds, his is smaller, all white, roses perhaps, though it's hard to tell from this distance. Jane doesn't stay long. She places the flowers on top of the grave, says a few words to her brother, hugs him and goes.

Left alone, he arranges both bunches of flowers in the bronze headstone vase. He gets down on his haunches, traces the simple lettering with a finger, rocking back and forth on his heels. She can hear the sound vaguely, and his lips are moving, but it takes her a moment to work out that he's singing. His voice is slightly out of key, but the tune is still recognisable. *Angie.* He only sings one verse, the chorus, and then sits silently, his head bowed as if in prayer.

When he stands, he looks up at the grey sky, puts his hands in his pockets and walks away without a backwards glance. There's something different in his walk, something's changed, he stands taller, straighter, and when he strides the bounce is more apparent, as if he's conscious of it. She is about to call out, let him know she's here, to go after him, when she sees him wave at someone in the distance. A small child runs towards him through the maze of headstones and he leans down and picks her up, swings her about effortlessly. When he reaches the iron gate there is another child waiting, and a woman. He holds out his hand—

Erin turns away before she has to see the woman's answering handclasp, or God help her, a clinch. *Happy endings*, she thinks. *They're way overrated.* They've never really been her scene.

She makes her way through the cemetery, heading past the trees towards the exit on the opposite side. She's just about to open the gate, when a strong hand grips her shoulder.

'Hey, Fury. What are you doing here?'

'I just—'

'And where do you think you're going?'

She closes her eyes for a moment, holds her breath, turns. 'I don't know,' she says honestly. 'I saw you with your wife. I thought ...'

'Ex-wife. She was just bringing the girls—it's my weekend. It's a bit weird, I guess, dropping them off at a cemetery.'

Erin can see the two little girls now, standing quietly behind their father, carrying backpacks. The smiles they give her are shy, but expectant, as if they're eager to be introduced.

'We thought we'd get an ice-cream. Go to the park. This weather's meant to clear. You can come with us, if you want. The girls would like that, wouldn't you?'

They both nod enthusiastically, their eyes wide, smiles even wider.

'They've got these really good new swings,' the youngest girl says. 'They go up really, really high. You can push us.'

The older one glares at her little sister, then addresses Erin solemnly. 'Grown-ups can go on them, too, you know. You don't have to push us.'

It has been a long time since she's had an ice-cream, a day in the park. The last time she'd swung on a swing was with Kelly. In another life.

'I'd like that,' she says. And she would. There's nothing she'd like more.

Mick doesn't speak, just pulls her close, holds her hard. She leans in against him, solid, warm. *Real.* She breathes out, squeezes her eyes shut. When she opens them again the day already seems clearer, brighter—the grey clouds beginning to thin.

Happy endings. She thinks that maybe they're not so bad. If she tries really hard she might even get used to them.

ACKNOWLEDGEMENTS

I have a feeling that the first draft of *The Lost Girls* would have been despairingly bottom-drawered (and kept there under lock and key) if not for the enthusiasm and confidence of my wonderful publisher, Belinda Byrne. Thanks for everything, bb— I'm missing you already!

My heartfelt gratitude to my remarkable editor (and fellow cardigan), Caro Cooper, for her help getting this novel shipshape and ready for the world—and for always, always seeming to know just what is needed.

A big thank you is owed to my agent, Alexis Hurley, for her constant encouragement, her efforts to get things happening internationally, and for putting up with all those late night/early morning missives.

Once again I'm hugely grateful to my sister Rebecca James for her early reading of the work, but this time more particularly for her eleventh-hour plot advice—all those trees, yet somehow I'd managed to disregard that forest. Thanks, too, to Heidi McCourt, Laura Thomas, Clem Edwards, Anyez Lindop, Ben Ball and all the folk at Penguin Australia whose behind-the-scenes efforts make all the difference.